Hyun Kil-Un

DEAD SILENCE

And Other Stories of the Jeju Massacre

Hyun Kil-Un

DEAD SILENCE

And Other Stories of the Jeju Massacre

translated by

Kang Hyunsook
Lee Jin-Ah
John Michael McGuire

with an Introduction by

John Michael McGuire

EastBridge
Norwalk

Signature Books
Copyright © 2007 EastBridge

All rights reserved.
No part of this book may be reproduced in any media whatsoever
without written permission of the publisher,
EastBridge
64 Wall Street, Norwalk, CT 06850 USA

EastBridge is a nonprofit publishing corporation
chartered in the State of Connecticut and tax exempt
under section 501(c)(3) of the United States tax code.

This book is partially supported by
the Korea Literature Translation Institute

Library of Congress Cataloging-in-Publication Data

Hyon, Kir-on, 1940-
Dead silence and other stories of the Jeju massacre / Hyun Kil-Un ; translated by Kang Hyunsook, Lee Jin-Ah, John Michael McGuire With an Introduction by John Michael McGuire. -- 1st Eng. ed.
  p. cm. -- (Signature Books)
Individual srories selected from various Korean collection.
ISBN 1-891936-80-8 (pbk. : alk. paper)
1. Korea--History--Chejudo Rebellion, 1948--Fiction. I. Kang, Hyon-suk, 1961- II. Title.
PL992.3.K57D43 2006
895.7'34--dc22
                    2006021277

Printed in the United States of America

Contents

Introduction	vii
The Dream of a Dragon Horse	3
The Dawn	20
Grandfather	53
Fever	68
The Homecoming	116
Fire and Ashes	134
Dead Silence	172
Chronology	189
Glossary of Korean Terms	190
Glossary of Other Terms and Names	191

Introduction

It has been called "The Jeju Secret," "The Jeju Massacre," and even "The Jeju Civil War." Koreans, if they speak of it, usually use less suggestive terms, such as "Jeju 4.3" or "The April Third Incident" (*Sa-sam Satae*). However, it is seldom spoken of at all, either within or outside of Korea.

The massacre of some 30,000 people that began on April 3, 1948, on Korea's southernmost island of Jeju has been shrouded in secrecy for more than half a century, and the truth about this tragedy is only just beginning to emerge. In 2000—some fifty years after the horror subsided—the Korean National Assembly enacted a law to investigate the case and compensate the victims. In 2003, Korean President Roh Moo-Hyun issued the first formal apology on behalf of the national government for its role in the brutal slaughter of innocent Korean civilians and the destruction of their homes and villages. He described the miserable event as "one of the worst episodes in modern Korean history," a rather remarkable claim considering that modern Korean history includes the Japanese colonization of Korea, the occupation of Korea by an American military government, the horrific Korean War, and a series of repressive military regimes that controlled South Korea for nearly four decades following the war—to say nothing of the horrors and tragedies north of the DMZ. With a history as woeful as this, an event that ranks as one of the worst episodes in modern Korean history must also rank among the great tragedies of the twentieth century. However, unlike the other twentieth-century slaughters with which we are more or less familiar, the human massacre that took place on Jeju remains largely unknown.

In an attempt to "bring closure" to this incident and to "restore the honor of the victims," President Roh said in his apology that he would consider establishing a memorial peace park on the island. Whatever one may think of the proposal for a peace park, it is certainly a mistake to attempt to bring closure to this tragedy that is only now coming to light. What is needed at this point in time is not a closing, but an opening of dialogue and debate on the causes and consequences of the massacre, its significance for the people of Jeju, and its meaning in the context of Korean society, Japanese colonialism, the Cold War, and American foreign policy. It was immediately after Liberation from the Japanese Occupation, while Korea was ruled by an American military government, that the horrible slaughter on Jeju occurred. A recent report prepared by the Office of the Korean Prime Minister claims that the U.S. forces that were stationed in Korea at the time played a significant role in supporting and advising the regime that carried out this atrocity. Thus, there are more than a few unpleasant truths hidden in the dark memory hole of the Jeju Massacre, and the exposure of these truths is sure to have ramifications not only within, but also beyond, the borders of Korea. Those who are responsible for the massacre as well as those who in any way benefited from it are understandably uncomfortable with any public discussion on the topic, and it is precisely because of the influence and authority of those very people that the incident has been shrouded in secrecy. However, there is too much at stake, in terms of our understanding of modern Korea and world affairs, to continue to remain silent about this dark horror.

The stories of the Jeju Massacre assembled in this book are purely fictional, but they too form an important part of the much-needed public discourse on the subject. Written in the 1980s and 90s, they are among the earliest efforts to draw attention to the tragedy. Given Korea's political climate in the 1980s—it was ruled by a military dictatorship with little tolerance for opposition and a history of human rights abuses—it is entirely understandable and appropriate that the earliest attempts to broach the subject of the Jeju Massacre would have come in the form of fiction. Indeed, even to this day it is difficult and dangerous to approach the issue in any form other than fiction. As recently as 1997, with the military rulers gone and the formal apparatus of democracy firmly in place in Korea, the organizer of a film festival that included the screening of *Red Hunt*, a South Korean documentary on the Jeju Massacre, was arrested and charged under the National Security Law. Outside of Korea there has been even less discussion, debate, or awareness of the massacre. This collection of stories, written in Korean and translated for the first time into English, helps to fill the lacuna in public consciousness by making this narrative on the Jeju Massacre available to an international audience.

The author of these stories, Hyun Kil-Un, was born on Jeju in 1940. He therefore experienced the Jeju Massacre as a young child and was subsequently raised amid the ensuing social chaos on the island. The events and issues surrounding the massacre have clearly haunted Hyun throughout his life and literary career, for they recur in various forms in many of the short stories and novels that he has written.

All but one of the stories in this collection relate directly to the Jeju Massacre. The exception is the first story, "Dream of a Dragon Horse," which is set on Jeju some time in the nineteenth or early twentieth century, prior to the Japanese Occupation. The story is a valuable addition to this collection because it paints a picture of Jeju in the *Joseon* period (1392-1910), providing a sense of the long-standing oppression of the islanders by the mainland government and the bitter relations between the two. Seoul (*Hanyang*), the capital of Korea in the *Joseon* period, was not only the seat of all government affairs it was also regarded as the locus of learning and culture. Even to this day, many Koreans disparage those people and institutions, for example "regional universities" (*Jibang Daehak*), outside of Seoul, but in earlier times such discriminatory attitudes were more intense. Being the southernmost region of Korea and separated from the mainland, the residents of Jeju Island experienced the most severe forms of this regional discrimination. It was common for the king in those days to send his opponents and other rejects into exile by awarding them with official positions on Jeju. Such is the fate of one of the main characters in "Dream of a Dragon Horse," a man who is sent to Jeju and positioned as governor of the island after receiving an earlier dismissal from office. At a farewell party before his departure for Jeju, his friends tell him that the islanders are wicked people and that if he expresses warmth toward them he will be "robbed of his bamboo hat, beaten by mobs, and will never make it home." In this story, the governor confronts his first challenge in office when Counselor Kang, a native islander admired by the people, cuts down some of his own tangerine trees in protest against the custom that requires islanders to give regular tributes to the king. The story, which nicely illustrates the islanders' disenchantment with the oppressive taxation policies of the mainland government and the mainlanders' distrust and contempt for the people of Jeju, provides a suitable backdrop for understanding the events of 1948-49 with which the rest of the stories in this collection are concerned.

The stories that follow "Dream of a Dragon Horse" present an interconnected and multifaceted perspective on the Jeju Massacre. Some of the stories are set squarely during the massacre; others move back and forth between the present and the past. One of the dominant and recurring themes in these stories is the futile quest for historical truth. How is history distorted? Why is the truth so difficult to reveal? In "Grandfather," this theme is brought to life in a fantastic but compelling manner. The spirit of the narrator's father, who was sentenced to death owing to a false accusation in the Jeju Massacre, transmigrates into the narrator's grandfather, who subsequently reveals the father's innocence. However, only the narrator, who was born after his father's death, is intrigued by the story of his father; everyone else—the narrator's extended family and the other villagers—are too disturbed by the return to this forgotten incident to accept the grandfather or his story. The transmigration of the father's spirit into the body of the grandfather, an interesting narrative device with Buddhist overtones, dramatically represents the idea that the truth of our past behavior often returns to haunt us. However, the real focus of the story is the attitude of the people around the grandfather, those who insist on interpreting his behavior as a sign of senility. They cannot accept or even entertain the idea of transmigration, not because of any empiricist inclinations, but because they are too afraid that the truth about the massacre might be revealed. The story thus shows how subversive the truth can be in a world that enforces deception and ignorance.

In "Fever," which was originally published as a novelette, Hyun illustrates some of the social forces that inhibit and suppress historical truth. The narrator in this story is a journalist working in Seoul who returns to his hometown on Jeju to write a story about a man named Kim Man-Ho, who has been nominated to receive "the award for pioneering citizenship." After learning about Kim's past behavior, the journalist realizes that he does not deserve the award, for he was merely an opportunist, a man who profited by collaborating with the Japanese during the Occupation of Korea. The journalist decides that it is rather Kim's former friend and rival, Reverend Kang Sung-Su, who deserves the award. Kang was a man of integrity who worked for the Korean people and his community. However, for refusing to cooperate with the Japanese authorities, Reverend Kang was forced to close his church, and after Liberation from the Japanese Occupation he was accused of communist activities during the Jeju Massacre and was killed. When he attempts to reveal the truth about Kim Man-Ho, the journalist receives threats and bribes and is ultimately forced to write a flattering story on Kim in the newspaper for which he works. Unable to report the truth, the journalist laments his powerlessness. The story shows how if it is difficult to discover the truth about the Jeju Massacre and the people in any way associated with it, it is even more difficult to reveal that truth in society.

The Jeju Massacre is sometimes described as an unfortunate and excessive but ultimately necessary crackdown on a communist uprising. However, the term "communist" needs to be understood carefully in the context of Korea following WWII; for there was then, and still is, a real tendency to confuse communism with the simple desire for independence. In *Korea's Place in the Sun*, University of Chicago historian Bruce Cumings relates the following information which is germane to this point. After liberation from the Japanese Occupation, a People's Committee set up on Jeju began operating as a de facto government. According to General John Hodge, commander of the U.S. military government in Korea from 1945 to 1948, Jeju was "a truly communal area ... peacefully controlled by a People's Committee without much Comintern [i.e. Soviet] influence." The majority of Jeju citizens were moderately leftist in their opinions, but many were relatively positive toward the United States, largely because of the latter's role in bringing an end to the Japanese Occupation of Korea. However, "the people were deeply separatist and did not like mainlanders; their wish was to be left alone." The governor of Jeju in 1948, Yu Hae-Jin, a mainlander with ties to two right-wing youth groups, was reportedly "ruthless and dictatorial in his dealing with opposing political parties." In an interview with Americans two months prior to the April third uprising, Governor Yu admitted that he had used "extreme rightist power" to reorient the Jeju people. In particular he had unleashed on the islanders the Northwest Youth, a radical terrorist group of anticommunist refugees from North Korea, a group that continued to work with the police and armed forces in suppressing the islanders after the April third revolt. Thus, the Jeju Massacre was less of a communist uprising than it was an anticommunist crackdown; it had less to do with the islander's ideology than it did with their basic and legitimate desire for freedom—from the Japanese colonialists, the mainland oppressors, and the American military government.

Nevertheless, it is true that Korea was in the grip of a fierce ideological struggle in the years following Liberation and that the communism that ultimately triumphed in the North also had some influence on Jeju. Two of the stories in this collection, notably "The Dawn" and "Dead Silence" illuminate some of the communist aspects of the Jeju Massacre. Ji-hyok, the main character in "The Dawn," is swept up in the ideology of communism partly as an escape from the Confucian traditions that restrict his autonomy. However, he ultimately realizes that as a communist fighting for the liberation of the Korean people, he was no more in control of his destiny than at any other point in his life, which has always unfolded "independently of his own volition." At the end of the story he finds himself chained inside a truck that is taking him to his death—a powerful metaphor for his, and our, lack of autonomy. And "Dead Silence," the final story in this collection, depicts one battle in the Jeju Massacre from the point of view of a guerrilla fighter. After the battle is over, and the communists are defeated, all of the local villagers are rounded up in a field and accused of being communists. Gyu-Min, the main character in this story, watches from a distance as the government soldiers fire their guns, and the innocent villagers drop to the ground, one by one.

The work of translating and editing this collection is what first brought the Jeju Massacre to my attention and compelled me to learn more about it. It also provided me with a deeper understanding of the Korean language, Korean literary styles, and Korean society. Finally, it left me with an appreciation of Hyun Kil-Un's writing and his courage in speaking out on the Jeju Massacre in a political context in which it was so difficult to do. I can only hope that others will have similar experiences in reading these stories.

—John Michael McGuire

Hyun Kil-Un

DEAD SILENCE

And Other Stories of the Jeju Massacre

The Dream of a Dragon Horse

1

"My lord, I have come to you at this hour of night with an urgent matter."

Ho-Bang, a low-ranking government official on Jeju Island, hastily entered the room in which the governor of Jeju was coping with homesickness by drinking with a *gisaeng*. The governor was angered by Ho-Bang's rude intrusion, but instead of revealing his anger, he merely straightened himself.

"What is the matter?" the governor asked.

Ho-Bang found it difficult to speak, and his hesitation irritated the governor. Instead of coming to the point at once, Ho-Bang glanced around the room with an uncomfortable expression on his face. For the last few days a northeasterly wind mixed with sleet had troubled the governor, who was so far away from his home. He was unable to sleep with the sounds of the waves washing over the pebbles on the nearby seashore. Even the *gisaeng's* flesh, trembling in his arms at night like a repulsive serpent, made him anxious. He had nightmares on such nights.

It was through a royal favor, three years after an earlier dismissal from office, that he had become governor of Jeju, a lonely island in a remote sea. He had wondered whether this position would be a good opportunity for him or rather his final employment, but he was unable to refuse the offer. Thus he came to this island, abandoning himself to the wild wind and waves. But even after two months at his new post, he could not adjust to being on the island at all. So he soothed his lonely heart by hunting during the day and drinking with women at night.

Tonight, as usual, he warmed his heart with clear rice wine served by a *gisaeng*, and just as he was about to forestall his troublesome dreams by warming himself with her body, Ho-Bang entered without any sense of courtesy. The governor was vexed by suspicions that Ho-Bang might be spying on him or trying to prevent him from neglecting his duty through his indulgence in sensual pleasures. However, what would be the use of revealing his uneasiness to Ho-Bang if he wanted to save face? He cleared his throat while glancing at the man. He had gone through all sorts of hardships to get to Jeju Island, and before assuming this new position, he had burned his ears with the stories of the previous governors who had ruined themselves through their mishandling of the low-ranking government officials on the island.

"What kind of pressing matter has brought you here so late at night in this foul weather?"

The governor spoke in a leisurely manner in order to conceal his uneasiness.

"My lord, I know it is too late to discuss government affairs, but this is so important that it can not be delayed."

Ho-Bang was only beating around the bush. He had a secret scheme of his own. He thought that he needed to make the governor feel edgy in order to achieve his objective. Who could surpass Ho-Bang in this kind of scheming?

"Go ahead and tell me what this is all about."

Ordering the *gisaeng* to leave, the governor glanced slyly at Ho-Bang. The governor was disturbed by the thought that this man might have news of the people's judgment on his corruption and dereliction of duty. Or perhaps he had heard disturbing opinions on the governor's competence, opinions voiced by the landed gentry or the Confucian scholars on Jeju.

"Mr. Kang, a counselor of Changgonae village, in the district of Daejung, has been criticizing your handling of government affairs."

Instantly, the governor became nervous. The people of Jeju, who were known to be troublesome, would ruin him. The governor would be responsible for a revolt, regardless of its cause.

"What? Counselor Kang? Isn't he a criminal? How dare he? Only a local counselor!"

The governor shouted at Ho-Bang in a rather agitated voice. This was unusual news. He wondered how the counselor of a village, someone who was supposed to advise and support the governor, could criticize the governor's handling of government affairs. Complaints about the new governor arose a couple of months after he had assumed the position, and he did not have a good relationship with the counselors. He wondered how he could finish his tenure in this insignificant office under these conditions. When the governor thought about it, he felt dizzy, and his eyesight became hazy.

"What is it all about? Give me the details," he demanded.

"Yes, my lord, let me tell you the whole truth."

In his peculiar manner of speaking, Ho-Bang began to explain the situation to the governor.

"Counselor Kang, who lives in the village of Changgonae in Daejung, owns rice fields that produce about 2,500 bushels of rice each year; he also owns 300 cows and 200 horses. He is one of the powerful landed gentry on Jeju. He once was a counselor of Daejung, so he is fairly influential in that area. Last summer he was ordered to present, as a tribute to the king, a gift of tangerines—a total of 13,567 pieces of fruit. He was ordered to present 8,912 pieces to the king by November and the rest by the end of December. A local official was ordered to determine whether or not the November tribute had been prepared yet, but when he tried to do so he discovered, to his surprise, that about 100 tangerine trees had been cut down. It was very strange! Anyway, this accident is an obstacle to the November tribute and will certainly hinder the December tribute. Upon hearing the news, I was at a loss, not knowing what to do, but since this incident seemed to me to be a complicated affair, I came to see you, my lord, at this late hour of the night."

The governor cleared his throat a couple of times while he was listening to Ho-Bang's tedious speech. "What trivial matters," he thought. He was expecting something far more serious, so he gradually calmed down as Ho-Bang spoke.

"Are the tangerine trees dead? Have they caught some disease?" the governor asked.

Indeed, the governor had not been listening attentively to Ho-Bang's description of the accident. Thinking that Ho-Bang was trying to intimidate the new governor, as someone might intimidate a child with a story of a tiger, the governor imagined that Ho-Bang's malicious intention was to put him through his first trial on Jeju Island.

"My lord."

Ho-Bang's eyes revealed compassion for the governor. He felt pity for him, wondering how such a childlike man could maintain his position of authority on this turbulent island.

"No. The trees did not die of some disease. Counselor Kang intentionally let them wither away so that he could cut them down."

"What? Intentionally? Only an idiot would kill valuable trees!"

Ho-Bang looked at the governor with contempt in his eyes, but the governor did not seem to notice.

"My lord, you may think so, but that is only because you do not yet fully understand the situation here. Traditionally, officials from the Department of Taxation and Finance visit every house on the island around June, when the tangerine trees bear fruit, and count the number of tangerines on each tree. Later, they collect a specific quantity of tangerines to present as a tribute to the king in the winter. If an owner of a tangerine orchard does not give the predetermined quantity of tangerines, he either receives a flogging or else pays a considerable amount of money for each of the missing tangerines. You know, my lord, the trees are nourished by sunlight from the heavens and water from the earth, and yet many of those tangerines fall down naturally and others are eaten by crows or other birds. So the people here regard the raising of tangerine trees as an unfortunate occupation, and they frequently choose to kill their trees by burying poison in the ground near the base of the tree trunks. However, never in the history of Jeju Island have so many trees withered away at once. Is this not odd?"

At first the governor was surprised to hear that people received floggings or had to pay money when they were not able to provide the exact quantity of tangerines that were counted during the summer. Then he felt ashamed of himself for having spent the last two months, his entire time in office, up women's skirts. The vague thought dawned on him that harassing people might be a pleasant diversion for him in this hellish place.

Ho-Bang continued, "You may think that the manner of collecting tangerines is too harsh, but the islanders are shrewd. If we weren't harsh on them, it would be impossible to give tributes to the king. If you are too concerned with people's distress under your administration, you will end up selling your own bamboo hat."

The governor gradually got a sense of the situation, while listening to Ho-Bang. It seemed to him that Counselor Kang was insolent.

"Are you sure that he did it on purpose?" the governor yelled, startling Ho-Bang.

"From the bottom of my heart, I can say that he did it deliberately. I am telling you this because this incident should be handled very cautiously. Moreover, this is the first difficulty that you have faced since coming here, and this may be a challenge to your authority …"

Ho-Bang began to say things that would offend the governor, thinking that the governor's increasing interest in Kang was a good sign.

"What? What an impudent fool to challenge the governor's authority!"

Exploding with rage, the governor recalled the advice he had received from his friends at a farewell drinking party before departing for Jeju. They told him that Jeju is a troublesome place and that when he is there he will either become a just and wise leader or else a wicked ruler who squeezes blood from the people. They also said that if he expresses a warm attitude toward the people, he will be robbed of even his bamboo hat, be beaten by mobs, and will never make it home. He became anxious with this memory.

"Ho-Bang, make contact with the mayor of Daejung as soon as possible and inquire into the details of the incident. Isn't this a refusal to give a tribute to the King? Isn't it a failure to do one's duty?"

The governor's loud voice reverberated throughout the room.

"This is not the first time that man, Kang, has done such a thing. Once, as a former governor was passing by his house, he saw Kang's handsome horse and decided that he wanted it for a tribute to the king. However, a few days later it was reported that the horse had run away. Kang fabricated an excuse that the horse was so intelligent that it knew it would one day be shipped to the mainland. So, not wanting to leave the island, the horse ran away. Isn't that a preposterous excuse? He is rich, powerful, and trusted by the lower people around him, so he looks down on the governor and mayor. But until now all governors have overlooked this matter in one way or another because they did not want it to become any more serious than it is. However, I think the present incident should not be passed over lightly."

Ho-Bang went on speaking without discretion in order to disturb the governor's irascible mind. Soon enough, the governor was indeed upset.

"To be disloyal to me on this island is to be disloyal to the King, which is equivalent to the crime of treason. How can I tolerate it?" said the governor.

This is the first time that the governor had displayed courage since being assigned to the island. His face was filled with shame at the thought that he had been dancing to the tune of a low-ranking official and chasing women's skirts. When he now, finally, resolved to demonstrate his authority, the cold air blowing into his coat sleeves kindled a fire in his heart.

After sending Ho-Bang away, the governor was consumed with rage. He wondered how this man Kang could deliberately kill tangerine trees whose fruits had been earmarked for a tribute to the King.

He asked himself, "How could Kang be so foolish, not fearing the heavens? Is it even possible to think so little of the King's tribute? And what did he think of the governor?"

With Ho-Bang gone, the *gisaeng's* flattering smiles could no longer comfort the governor's angry mind, so he continued to empty the blameless bottles of wine.

"My lord," the *gisaeng* asked, "what's the matter with you? Why are you so pressed by business even at night?"

The governor could not calm down, so he vented his wrath on the wench.

"Why are the natives of this island so insolent?" he yelled. "How dare they do such things!"

"What's the matter?" she asked again.

She put her arms around his neck and flirted with him.

"It's humiliating to be assigned to this island. And to make matter worse, such a rat dares to challenge me ..."

Men become childlike with women. So disturbed was the governor by this situation that he wanted only to rest, even with this kind of woman. So he revealed to her everything that he had talked about with Ho-Bang.

"Oh, my Lord," she said, "you should strike such rats dumb. Islanders are by their nature so rude and wicked that you will not be able to keep the strings of your bamboo hat and the hem of your garments if things go wrong."

She even suggested that he might be discharged from his office.

"So, you say that islanders could do such harm to me?"

Recalling that Ho-Bang had said the same thing, the governor suppressed the obvious question of whether or not she too was an islander. Their words confirmed for him that islanders were crooked people.

That night the wind blew more furiously than ever, stirring up impetuous sounds from the sea, as the waves washed away the pebbles on the seashore.

2

The mayor of Daejung was upset by the governor's message, which he received early in the morning. He was on friendly terms with Counselor Kang and regularly discussed local matters with him. He himself could not control Kang, who was a sensible man in both public and private affairs. Moreover, Kang was a moral authority for the people in Daejung. To mishandle this matter would be like jumping into a fire with an oil cask on one's back. Furthermore, the people in Daejung were tough and strong-willed; they would even walk through fire once they had made up their minds to do so. Ho-Bang discussed this matter with the mayor of Daejung.

"I thought this situation was odd, but I intended to overlook it, pretending not to know about it. If the truth were revealed, wouldn't it be more troublesome to us? I could neither blame Counselor Kang nor resolve the issue, so I tried to ignore it. But now that the governor has become furious, the situation is beyond my control."

The mayor remained silent with his eyes closed, which made it difficult to judge whether or not he was listening as Ho-Bang continued to speak.

"The governor seems to be responding to this matter harshly, and I wonder whether such a response is the best way to handle the issue. Even if it were proven that Kang deliberately killed his tangerine trees, the governor would not convict him of the crime. Maybe Kang wants this situation to become more serious. It might be an opportunity for him to publicize the exploitation of islanders by public officials. The new governor has not been in his position very long and, moreover, he does not seem to be a just ruler. A rumor has spread that he indulges in drinking and buries his face in the bosom of young women every night. So how could he blame Counselor Kang for deliberately killing some trees? The real problem is the public officials who squeeze blood from people, collecting much more fruit than is necessary, on the pretext of giving tributes to the king."

The mayor frowned several times while listening to Ho-Bang, but he did not interrupt him. As a mayor and native islander of Jeju, he knew the people's sufferings and could not ignore them. Ho-Bang was quite right, and Kang was an honest official who would never take even one tangerine from the people.

"Nevertheless," said the mayor, "we are in government service, so we should deal with this matter first and discriminate what is right and wrong later. You yourself had better visit Kang and take care of this matter. I hope everything goes smoothly."

The mayor did not say any more. The situation was beyond his ability to control, and it might become worse if he tried to get involved. Kang had been a fellow student in his youth, and it was the mayor himself who recommended Kang for the office of local counselor. As mayor, he had tried to manage the district affairs as he had learned from books, and he soon discovered how difficult it was. Recently he came to regret the fact that he had entered government service.

Ho-Bang rode a horse alone to Counselor Kang's house in the village of Changgonae. The wind raging through the Daejung fields struck his cheeks. His horse hesitated several times, pulling its head back from the violent wind. Snow fluttered about in the wind, the sky became darker, and snowflakes grew larger. Sitting up straight on his horse, Ho-Bang wielded his whips, but it seemed to him that he struck his horse in vain, since this visit was not a pleasant one.

After passing Mount Sanbang, he came to a wide open plain and saw in the distance fields deeply buried in snow. But the thick forests of Changgonae were still green. The peak of Mount Goon could be seen more clearly through the snow. During his previous comings and goings, he had never paid much attention to the beauty of the natural surroundings here. Wondering why he was concerned with nature on this day, he felt a bitter taste in his mouth. He saw fields with stalks of grain standing like cottages as well as other black fields that were sown with barley seeds. It was Kang's grandfather who had cultivated this spacious plain into paddies and dry fields. The work had provided the villagers with considerable power and strength. When Kang's grandfather first moved here and settled the land, he brought several stout young men with him. The story was often told of how he had turned the wide plain below Mount Goon into rice fields by supplying it with water from Changgonae. Three generations later, Kang had become one of the richest men in Jeju. It was generally thought that the rich strive to get richer through the sweat of the poor, but Kang was different. During the spring poverty that recurred each year, he donated a substantial amount of food to the people of Daejung. Sometimes, if a poor man asked to borrow some grain, he would give it to him without any questions. A common complaint, that a rich landlady's stingy measuring of grain causes the poor people's joints to shake, had never been uttered by the women who frequented Kang's house. Furthermore, he never pressed the poor people to pay him back in the fall harvest. They paid him back if they could afford to do so; otherwise, they would work for him the following year. So the local people were more than willing to look after things in Kang's house.

Not only did Kang increase his wealth, but he also won the hearts of people in this way. He was neither arrogant with his wealth, nor a nuisance with his power. His modest way of living was a model for the people, and his servants were like his family members or relatives. But even though he was such a generous man, he was critical of public officials. None of the successive mayors of Daejung could boast in front of him due to his hidden power and authority, for he had protected the lower-ranking officials and none of the noblemen were equal to him in terms of moral stature. No one knew much about his ancestry, except that his grandfather had settled here and cultivated the land. So even though he did not belong to the noble class, everyone sensed that he was of uncommon origin because of his way of handling affairs.

Ho-Bang rode his horse slowly through the falling snow and the northeasterly wind that penetrated into the marrow of his bones. He was thinking many things while riding his horse. He even wondered whether he should continue with this visit to Kang. Maybe the incident with the tangerine trees was a deliberate act, Ho-Bang thought. From the time of Kang's father's generation, his family had grown enough trees to produce all the tangerines for the tributes to the king so that the local people would not have to give gifts with fruit from the orchards run by the government. Produce from his orchard could supply the designated amount for Daejung. However, exploitation by the public officials became increasingly worse. After the number of tangerines had been counted in the summer, all of them were regarded as belonging to the government. If the exact number were not presented, the guilty people had to pay for the missing tangerines, which were regarded as stolen property.

A man named Choi Pung once picked some tangerines from his trees in order to prepare for a ceremony to worship his ancestors. When the government officials discovered this, they flogged him as a criminal, as someone who had stolen a national treasure. There were many incidents of this sort.

"Ah, his luck has come to an end," old Ho-Bang sighed. While he was lost in thought, he arrived at Counselor Kang's house. Alongside the long walk to the house, densely planted camellias were already blooming. When he entered the big gate, a dog started to bark. A couple of strong young boys, alerted by the sound of the bell hung around Ho-Bang's horse, ran to him and greeted him with bows. Counselor Kang received Ho-Bang in a room detached from the main part of the house. In front of Kang there were some brushes, paper, and Chinese ink. Discarded paper was scattered in one corner of the room. He had been drawing orchids.

"Please come in," he said. "I knew that you would come."

Ho-Bang was surprised that the counselor had been drawing orchids, and even more surprised by his friendly disposition. They were close friends, but they were not of equal social status: Ho-Bang was a low-ranking official, while Kang was a counselor and a powerful local landlord. So, until now, they had usually addressed each other formally when they met.

"I had a dream about you, one in which you turned your back on me. So I have been thinking of you, wondering when you might come here. I've been drawing orchids, which is unusual for me."

When Kang was a child, he learned how to draw and write from a guest who stayed with his family in that detached room. However, Kang was more inclined as a child to ride horses or shoot arrows than he was to draw orchids.

They sat down together over a drinking table. As they were both over fifty years old, they had plenty of experience and were familiar with the ways of the world. Though he was the son of a rich man, Kang had never been lazy, even at this age. He would rather reread old books that he had already read several times, write, draw, or strand ropes as servants did, than waste time sucking on a long tobacco pipe while shouting commands at the servants.

After closing the door of the room, they began to drink without saying a word. Ho-Bang was not an ordinary person either. For more than ten years he had worked as an official in the district of Daejung, and he could have become wealthy by acquiring illegal income in connection with his job. However, because of his moral integrity he had remained poor. So Kang would secretly send sacks of grain and meat to him at the end of every year. Thanks to Kang, Ho-Bang had managed to keep his position while several mayors had come and gone. Kang had taken care of almost all of Ho-Bang's difficulties.

"What brought you here in this foul weather?" the counselor asked, even though he already had an idea about the reason for Ho-Bang's visit.

"I came to look at your drawings."

Ho-Bang blushed and smiled like a child as he spoke. Kang was so astonished by that innocent smile that he put down his glass and looked again at Ho-Bang's worn-out face.

"I would like to hear about your dream," Ho-Bang remarked, with a serious look on his face.

Suddenly, the fading dream vividly flashed across Kang's mind.

"It was strange. Those severed tangerine trees began to grow taller than the height of a man, and then they blossomed. But they bore no fruit and soon began to wither and die. While I was watching those sorrowful, withering trees, I saw you turning your back on me. I tried to call you, but you didn't answer me."

Finishing his story, the counselor laughed by himself.

Ho-Bang replied, "Last night a man from the governor's office came to me. The governor sent him to inquire into the incident of the withered tangerine trees …"

Although Ho-Bang tried to speak as if this were trivial matter, Kang was keen enough to sense the seriousness of the situation.

"I expected as much. A couple of stolen tangerines are grounds for a flogging, so I did not think this incident would go unnoticed. By the way …"

The counselor paused for a moment, and just as he was about to continue, Ho-Bang interjected: "I am going to quit my job."

"It would be nice if your resignation would bring a conclusion to this situation. However, if this incident brings calamity upon you …"

"Let's just drink," Ho-Bang suggested.

The two of them paused momentarily for a drink. Then the counselor continued the conversation.

"Look, report that I did it on purpose."

Ho-Bang thought about it, and then said, "I would like to know the truth."

"It is true," the counselor responded.

Ho-Bang wanted to talk about this, but he closed his mouth instead.

The counselor continued, "What's the big deal? I simply cut down my own tangerine trees! Consider this: if this incident will eventually relieve all of the suffering caused by the Jeju custom of giving tributes to the king, then I will be quite satisfied. There is nothing in this world more ridiculous than this custom. If the king came to know the truth about the tangerine gifts, I wonder whether he would even accept those tributes."

The voice of the counselor was very calm as he spoke.

Ho-Bang realized that this incident was a deliberate act by Kang. He blushed with the thought that he had worried pointlessly about whether the situation would get out of control. He acknowledged that Counselor Kang was truly an important man.

They continued to drink together as the night grew darker. When they finally parted company, the snow outside was being pushed about by the wind.

Ho-Bang was quite drunk as he mounted his horse. The counselor gave a large sum of money to the servant who led Ho-Bang's horse down the road from the house.

"Give this money to Ho-Bang's wife without letting him know about it. Let her know that it is a gift from me."

He thought that whatever might happen to Ho-Bang, his friend should not starve. Ho-Bang would soon know that this was the last expression of the counselor's generosity, for before long he would lose all of his riches. Thinking to himself as he stood outside the gate of his house, Counselor Kang watched Ho-Bang and the servant disappear in the snowy night.

3

While drinking with the *gisaeng* and holding her in his arms, the governor received the news from Ho-Bang that no deliberate intention was found in the incident of the severed tangerine trees. This brought the governor some relief.

"I think this incident is intended to make a fool of you, my lord."

Ho-Bang then tried to irritate the governor further by insisting that he could not believe the report of the mayor of Daejung. However, the governor suppressed his anger in order to think about this matter carefully.

"If they knowingly allow the tangerine trees to die on purpose, there must be some reason."

With these words, Ho-Bang cast his pitiful gaze on the governor's face for a moment, and then continued to speak.

"I hesitate to mention this, but a terrible scheme by Counselor Kang may be coiled behind this incident. After closely observing how you deal with this matter, he intends to take further action. If you treat the incident with leniency, it will be very difficult for you to collect tangerines for future tributes to the king. If you react harshly, Kang may provoke other people to join in an uprising. If the situation is made more serious in that way, the public's grievances about tributes will reach the royal court, and you may experience great troubles. To make matters worse, presenting tangerines as gifts to the king will become more difficult in the future. This situation is a delicate one. In my opinion, Kang has probably done this intentionally, expecting that you will react harshly. He's probably waiting for some punishment from you."

Ho-Bang's incessant chatter irritated the governor. However, his irritation was of no help in solving the problem. He did not know what to do.

"I will fetch Counselor Kang and talk to him myself," the governor said, as he began to sense a sinister plot bundled up in Ho-Bang's lengthy explanation.

The governor sent a man named Kwon, one of his friends, to visit Counselor Kang. He ordered Kwon to dress himself poorly and obtain some personal information about the counselor. However, after receiving Kwon's report, a couple of days later, the governor became tense. He was informed that Kang was deeply trusted not only by his neighbors, but by all of the people in the district of Daejung, that he was so influential that people would rather follow him instead of the governor if something might happen, and, moreover, that he was an extraordinary person. Kwon also claimed never to have seen a finer person, even though he had associated with plenty of people in Seoul. As for Kang's house, it too was out of the ordinary. In the first place, its appearance was majestic and its pillars were peculiar. The pillars of most private houses were cut square, but the pillars of Kang's house were like those of government buildings. However, what disturbed the governor most was that in Kang's detached living room a folding screen autographed by a man named Kim was openly displayed. Kim had been exiled to Jeju, released a couple of years ago, and then executed as a traitor. After having spent seven years in exile on Jeju, he was set free with the king's pardon and positioned as a high-ranking official in the Ministry of Education. However, only two months later, he received the death penalty for his deep involvement in a conspiracy to usurp the throne and was executed.

"It proves," said Kwon, "that Kang was closely connected with Kim. He certainly knows about Kim's death. He's probably plotting to take control of this island."

Kwon concluded his long report as if he were certain of Kang's treason.

The governor was rightfully anxious about Kwon's report, which revealed that the situation was becoming increasingly serious. Sensing that this whole thing was a challenge to his newly acquired authority, the governor became exasperated.

He dismissed Kwon and then called for Ho-Bang. He asked him about Kim and his sentence of exile.

"Yes, my Lord. Kim spent several years in Kang's house in Changgonae. However, at that time Kim was not a serious criminal. He was a learned man and skilled in calligraphy, so many people flocked to him. And he received great financial support from Kang."

After listening without any comment, the governor sent Ho-Bang away. Everything was becoming clear. The governor decided to find a more serious offense committed by Kang, something more serious than the deliberate killing of tangerine trees. Through this scheme, he wanted to display his authority and to bring about a complete resolution of the situation.

He summoned Kwon once again.

"My lord, feel at ease," Kwon began. "I have a way to deal with this matter. If you are going to flog or fine Kang for cutting down the tangerine trees, you may disgrace yourself by falling into a trap set by those cunning people, so allow the situation to unfold in this way."

Kwon then whispered something into the governor's ear. The governor's eyes glared for a moment, and then he nodded in agreement.

A few days later, a strange rumor went around Daejung that the site of Counselor Kang's house belonged to royalty. Those who heard this rumor turned pale, but nevertheless helped spread the rumor further. When it finally reached the mayor, he called Ho-Bang in to hear the whole story.

"How on earth could the site of Counselor Kang's house belong to kings and princes?" asked the mayor.

Ho-Bang closed his eyes and did not answer at all.

The rumor then made its way to the governor. Pretending not to know about it, the governor summoned the mayor of Daejung.

"What an outrageous rumor! Have you ever heard this kind of story before?" the governor asked.

"Yes, my lord, it's an old story. The place called Dragon Head, below Mount Sanbang, was the site designated for future royalty and thus deliberately ruined by a Chinese man named Go Jong-Dal. Such stories are scandalous."

The mayor looked perplexed as he spoke.

"Then let's think about it," the governor said. "His family settled in Changgonae only three generations ago. How did they become so prosperous? Moreover, they say that Kang is an extraordinary person and that even his servants are outstanding in their appearance. There must be some reason for that."

The governor's question seemed reasonable.

"Furthermore, he had been very close with Kim while he was in exile, and people say that he proudly displays the folded screen on which Kim had painted. By doing that, doesn't he intend to say something to those who frequent that detached living room?"

The mayor of Daejung merely listened to the governor, afraid of what might happen next.

That evening, Ho-Bang secretly visited Counselor Kang. A young man who was sweeping the snow in the yard saw Ho-Bang approaching and quickly went into the house. After a while, he came out and led Ho-Bang into the detached room.

"He wants you to wait for him for a moment."

A short time later, Ho-Bang was instructed to enter. When he came into the main wing of the house, Kang was waiting for him on the floor. The two men sat for a while, face to face, without saying anything. Then Kang spoke first.

"The snow is likely to pile up quite high."

"This year's snow came earlier than last year," Ho-Bang answered.

After another brief silence, Kang said, "I am sorry to make you worried."

Ho-Bang could not understand what he was talking about.

"I know all about the rumor going around in the town. I have already prepared myself for the consequences. I am ready to let my servants leave."

Ho-Bang was not expecting this.

Kang continued, "I know what's going to happen to me. I made an earnest request to the men in the house. I also asked the head of the villagers to behave prudently and refrain from any rash acts. I do not want innocent people to suffer if things go badly. I know that many men in the past incited innocent people into political turmoil in order to satisfy their own desires. However, whatever great goals they might have, if the cause is not for the benefit of the people, it is a serious crime. Making fools of ignorant people and stirring them up in the name of false righteousness are crimes. So I decided to give all of my servants their identification documents and to set them free with some money or sacks of rice. I told them that if they lead a diligent and honest life, hidden away on some mountain, they will find a way to live on. Thanks to them I was able to make a considerable fortune."

Kang's words gradually made sense to Ho-Bang.

"I already told my family what to do, and to not be upset, whatever may happen."

A drinking table was set up and brought in.

"Let's drink. This may be our last chance to do so. So let's just drink without talking," said Kang.

He poured the wine into Ho-Bang's cup, but he himself did not swallow it.

The two men exchanged cups without any talk.

As he gave Ho-Bang the last cup, the counselor said, "Ho-Bang, I have a favor to ask of you. It's about my second son. He's got a temper. I'm worried about what will become of him if anything happens. I want to send him far away or have you take care of him. You may provide him with a learned tutor and teach him to be detached from things in the world. It won't be easy."

Ho-Bang nodded, and without revealing his thoughts, he left the house. As usual, despite the falling snow, the counselor stood at the top of the road to his house until he could no longer hear the ringing of the bell hung around the neck of Ho-Bang's horse. Then he returned to the house. In the front yard, about twenty young servants wept as they gave their final bows to the counselor. With heavy bags on their shoulders, they sobbed as they lay prostrate in the snow-covered yard.

"Leave this house as soon as possible. No one can predict what will happen to me next. Wherever you go, take care of yourselves and live with diligence and kindness. A better world will open up to you."

Counselor Kang then entered the main room of the house and locked the door behind him. Snow fell silently on the backs of the young servants as they continued to cry.

4

A little while later, another rumor about Counselor Kang of Changgonae was spread. Now it was said that he had wings under his arms. More and more stories were added as the rumor passed from one person to the next. They said that the wings had been growing since his early childhood, that his father had raised him with the wings hidden from people's sight, and that Kang had also hid them, waiting for his chance to change the world. The rumor itself seemed to acquire wings as it spread. The governor and the local officials would not take any measures against the rumor, so they pretended not to know about it. The mayor of Daejung and Ho-Bang were the only ones who were distressed by the rumor, and yet there was nothing they could do about it. So they too pretended not to know about it.

The rumor had almost been accepted as truth when the governor officially raised a question about Counselor Kang to the six low-ranking officials of Jeju Island.

"I was informed of the outrageous rumors about Counselor Kang in Changgonae. Are these rumors true?"

No one denied them.

"Do you have any suggestions about how to deal with him?" the governor asked.

Ho-Bang came to admire the governor's composure at this time. When he recalled that after having been absent from the Machiavellian world of government for three years this man was capable of returning to public service as the governor of Jeju, Ho-Bang felt ashamed for having once thought so poorly of him.

"Yes, my lord. It is right that the national law punish him."

All of the low-ranking officials gathered there agreed with this, feeling a sense of shame for their negligence.

"We have often heard such stories on this island—that children with wings were hidden from the local government," one of the officials said.

The officials were seeking loopholes. Whether or not they acknowledged the truth in the rumors about the counselor, they felt responsible for the matter, since they were natives of the island and were paid by the government.

That night, Counselor Kang was arrested and, under tight security, tried for a grave offense. As flames from firewood in the front yard of the local government building darted their tongues toward the heavens, the governor tried Kang, who was already half-dead at that point, for his offense. The trial was held in the presence of the local ministers and the six low-ranking officials. Those who had gathered around were startled at the governor's sonorous voice and Kang's screaming as he was flogged. It seemed as if they themselves were on trial since they too felt responsible for Kang's crime.

"You villain, how dare you plot to overturn the country? Do you not know the gravity of your crime?" the governor yelled.

"I have not committed a crime," Kang responded.

"You liar! Is it with no shame that you seek to usurp the throne?"

The flames from the fire carried the governor's loud voice to the stars in that dark night.

"I never tried to usurp the throne. How could I have even thought of it? Those rumors were fabricated. It's scandalous! Somebody deliberately made up those stories and spread them."

Counselor Kang plainly knew that such an explanation would be useless, but he tried his best to disclose the truth.

"You scoundrel, you have won over people's hearts by giving them food for free, devised a wicked plot to instigate them, tried to extend your power by means of bribing poor officials, and plotted a villainous scheme to seize this island on which the king's abundant favor has been bestowed. I know all about these plans. How dare you wag your tongue at me? It is right that you be punished according to the national laws for a heinous felony, and yet I gave you the chance to admit your own faults and to reform yourself as one of the king's faithful people. But far from repenting your sin, you dare to spew such disloyal words ..."

The governor pretended to tremble as if he could not tolerate Kang. If he beheaded him now, that would conclude the situation. But the governor continued the trial for the additional purpose of demonstrating his authority in front of the people of Jeju. The governor thought that he had no choice but to be a tyrant from now on. He was sure that the attitude of the islanders toward him would change after they witnessed him punishing this man.

"You villain, won't you tell the truth?" the governor stormed at him with an angry glare.

"I am innocent. Kill me as quickly as possible," Kang replied in a deep, quiet voice.

"You rat! This has not been enough for you. Until this villain confesses more of the truth ..."

Hot iron prongs were then inserted into Kang's shins.

"They are not hot enough. Make them hotter!" Kang shouted.

The guards with the iron prongs in their hands hesitated. The governor too was startled. While smoke with the smell of burning flesh came off his shins, Kang remained composed, staring fiercely at the governor.

"What a wretched villain!"

The governor suddenly stood up from his seat and was about to charge at him, but just then he was taken aback by Kang's keen glare. They were dreadful eyes indeed.

"You villain, how dare you glare at me? I was appointed as governor by the king's command. I am a representative of the king, and my order is the king's order. At whom do you think you are staring? What a disloyal villain you are, an utter scoundrel!"

Suddenly the governor's face became distorted as Kang spoke.

"I know all about your deceitful scheme. This is my last request. All you have to do to become a loyal servant to the king is to bestow the king's mercy on this island. Ask the islanders whether any of them are grateful for the king's favor. Man is destined to die, so I am not afraid of my death. But I am sorry for the people of this island who will live in hunger until the end of their lives."

Kang's quiet voice frightened the people who were gathered in the yard of that government building.

"What a disloyal scoundrel! How dare you ..."

The governor emphasized the word "disloyal." His red eyes were bloodthirsty, and yet he did not know what to do. Again the hot prongs began to dance on Kang's thighs, and smoke from his burnt flesh spread through the air. It moved over the floor of the government building, under the tiles of its roof, into the rafters, under the stone steps, into the clothing and, finally, the nostrils of those who were gathered there.

5

After the execution of Counselor Kang of Changgonae, the local government officials confiscated his fortune, and his family members became slaves in the district of Daejung.

A little while later, another strange rumor began to spread. One night Counselor Kang's second son, riding on a swift dragon horse, appeared in front of the family house, wailed toward the heavens, and then disappeared. Some said that the dragon horse with the second son on it ascended into the heavens and soon would descend. Others said that they saw with their own eyes the second son return as a general, riding on a dragon horse. They added that Counselor Kang was in fact a general with wings, that the site of his house had been destined for a royal birth, that his death was caused by his untimely birth, and that someday his son would return on a dragon horse in order to fulfill his father's unrealized destiny. The story went on in this way. The guards who were watching over Kang's house saw these things with their own eyes. And people nearby could hear, but not see, the soldiers being disciplined every night. Some said the voices of the soldiers were actually those of the young men who used to work as Kang's servants before the incident of the tangerine trees. Others said that the governor stayed one night in the house and that, upon waking up to the sounds of the soldiers being disciplined, he saw the second son on a dragon horse, and took flight for his life.

People in Changgonae, whether in groups or in pairs, talked about the story of the dragon horse in secret excitement. They came to regard the story as fact, and remembered Counselor Kang waiting for a general on a dragon horse.

The Dawn

1

"We're almost there."

Faintly hearing an unfamiliar voice in his sleep, Ji-Hyok opened his eyes. A low ceiling blocked his view. Looking to his right and left, he saw people lying close to each other. He wondered whether he was still in that narrow prison cell. Then he heard the sounds of an engine and waves. Suddenly he remembered having boarded a ship in Busan the previous afternoon. He also remembered getting out of the red brick house in Incheon, leaving his companions, and enduring the heat and hunger as he traveled down to Busan by himself. His heart began to beat with joy—now he was free, alone, completely unfettered. He was relieved by the fact that the deadly situation that had been weighing on him suddenly turned out to be a dream. Ji-Hyok stood up while those around him were still sleeping soundly. They were scattered about on the floor of the third-class passenger quarters. Just then, a middle-aged man near an exit asked a young man entering the room about the situation outside.

"You can see the island," he answered.

Ji-Hyok was pleased to hear the familiar sounds of the local dialect—they reminded him of his uncle's voice. He was also pleased to hear that he was close to the island. He headed for the exit, leaping with big strides over the people lying on the floor.

"The sea is rough," said the young man standing in front of the exit.

The young man inspected Ji-Hyok's appearance and tried to persuade him from going outside, but Ji-Hyok ignored this advice and exited the room. The sound of the waves rang in his ears, shaking the dark space. The slightly bent upper part of his body was being pushed about in all directions by the strong wind. Though it was the middle of summer, his whole body shivered with the cold air coming from the sea at dawn. Turning his face away from the wind, he clumsily mounted each step of the stairs that led to the upper deck, where the wind blew even more violently. Deck lamps whose brightness seemed to be fading with the wind guarded a lonely flagpole that soared high up into the air. Sailing on the rolling sea, with the front of the boat bobbing up and down, the ferry cut through the white waves like the teeth of a beast. Ji-Hyok couldn't see the island yet.

"It's dangerous to be here. We have one more hour before we reach the island."

Ji-Hyok turned back on hearing a young man's voice behind him. The man was advancing toward him, step by step, remaining upright by clutching an iron rope. Ji-Hyok thought he had seen the man once before, but he could not remember him clearly. Thinking that this man might know who he was, Ji-Hyok was on his guard. He didn't like it when others remembered him. Perhaps he and the man had seen each other once or twice while waiting for the ferry at the quay in Busan. Whereas other people were panic-stricken by the news of war, Ji-Hyok was happy, for he had just been released from prison. While waiting for the ferry at the quay, he had felt as though he were embarking on an exciting trip.

"You're lucky to have gotten on the ferry. People are clamoring to get back home. By the way, I was told that you're from Seoul. Do you know what has become of the war?"

Ji-Hyok was not interested in the man's question. Instead, he thought to himself,

"War? Yes, a war has broken out. That is why the prison gates were been opened and why I was set free. War can liberate people, and it can also excite them, but it's like gambling—the outcome can be known only after it's all over. Why do people engage in such unpredictable wars at all? The muzzle of a gun has no clear purpose."

"Are you from Busan? Or did you go to school in Seoul and then return home?"

The young man asked these questions tenaciously. Ji-Hyok, who had already begun to think about himself, remembered how, as a student, he would return home by boat. He looked at the young man and then turned toward the sea. He recalled the faces of the people who had been released from prison with him.

"Where are they now?" he wondered. "And what are they doing? They're probably carrying guns and running around the country as 'heroes fighting for the liberation of the Fatherland.'"

"Living on an island wouldn't be so bad if you didn't have to take a boat to get home," the young man shouted, trying hard to keep his balance as the boat rocked violently.

To Ji-Hyok the young man's words sounded like the wind.

"Taking a boat is a death-defying adventure. What distress! You should be careful, since it will be another hour or so before we arrive at the Island."

As he could not get any response from Ji-Hyok, the young man went back down the stairs. His warning of danger did not get Ji-Hyok's attention. Ji-Hyok had experienced countless crises and lived as if to scorn those moments. He would not be afraid even if the waves capsized the boat. He was at peace and free. Could a mere boat on the vast sea really make him feel so free and comfortable? Suddenly he remembered that on his way home during every vacation he would climb up onto the deck to relieve himself from seasickness and be glad to see the vague outline of the island. Yes, now was such a moment. He was even more delighted and happier than at those times in the past. When he turned thirteen, his grandfather had sent him away from the island to K city on the mainland in order to get an education. His grandfather, who was rich but illiterate, always wanted to look noble to others, so he counted on his first grandson. Though Korea was ruled by Japan, Ji-Hyok had learned *hanja*, the Chinese script, from a private tutor in a separate room of their house before he entered elementary school. By the time he entered elementary school, his grandfather had expected much of him. The old man always asked his young grandson to live up to his expectations for the honor of the family. The boy had carried this burden since the age of four, when he read words to his private tutor and then proudly recited them to the old man.

As a student in K city, Ji-Hyok increasingly felt the weight of this burden that he couldn't bear. He felt it acutely when he returned home with a heavy heart on his first vacation and met his family. He felt the role of the eldest grandson to be too much for him. He could not have his own way in anything, even in the choice of food. For his grandfather's sake he had to take traditional Korean restoratives, which he did not want, and his manner of greeting people had to please his grandfather. Outwardly he accepted his grandfather's standards, but inwardly he hated them. He felt suffocated by them. Nevertheless, he was always delighted and sometimes excited to see Mount Halla. It was the first thing he saw from the ship on his way home every vacation. But the excitement that he had felt in the past could not compare to what he was experiencing this time.

The sea that had been overwhelmed with darkness began to reveal its features. The eastern sky slowly separated from the sea as day began to break. The dim outline of the island, surrounded by a light fog, appeared in the distance. The mountain that now revealed itself to his eyes was the only thing this island has. The mountain! He had once buried his vain desires in that mountain. Gradually his eyes became misty, for the happy memories of his birthplace had all been blown away. He once had been in the grip of a mysterious power, an intense flame. In retrospect, it was not something that he had chosen—just as it had not been his own choice to study in K city.

2

From the time that he entered middle school in K city, Ji-Hyok had felt stifled; his life unfolded independently of his own volition. Moreover, the desolate atmosphere near the end of the Japanese Occupation made his situation even more unbearable. As a means of escape, he neglected his studies and immersed himself in reading other books. When he received unusually low grades in his first year of middle school, he was severely scolded by his grandfather. But during these times, when no one could predict what would happen the next day, the grandfather did not worry about his grandson too much. Korea was then liberated from Japan, giving Ji-Hyok a chance to make a new start.

Before long he turned into a model student. After Liberation, students and teachers regarded his exceptional behavior with curiosity. His friends asked him to discard the remnants of the Japanese rule at school, but he sternly refused. Indeed, he had no opinion on that matter, and he wasn't interested in it. He turned his face away from such issues and observed with scorn the changes taking place at the school. He was absent from his classes almost every day, buried among books in his lodging house. Occasionally, in the early fall, he would go for walks at the school, ridiculing people who tried to behave wisely in this whirlwind of history, and thinking that the books he read were his only guides in this situation.

Around that time Ji-Hyok came to know his history teacher, Mr. Song Gwang-Cheon, who had been hired in the fall right after the Liberation. Song was said to have hidden himself in the mountains in order to evade military service under the Japanese rule. Other rumors were also spread about him.

One day Song, who came from an influential family in K city, invited Ji-Hyok over to his house. Ji-Hyok was overwhelmed by the size of the house. Ji-Hyok's family owned a considerable amount of land, and because of their diligence and frugality, the family was considered by the other villagers to be rather rich. But the size of his own house was nothing in comparison to Mr. Song's.

That night, Song treated Ji-Hyok to a large dinner and lent him some of his books.

"Behave cautiously!" Mr. Song said. "We will not achieve independence simply by shouting. We must have the strength to fight. When have we had the chance to acquire that sort of strength? All of those who are excitedly raising their voices, introducing themselves as patriots—they're all fakes. They lack the ideas that are needed in order to carry out a revolution. So we don't know to whom we may sell our country again."

Mr. Song talked about many things that seemed difficult for Ji-Hyok to understand, but he had never heard such powerful words, and they left a deep impression on him.

From that day on, Ji-Hyok read avidly and rarely went to school. He spent the winter that way, alone in his lodgings. Those books, which he read out of intellectual curiosity, made him a young thinker.

Strangely, things that had nothing to do with Ji-Hyok's volition kept happening. At school there were many incidents: students were frequently going on strike, and the police were bringing teachers and students to the police station for interrogation. There were no significant political changes, but general confusion was increasing. Ji-Hyok did not want to be involved in these situations, so he spent his time alone, reading books in the lodging house.

One day Ji-Hyok was summoned to school by Mr. Choi, the teacher in charge of his class. Ji-Hyok was not the kind of student who would go to school just because his teacher ordered him to do so. However, the situation with Mr. Choi was a little different. There was a rumor that Choi had been dispatched by a radical right-wing organization in order to shatter the communist influence lurking in the school. Mr. Choi was not an open-minded person, and the students were afraid of him. He was as stout as a high-ranking Judo expert and handsome too. His eloquent lectures fascinated the students, but he was too self-righteous. He was the son of a well-known and wealthy family in one of the provinces in North Korea, but the family fortunes had been confiscated when the communists came to power. Mr. Choi was the only one from his family who managed to cross the border into South Korea, so he was strongly opposed to the communists.

Ji-Hyok did not go to school when he was summoned. He thought Mr. Choi would ask him about his absence, and he did not want to make clumsy excuses about it. But one day, just as he was finishing his dinner at his lodging house, he had an unexpected visit from a couple of strong young men. They were the key members of a right-wing organization in K city. They turned his room upside down, confiscated several books that he was reading, and ordered him to leave with them. He followed them obediently.

After three days Ji-Hyok was released. He had managed to endure the horrible suffering he experienced at their hands by remaining mostly silent, except, when he was forced to speak. The men repeatedly asked him where he had gotten the books that he was reading, but Ji-Hyok never mentioned Mr. Song. Eventually he lied, saying that a relative in Japan had sent them to him before Liberation.

Shortly thereafter Ji-Hyok was stigmatized as a communist sympathizer, and Mr. Choi summoned him again. At the time, Ji-Hyok was hiding out in his lodging house, occupied with thoughts of those nightmarish days. He was falling into a boundless indolence and felt a sense of futility, thinking that he would never be able to make his own choice in this world. Even though he did not feel well enough to walk, he went to see his teacher, for he was afraid that something might happen to him again.

"Don't be swept away by vain intellectual curiosity. You should understand the world with a sober mind or you may ruin yourself. This is a chance for you to break ties with them. I know everything about this incident but I will overlook it."

Mr. Choi spoke kindly to Ji-Hyok, but also gave him a stern warning, which left him feeling somewhat annoyed.

Ji-Hyok replied: "Have I done something wrong? What's wrong with reading books that I want to read? I don't understand."

"Are you going to deceive me? I know where you got those books. Do you think those books can save you? This is my last warning: you are being manipulated. It's not your choice to make. You must return to your senses."

That was the end of his encounter with Mr. Choi. A couple of days later, he was invited to dinner by Mr. Song. A sumptuous meal was served, and there were some familiar faces at the table that night.

"Well, let's have dinner together to console Baek Ji-Hyok, who suffered for several days," Song said, with a gentle look, to all those gathered at the table. As the delightful meal began, everyone comforted Ji-Hyok.

"Iron should be placed in fire to become strong. You should be disciplined through suffering in order to do great work in the future. So be courageous rather than pliant."

Song's encouraging words were followed by consolations from his friends. It had been a long time since Ji-Hyok felt warmth from people. Having lived such a dreary and lonesome life, he was touched by these people. They seemed like old friends to him, and he compared this meeting to the one with Mr. Choi.

Ji-Hyok continued to skip school, and his aversion toward Mr. Choi grew stronger. A rumor spread that it was Mr. Choi who had sent the young men from that right-wing organization to scare Ji-Hyok.

Then another big incident occurred at the school. In the middle of the night, Mr. Choi was terrorized. Three masked youths attacked him while he was sleeping in his lodging house. There were fisticuffs and Mr. Choi suffered several blows with iron hammers. He struggled against the assailants for his life and barely managed to survive. Ji-Hyok, who didn't know about the incident, later received a notice from Mr. Song that he should leave K city, so he slipped out of the city early one morning and went to the countryside.

A couple of days after that Ji-Hyok came to learn about the incident concerning Mr. Choi. He was surprised that the police wanted to arrest him for leading the attack, but it was already water under the bridge. With Mr. Song's help, he hid himself in a temple. In doing so, Ji-Hyok found that he had become inextricably linked to Song. He remembered what Mr. Choi had said to him, but he felt that he could not betray Mr. Song.

One year passed in this way. Ji-Hyok had already been expelled from school, and could not freely move about. In the quiet mountain temple, he tried again to read the books that he had once pushed aside, but he could not concentrate on them as much as he used to. He suffered from bad sleep due to disturbing thoughts, and yet there was nothing he could do about it. He waited for a turning point, a way out of this tedium.

One day a middle-aged woman came to see him with a message from Mr. Song. She told him about the situation in K city: Mr. Choi had left the hospital and had a strong hatred toward Ji-Hyok. In her detailed story, she first expressed concern about the future of Korea, but then revealed her true colors. She said that she had struggled in the underground movement during the Japanese Occupation. Ji-Hyok stayed up the whole night listening to the vicissitudes of her life and thinking about what he should do.

Before dawn, Ji-Hyok left the temple to go to K city with the woman. There he stayed in her house and served as her errand boy. She was running a meat factory and, to his surprise, she provided meat to right-wing organizations, the military, and the police. At the same time, she collected all kinds of information from them. Many of her employees were so-called revolutionary combatants. Ji-Hyok worked in the daytime and was indoctrinated at night. The books that he had read up until then became textbooks for reestablishing the basis of his thoughts; he now came to understand them from a new perspective. When obscure theories were applied to the structures of reality, they came alive with clearer meanings, and were strongly impressed on him, not as knowledge, but as living powers. Ji-Hyok felt that he had been transformed into a new being and thus experienced a strange joy. After staying in the woman's house for two months, he met Mr. Song again.

"I appreciate your work. The time is near when your pains will be rewarded. Go to your birthplace, Jeju Island, where the time for insurrection is ripening. But there will be more than just an insurrection; there will be a great opportunity for a revolution throughout Korea. For that purpose, we need a comrade who will be in charge of ideological education on Jeju. Go and work there to your heart's content. You will have ideal conditions in which to work."

With those words of encouragement, Ji-Hyok traveled to Mokpo that evening and, the next night, took a ferry to Jeju. While on the boat, he experienced emotions that he had never felt before. On the one hand, he thought this would be a way to honor his family, as his grandfather had always commanded him to do. On the other hand, he criticized himself ruthlessly, for he found within himself the bourgeois sentiments that were contrary to the logic of the revolution.

* * *

The outline of the island became increasingly clearer. People with swollen faces due to light sleep came up to the deck and looked toward the island in the distance. Strangely, Ji-Hyok could not feel any excitement. His heart was as calm as the sea in mild weather. The feeling he had at that moment was totally different from the one he had while entertaining revolutionary thoughts. He wondered about the cause of this change of heart.

Those gathered on the deck went back down to the passengers' quarters to collect their baggage. The aggressive faces that had been in a hurry to board the ferry at the quay in Busan now looked so pure and innocent. Ji-Hyok wondered if people could look so different just by being close to their birthplace.

"The island is so quiet, but the mainland is in such turmoil."

"But Jeju has already suffered from the Insurrection. It's suffered like a child with the measles. The Insurrection was even more tumultuous than the war on the mainland."

People talked like this as they watched the approaching island. Listening casually to their conversation, Ji-Hyok became nervous.

"The Insurrection is a thing of the past, isn't it?" he wondered to himself.

"Since war has broken out on the mainland, there may be another uproar on the island. They say there are still communist guerrillas on Mount Halla."

"Are there many of them? How could they survive?"

"The guerrillas already have information about the war and will soon go wild, like a pack of mad dogs. The right-wing government may rashly launch another attack on the guerillas. On the mainland, those who were suspected of treason on ideological grounds have already been arrested and are now being interrogated."

Ji-Hyok did not have much interest in their conversation.

3

What he had done on the island seemed to him now like child's play. He had realized too late that he could not be a leader for such a task. Unwittingly, he had become a key member of the communist revolution, although he was too young to bear its enormous consequences. His desires and wishes were but fires, swept over dry fields by the unimpeded wind.

After returning home from K city, he took advantage of his weak, pale appearance by spreading a rumor that he was on a leave of absence due to illness. He felt sorry for the elders who were so worried about him, but for the sake of the great task ahead he had to ignore those feelings. He spent two days at home and was hospitalized in the Namgook Clinic in the town of Namdo. A Dr. Yang Jae-Sung of that clinic had already been recruited as a cell member. As a student, Dr. Yang had left college because of tuberculosis. While he was lost in a dungeon of despair, he came into contact with the revolutionary theories of communism, and acquired courage and affection for his decaying body. First, he taught himself to be a doctor in order to overcome his own illness. With his health restored and having attained an affluent lifestyle, his ideological commitment grew weaker; he hesitated to participate in revolutionary struggles and began to doubt the success of a revolution. The Communist Party therefore appointed Ji-Hyok to be his ideological instructor and sent him to Jeju to command and strengthen the left-wing student organizations there.

At that time, Jeju Island was panic-stricken by the shortage of food due to successive bad harvests and the waves of immigrants returning from Japan. Furthermore, small businessmen or those who served as government officials under the Japanese rule held most of the economic power. After liberation from Japan, young people began returning home from the mainland and started a popular movement for the transformation of the island. The islanders, who had been always exploited by alien powers, thought that the time had come to search for the means of self-survival. The Communist Party ordered its members to take advantage of this opportunity and use it for its own ideological purposes. Their strategy was to turn the longings for existence, latent in the popular consciousness, and the instinctive desires for survival into political consciousness, and to then use that consciousness to spark the revolution. Thus Ji-Hyok was dispatched to Jeju as the Party realized that the people would need an ideological education in order to develop the will for reformation.

During the day Ji-Hyok pretended to be a tuberculosis patient. Because he was hospitalized as a patient with third-degree tuberculosis, visitors to his ward were strictly regulated. Only the doctor, nurses, and his relatives could visit him. The clinic had about ten wards and only a few patients. Since tuberculosis was generally considered to be life threatening, Ji-Hyok was quarantined in one ward.

During the day, he gave private tutoring to students who disguised themselves as visitors. The tutoring time did not go beyond thirty minutes. He confirmed each student's preassigned task, examined and evaluated the work that was already carried out, and then gave new orders. In addition, he indoctrinated those students, including Dr. Yang, whose ideological commitment had grown weak.

He was excited about what he was doing. It was the first time in his life that he had totally given himself to a cause. He had some experience of staying up all night to pass the entrance examination for middle school, but that was for the sake of his grandfather, who had spent his nights coughing, worrying over his grandson's studies. For Ji-Hyok, those experiences were neither interesting nor were they expressions of his own will.

Early in the morning of April 3, 1948, Jeju Island was turned upside down. Cell members who had penetrated organizations or administrative offices had begun a planned insurrection. The police stations in each town were raided, and the former government officials under the Japanese rule, the objects of popular enmity, were ruthlessly terrorized. There had in fact been a secret plan to take over each government office peacefully, but because the information had been leaked in advance by a couple of betrayers, the situation necessarily turned violent.

"Our undertaking has ended in success. Thirteen police stations and substations on this island were attacked by our comrades, and seventeen vicious reactionaries were executed," Dr. Yang reported to Ji-Hyok in an excited voice.

But Ji-Hyok was not so enthusiastic about the doctor's confident report. Instead, he asked,

"Do you think the result of this undertaking will help liberate the Island?"

Even though Ji-Hyok himself often emphasized the need to struggle, he always felt strange when he heard that people had been killed and fires had been set.

"We cannot expect to carry out a revolution without spilling blood," Dr. Yang replied.

Ji-Hyok's heart was shaken by the doctor's sullen response. A fear came over him that while the revolution was intended for the happiness of the people many people would be sacrificed, unwillingly swept up in its vortex. He had emphasized in his teachings that this is a weak point of the revolutionary ideology, one that should be guarded against for the success of revolution. Now that he himself was in the center of the affair, an unbearable conflict arose in his mind.

"I need to observe the state of things with my own eyes. We may have to revise our strategy," Ji-Hyok announced.

Dr. Yang became suspicious of Ji-Hyok's remark, for this was not his responsibility: Ji-Hyok's duty was only to teach students.

"Please arrange for me to go back home today or tomorrow. I want to see what's happening for myself."

"It would be too dangerous," Dr. Yang replied. "Everything has been carried out as planned. The revolution has already begun and it cannot be contained by the strength of a few people. What we have to do now is entrust everything to history."

Ji-Hyok sensed self-scorn in the doctor's words.

"Do not start a new course of action. You must deliberate on how to conduct yourself. You cannot live long pretending to be a patient. If another doctor were to appear right now, everything would be exposed. Neither I nor this clinic is safe."

With these blunt remarks and without finishing the conversation, the doctor left the room. Instantly, Ji-Hyok recalled Mr. Song. Whenever something big happened, Mr. Song would order him to leave from wherever he was staying and go to another place. So Ji-Hyok thought it was time for him to leave the clinic.

That night, Ji-Hyok slipped out of the clinic and returned home. He was thin and sickly looking.

The state of affairs at his birthplace was far worse than that in the town. Left-wing activists had raided the police substation in the village, set it on fire, and killed three police officers. The family members of the chief of the village had been stabbed to death with iron spears. The villagers who visited Ji-Hyok spoke with fearful sighs about the state of things around them.

"What will become of the current situation? Things that have never happened before are happening now. How can we relax?"

"It is understandable that someone might want to attack the chief of the village, but what have the members of his family done? Even young children, younger than ten years old, were killed."

"A policeman was stabbed to death with iron spears and his corpse was burned with gasoline. How can human beings be so vicious?"

"I was expecting a happy life after Liberation, but what will happen in the current situation?"

Whenever people gathered together, they worried about the 4.3 Incident. Their faces were constantly clouded by dark fears.

The Incident did not end with the attack by the communists. With blood in their eyes, the police began to search for the communists. After the attack, some educated young men in Namdo were summoned to the police substations, almost beaten to death, and then released. Both the communists and anticommunists became fearful. And since Namdo, a village on the seashore with a police station and a village office, was deeply rooted in governmental culture, the villagers were very bitter about the Incident. After witnessing these circumstances, Ji-Hyok became anxious.

Ji-Hyok was told about the current sentiments and the present circumstances by Ko Sang-Ho, who was in charge of cell members of Namdo Middle School. He was the most enthusiastic of those who had been indoctrinated by Ji-Hyok. As Dr. Yang had said, these things were not part of Ji-Hyok's duty. Nevertheless, Ji-Hyok wanted to be involved in matters beyond his own responsibility. He immediately perceived the complexity of the situation by the anxiety evident in his family members' daily conversations. The government and the police had begun rounding up communist sympathizers on a large scale. After the identities of the cell members who were hiding in governmental offices were disclosed, their underground organization collapsed. At that time, the primary task of the Communist Party was to hinder the establishment of an independent government in South Korea. For that purpose, the Party ordered its members to use concrete strategies, such as terrorizing right-wing officials or raiding public buildings. Administrative officials responded by dividing residents into two groups, the right and the left, according to their ideological inclination. Based on that division, those whose ideological disposition was not clear were categorized as wobblers. Wobblers were those who had the possibility of turning red someday or those who had already begun to turn red without revealing it. Under these circumstances, those who were not much interested in political matters suffered great hardships. Moreover, educated people were forced to choose between the political left or right.

It was two weeks before the election of May 10, 1948. The Communist Party in North Korea judged that given the political consciousness of ordinary citizens it would be difficult for the communist sympathizers in South Korea to prevent the election. The slogan that a democracy would be established in South Korea seemed appealing to most citizens. That the establishment of an independent government in South Korea would permanently divide Korea into two countries was not a justifiable reason to refuse to vote. Only the educated few, those who had a deep understanding of politics, would be concerned with the possibility of a divided country. Under these circumstances, the best way to resist was to interfere with the election. As the election approached, confusion grew worse, and attempts by different groups to control each other made Korean society combative. Ji-Hyok was secretly concerned about this situation, but in reality he did not have the guts even to wring the neck of a chicken. In his teachings, he had emphasized that a proletariat revolution could be achieved only through struggles, but those teachings were not reflected in the way he lived his life.

In the middle of one night Ko Sang-Ho came to see him.

"You have to escape from this place," Sang-Ho urged.

Ji-Hyok thought that something was about to happen.

"Dr. Yang of Namgook Clinic was taken away by the police. The Party ordered us to go to the mountains."

Sang-Ho explained that since Dr. Yang was arrested, it would be just a matter of time before he confessed everything. The Party judged that being alone for long would not be good for the revolutionary task. He added that cell members hiding in various organizations or schools were also ordered to the mountains and that the Party had decided that now was the time for all of them to fight with arms.

"Probably on election day, or the day before, there will be another insurrection on the island."

On hearing this, Ji-Hyok had strange feelings. He guessed that the original plan had reached a dead end or that the Party would criticize what he had achieved. And yet, on reflection, there was nothing to criticize. The present situation did weigh on his mind, and he had some doubts about the revolution. But his conscience was clear, for whenever doubts about the revolution had occurred to him in the past, he had severely scolded himself.

Seeing her son change into work clothes and collect his belongings hurriedly, his mother alerted the other family members. His grandfather came to his room with a pale look on his face. After a while, he said a few words to Ji-Hyok, who at that point had no concern for other people or things.

"Whatever may happen to you, you have to survive. There is nothing more precious than life," said the grandfather.

He then went into his own room and returned promptly with some money and personal treasures, giving them to Ji-Hyok.

"Use them if it is necessary to exchange something for your life. Money or gold may not be needed, but you never know what may happen in this world."

With this advice, he asked his daughter-in-law to make a money belt for Ji-Hyok to wear around his waist.

As he walked into the dark night, unable to see even an inch in front of him due to the dense fog, Ji-Hyok suddenly wanted to look back. Images of his grandfather, grandmother, mother, and father, who rarely showed his feelings, came across vividly in the darkness. But he could not look back, for it seemed to him that to express such a bourgeois sentiment would be an act of self-betrayal. Following Sang-Ho, he slipped out of the village and went toward Mount Halla.

Living in the mountain, living a life he had never imagined, Ji-Hyok came to realize the futility of knowledge, ideology, thought, and even his position in the Communist Party. Though the Party tried to obstruct the election of May 10 by force, it was held nevertheless throughout the country as scheduled. North and South Korea then came to have separate governments. As the situation became unfavorable for the communist sympathizers on Jeju, the main revolutionary group rallied together and organized the People's Liberation Army of Jeju. It secured its stronghold halfway up Mount Halla and prepared itself for long-term battles. The government in South Korea incorporated the military and police forces to subjugate these guerrillas, and they mapped out a plan to isolate the Liberation Army's stronghold. They evacuated villagers living in the middle area of Mount Halla to villages on the seashore. They considered those who had not been evacuated as guerrillas, killed them at random, and totally destroyed their villages by fire. Some of those who had not been moved to the villages by the seashore entered deeper into Mount Halla and stayed there, hiding themselves from the subjugating army. Those who went to live on the mountain sometimes raided villages at the seashore to secure food for winter. But their main problem was that plans for a long-term struggle, especially plans for the handling of the elderly and women during the winter, had not yet been made. Some worried that if the Liberation Army provided protection for the women and the elderly, it might weaken the military capacity of the armed combatants.

From a rather high place in front of a cave that was the headquarters of the Liberation Army, Ji-Hyok could see his village. He was depressed. Around his waist he could feel the money belt that his grandfather had given him. Regarding the money and gold as useless, he felt lonely and afraid of the mountain life. Whenever he thought of the approaching winter, he became dizzy. He thought that his previous stay in the mountain temple was completely different from his present situation. It was hard for him physically to endure this life.

The temperature at the end of October on Mount Halla was below freezing. The headquarters of the Liberation Army was located in a cave near the small Han River that runs along Red Hill in Namdo, which is about seven hundred meters above sea level. Neighboring villages in the mid-area of Mount Halla, those that had been overtaken by the Liberation Army, had not been severely damaged by the military and police operations.

A meeting of the directing comrades of each post was held and there was a report about Comrade Kim Dal-Sam, a deputy leader of the army and a representative for Jeju Island in the People's National Assembly. Those in attendance at the meeting heard that the Assembly had guaranteed that the People's Republic of North Korea would actively support the revolution on Jeju. However, Kim Dal-Sam never returned from the mainland.

The next item on the agenda at that meeting was the issue of the noncombatants—the women, the elderly, and the children. At that time, the government in South Korea was attempting large-scale pacification work to persuade guerrillas and others in the mountain to defect. The People's Liberation Army also judged that it would be advantageous in the long run to have the noncombatants pretend to defect. However, there was no excuse to discuss that subject openly.

Moon Sang-Deuk, another deputy leader and former Japanese soldier, was the first to sense the mood of the assembled group and resolved to change it.

"From a short-term point of view, it would be effective for the maintenance of military forces to have the noncombatants go down the mountain as the enemy desires. But we, who willingly participate in the revolutionary task, have survived all kinds of suppression and threats. We even moved to this mountain. Sending those people down the mountain due to temporary hardship is an easy, bourgeois idea that ignores the important historical lesson that revolution is achieved through the people. The people are its main axis and power. Therefore, let's persevere in this hardship. Our duty is to be united with the noncombatants and to equip them with teachings in order to systematically strengthen their weak ideology. If they were given guns or spears, they would fight more courageously than combatants."

Ji-Hyok was strongly opposed to this impractical viewpoint.

"Why don't we let Comrade Baek Ji-Hyok take charge of their education?" Sang-Deuk continued.

Sang-Deuk made this suggestion with ease, as if it had been discussed beforehand. After the move to the mountain, Ji-Hyok had become the vice-director of education.

"I have just listened to Comrade Moon, but discussing the matter of noncombatants simply from the viewpoint of obligations, without considering the present conditions, will result in the weakening our military force. I think we have to mobilize all strategies regardless of the likelihood of their success. If we weaken our pragmatic tactics or incur inefficiencies in our struggle, then, no matter how justified our actions may seem, we will have made an irreversible error."

In this speech, Ji-Hyok disclosed everything that he had kept in his heart. Indeed, he wanted the women, the children, and the old people who did not strongly embrace communist ideology to get out of this battle. Those gathered there inwardly agreed with Ji-Hyok's words.

"Comrade Baek's speech contains a contradiction; it devalues our people. Why are they noncombatants? Let's give them arms. They will probably fight more courageously than you would."

Ji-Hyok felt defeated by Sang-Deuk's refutation of his argument. He had nothing to add, and the audience knew that Ji-Hyok was himself too weak to wring the neck of a chicken.

"Our comrade Kim Dal-Sam reported to the People's National Assembly about the heroic struggles of the people on Jeju Island. So how could such courageous people show a white flag?"

"You are right."

"Let's give them guns and spears."

Each comrade spoke in turn after trying to assess the atmosphere of the meeting. Ji-Hyok was now in a position to admit that he had made a mistake. At the meeting that day it was decided that noncombatants should be involved experimentally in an attack on the seashore villages in order to give them an opportunity to strengthen their fighting capacity.

However, an incident then occurred that caused Ji-Hyok to become more perplexed. The division of military affairs in the People's Army made a plan to mobilize about fifty people from among the residents of four mid-mountain villages in the area of Namdo to attack Namdo and the neighboring town of Nasung. Thirty combatants of the division of military affairs were given guns, the men from Namdo were given iron spears, old folks and young boys were given bamboo spears, and the women were ordered to carry the spoils. The division ordered them to attack the seashore villages, destroy the food and daily necessities, set the houses on fire, and ruthlessly kill any villagers in sight.

* * *

Two days later, early in the morning, the military campaign began. Ji-Hyok was astonished, but there was nothing he could do about it. Fortunately, he was not ordered to participate, but the campaign did turn out to be a great success. As the deputy leader had suggested, when the noncombatants were given arms and duties, they displayed a surprising show of strength. On that day, the spoils were so abundant that much was left behind, and two seashore villages were almost completely ruined by fire. Only the police substation and a few houses remained. In total, ninety-six people from the enemy side were killed. During the day, Ji-Hyok watched in moral anguish from the tower in front of the headquarter cave as the two villages and the surrounding area burned.

The next day, elated by the joy of triumph, the people who had gone to live on Mount Halla held a victory feast. While they were cooking the stolen rice and butchering cows and hogs for the feast, about two hundred of them were massacred by a counterattack from the incorporated forces of the military and police. On hearing the news, Ji-Hyok felt that it might have been a plot premeditated by the deputy commander of military affairs for the Liberation Army. With his one word, about three hundred people had died. Did the revolution need their blood? After that, the people of Namdo who remained on the mountain could not possibly defect even though they wanted to do so.

Ji-Hyok gave an order to the deputy leaders in charge of education in each village. He then came out of the cave, the headquarters of the Liberation Army, to see them off as they left for their respective regions on the mountain.

"Do as you have been ordered in spite of the difficulties, since it is the Party's command," he said.

When they came out of the mouth of the cave where chestnut trees grew thick, cold air rushed toward them through the grayish bark of the trees. Already leafless, the trees in that deciduous forest soared high into the sky. Ji-Hyok shivered as he looked at the desolate landscape of the naked forest that spread before him.

"As winter approaches, hunger and cold are indeed the biggest problems. Cattle in the field are already scarce, and so is horsemeat. It is difficult to give an ideological education to the hungry."

As they parted from him, the deputy leaders of the villages frankly revealed their hearts. Ji-Hyok could not respond. Ko Sang-Ho, who was in charge of Namdo, nervously approached Ji-Hyok and mumbled something. Ji-Hyok also wanted to speak to Sang-Ho to inquire about his own family and village.

"Now the government is engaged in pacification activities, and the remaining comrades want to go down the mountain in order to protect themselves. Since they cannot survive the hunger and cold in the mountain, it would be better for them to go down as soon as possible. We have already missed our chance. Our struggle should have ended either just after the 4.3 Incident or at least before autumn came, but it has continued until now. When winter comes, it will be a big disadvantage to us. Therefore, from a military point of view, it would be effective to use a two-pronged strategy: let the noncombatants go down the mountain and order the remaining comrades in the mountain to continue to fight."

Ji-Hyok's heart began to beat violently. What was on his mind? How could he say such a thing without any hesitation? He was right, however. To handle this situation, the Party controlled its members in the mountain with a stronger ideological education. As more people went down the mountain, the possibility that those in charge of education would be blamed for being ineffective became greater. Ji-Hyok was confused: he believed that Sang-Ho was right, but at the same time he could not accept his opinion.

"It would be reactionary to disagree with a matter already decided. The pacification work is all a lie. Go down the mountain if you want. People down there are also suffering from a shortage of food, feeding themselves with rotten sweet potatoes. Do you think they would welcome us and share their food and clothes with us? Re-arm our comrades so that they can awaken from this illusion. If you yourself are so weak, how on earth can you be responsible for the ideological education of the people?"

Ji-Hyok scolded his comrade so that he could not say any more. And then he added,

"I will disregard your words, but don't you dare utter such a thing to others."

Filled with shame, Ko Sang-Ho stopped talking, but soon added:

"As far as I know, the shrewder comrades have already escaped from this island. Kim Dal-Sam went to the People's National Assembly and never returned. And have you heard of anything from the high-ranking comrades who went to the mainland to let others know about the heroic struggles of the Jeju people and to seek support from them? They are now resting in safe places, but what about us? Kim Dal-Sam is said to have been welcomed as a hero in the Assembly in Haeju, North Korea. The people who have turned these men into heroes are suffering from hunger and cold, and yet those so-called heroes are applauded and live in great honor. Our struggles for the people have ultimately become struggles to make those few comrades heroes. Isn't that true?"

Paying no concern to Ji-Hyok's nervous response, Sang-Ho spoke his mind. Ji-Hyok had actually thought a lot about the fact that no one knew the whereabouts of the high-ranking members who had left the island. Once in a while he felt betrayed by them, but now he was surprised to learn that he was not the only one with such thoughts.

"We have already chosen this way. The ultimate meaning of our choice will depend on history."

Taking a deep breath, Ji-Hyok tried to comfort Sang-Ho, even though he himself was not confident.

"I did not just choose this way. I believed it was the only way, but in the end ..." Sang-Ho sobbed.

"Shut up!" Ji-Hyok shouted.

Ji-Hyok could not spit out the next words. He should have said, "You are a reactionary element," but such words would have made him look foolish.

"Take good care of yourself," Sang-Ho said. "It seems to me that our struggles have come to a dead end. By the way, elder brother, your family has moved to Jeju City, and my family is all scattered about."

When he heard the words "elder brother" tears came to Ji-Hyok's eyes, but he pretended to be stern, not saying what he wanted to say. "How could Sang-Ho reveal his own heart?" he wondered. Ji-Hyok was in a position to console and encourage him, but it was Sang-Ho who was actually comforting Ji-Hyok.

Sang-Ho added, "The headquarters and people here are lucky. The people in those areas allotted to each village are in a much worse situation."

Ji-Hyok knew about the situation.

Watching Ko Sang-Ho turn his back and walk away with drooped shoulders, Ji-Hyok felt an ache on the bridge of his nose. He thought to himself,

"Sang-Ho did not choose this way. He simply believed that this was the only way. How could there be only one right way? And could that way be precious enough to be exchanged for one's life?"

Ji-Hyok's eyesight was troubled; he looked on at illusory appearances of Sang Ho as he disappeared among the thin branches."

"What would become of this fight?" he wondered. "Why have we not heard anything from the comrades who left the island?"

4

Ji-Hyok looked up at the sky with a blank expression on his face and yawned as the ferry blew its horn, giving notice of entry into the harbor. The sound of the horn resonated far into the distance, caressing the calm surface of the sea. Ji-Hyok felt himself fly over to the island on the wings of that sound.

Though they were fatigued by the overnight trip on the boat, the passengers were smiling as they waved their hands to the people standing on the dock. The quay and surrounding area looked the same as before—there were the tin roofs on the low warehouses of the Dae-Han Transportation Company, the dismal appearance of the Japanese-style houses whose outer walls were paneled with black boards, the torn flags on the small fishing boats, the chimneys of a boat-building factory that occupied a broad empty lot behind the quay. The scene looked duller now because of the smokeless chimneys. Ji-Hyok had many memories about those chimneys, memories that he did not wish to recall. Nevertheless, the chimneys seemed rather peaceful now. Ji-Hyok had spent several weeks in those dark, gloomy buildings. His life at that time was a living hell. When a military campaign to suppress the guerrillas on Mount Halla began in earnest, the armed men who called themselves "revolutionary combatants" and the others living on the mountain were all captured and, without discrimination, taken to that boat-building factory. Occasionally, some of those people were taken from the factory in the middle of the night, never to return. The inmates of that makeshift prison thus became terrified of having their names called. But that dismal building blackened by the smoke of coals now touched his heart. It looked like an old country house from his hometown.

As the ferry entered the inner harbor, it emitted another long blast of its horn. The bustling passengers prepared to disembark. With the sound of the horn, people in fishing boats anchored in the inner harbor shouted greetings to those on the ferry. The fishermen waved their hands, as if stretching themselves in the morning. Their darkened faces, weathered by the sea wind, grinned, revealing white teeth. Knowing that they would not get any response, those who had come to welcome the passengers shouted names with their hands cupped around their mouths. The passengers did the same. With his eyes peacefully closed, Ji-Hyok continued to take deep breaths from the empty air as if to embrace the harbor at dawn. He welcomed the sense of a mysterious, dreamlike metamorphosis in which a place steeped in hatred, resentment, and terror was suddenly transformed into one of joy. Feeling as though he were resisting being awoken and taken from his mother's bosom, Ji-Hyok remained on deck while the other passengers competed with each other to be the first to disembark.

"Why don't you get off?"

The young man with whom he had spoken that morning approached Ji-Hyok. It appeared as though the man had been searching for him.

Leaning on a rope and looking down at the noisy quay, Ji-Hyok smiled at him without speaking and then moved.

"When you have too much sentiment about your birthplace, you become rather sober," the young man said.

Ji-Hyok had no idea what he was talking about. As soon as this man showed an interest in him, Ji-Hyok became nervous.

"Don't misunderstand me. It is my duty to escort you to the police station in Jeju. In coming this far, you have done a great thing."

Finally Ji-Hyok came to know the true identity of this person. When he realized that it was this man's duty to be interested in him, he felt a sense of disgusting betrayal. But on second thought, he was relieved that both of them had revealed their true colors to each other.

Ji-Hyok wondered how he could be free from this man in his mind and in his heart; then he resolved to shake that thought. There was a time once when he thought that if he threw himself into the sea, he would enjoy the boundless freedom of an infinite, open space. Now he wondered if that freedom was merely the absence of a fear of death. The freedom that he had never enjoyed he now considered to be a luxury.

"But why now?" he asked himself.

Just then the face of Ko Sang-Ho came to his mind.

"Is jumping into the sea the only virtuous course of action? Or would it be a final attempt to make up for never having chosen anything for myself?"

* * *

It was the winter of 1948. As a result of the attacks by the subjugating forces throughout that winter, the People's Liberation Army broke up into splinter groups. Taking advantage of that opportunity, they approached some private homes that had not been destroyed by fire and obtained food. Sometimes they raided secluded houses along the seashore to secure food and clothes, but they risked their lives in doing so. Not having any network of connections was a major disadvantage, and they were exhausted mentally. They could not hear any news from high-ranking members, and the government in South Korea was carrying out a carefully planned, large-scale military campaign to suppress them. The Korean Army had built posts in the mid-mountain area of Mount Halla and was ready to fight whenever members of the Liberation Army appeared. So unless it was resigned to accept the consequence of disclosing its location, the Liberation Army could not raid villages for food.

On the last night of that lunar year, Ji-Hyok was captured by the subjugating forces while he was eating a New Year's Day meal. The food had been sent by a cell member who had already gone down the mountain to live in Songdang, a village on the eastern side of the mountain. The police had received information about their connection, and won the cell member over for their campaign. Ji-Hyok thought that it all worked out for the best. As he did not have the courage to go down the mountain with a white flag and endure humiliation, he just wanted his situation to be brought to a conclusion, regardless of whether he ended up dead or alive.

Once he was captured, the police were surprisingly lenient on him. The subjugating forces usually treated the men of the Liberation Army with less respect than they would treat insects, but they handled him differently.

Ji-Hyok responded frankly to their questions. There was nothing to hide now. He told the truth about what he had done while living in K city. It was rather strange to Ji-Hyok that the police wanted to know about such trivial matters. However, judging that the situation was already over, and that the information he was giving would not be of any use to them, he confessed everything freely so he was not agonized by the investigation. Sometimes he had no choice but to say things that would harm others. However, the doctor at Namgook Clinic, with whom he had had some connection, and Sang-Ho, who was in charge of the cell members of Namdo, had already gone down the mountain and confessed everything related to Ji-Hyok so he did not feel any need to remain silent.

Sang-Ho had defected to the police in Jeju on his way back from the meeting of the leaders in charge of education in each village. This was something that Ji-Hyok came to know about much later. He ascribed the motivation for his defection to Ji-Hyok, though this was unimaginable to Ji-Hyok. Sang-Ho claimed that through his conversations with Ji-Hyok he had come to have doubts about communism. As things improved, Ji-Hyok came to think that he could not die in such a meaningless way. An ardent desire for life, which he had never had while living in the mountain, had arisen in him. And he was suddenly reminded of what his grandfather had said, though he did not know whether his grandfather was dead or alive now.

On the third day of the interrogation, Ji-Hyok sat with a man who recorded his testimony, though there was no need for a deposition since Ji-Hyok had been a commanding member of the guerrillas on Mount Halla. Ji-Hyok gazed directly into the man's face.

Handing him his money belt, Ji-Hyok said, "Please, save my life. I cannot die this way, as a victim."

He then turned his face away, as if nothing had happened.

A couple of days later, Ji-Hyok learned from this man how things were going. Among the various things that he heard, Ko Sang-Ho's confession and news about Dr. Yang gave Ji-Hyok some peace of mind.

After the interrogation, he was moved to the boat-building factory. Men and women were held there just like stored goods: they were divided into different buildings in which the floors were covered only with straw bags. Once in a while other prisoners were summoned out for interrogation. Some of them returned looking half-dead; others never returned. A boiled barley ball once a day or two steamed sweet potatoes was all they received for their meals. The inmates panted in extreme anxiety and despair, not knowing what would happen to them. They buried themselves under the cold, hunger, fear, and the dubious rumors that drifted about incessantly. And when they were overtaken with nervousness, they suffered even more.

It was there that Ji-Hyok was reunited with Ko Sang-Ho.

Ji-Hyok felt a sense of relief after being moved to this factory, and he began to think of a new start following this climax to the crisis. On the morning of his third day in the factory, after eating a boiled barley ball, Ji-Hyok was crouching among other prisoners when someone called him by his name, "Baek Ji-Hyok." Hearing his own name, he stood up. At that moment, he was frightened by something behind him. It was a strange feeling. When he turned around, a young man with a sickly appearance was staring at him. The young man, who seemed vaguely familiar, had disheveled hair and was wearing a black student uniform. The uniform instantly reminded Ji-Hyok of his fleeting life in K city. Pressed on by the shouts of the inspectors, Ji-Hyok had to just pass him by.

On that day, a court-martial passed a sentence of fifteen years of imprisonment on Ji-Hyok. To his surprise, he was relieved to receive that sentence.

"It's only a fifteen-year sentence. You can survive it," someone muttered, as Ji-Hyok was being escorted out of the summary court that had been temporarily set up next to the police station.

Furtively turning his face, Ji-Hyok saw the man who had recorded his testimony. Looking at him, he felt strangely calm.

When he came back to the concentration camp in the factory, prisoners flocked around him, avoiding the inspectors' eyes. The young man in the black student uniform, who had left an impression on him that morning, was also among the crowd.

"Don't you know me?"

The man in the student uniform made the first effort to communicate. On hearing his voice, he recognized it was Ko Sang-Ho.

"You are alive!" Ji-Hyok said.

That was the first meeting between them after such a long time apart. Though he had thought that he would have a lot to say to Sang-Ho if he ever met him again, he never imagined meeting him in this kind of place. Ji-Hyok remembered hearing news about him once. Looking closely at Sang-Ho now, he found that he had changed so much. Ji-Hyok had always treated him as a member of the Party, but Sang-Ho now seemed as young and innocent as a middle school student.

The other prisoners welcomed him, saying that they thought they would never see him again after he was summoned.

"How did you manage to return alive?"

Ji-Hyok closed his mouth. He did not want to disclose any of his thoughts, and the others, sensing something ominous in his inexpressive face, did not ask any more questions. Ji-Hyok just let himself fall into the sleep that was creeping over him.

When he awoke, the first thing he saw was Sang-Ho's black student uniform.

"You have been tried, they say."

Ji-Hyok nodded and smiled.

"I have not been tried yet," Sang-Ho replied. "Those who have been tried have the possibility of receiving a life sentence, unless they get the death penalty. However, sometimes, people are executed without a trial."

Ji-Hyok was astonished that he had an interest in such matters. He envied Sang-Ho for confronting his own situation so earnestly.

"I am nervous about it," Sang-Ho said. "I cannot be sure of anything at all. If I were summoned out tonight, it might mean the end for me."

The word was openly spread that those summoned could be either released or executed.

"How many years did you get?"

"Fifteen years."

"If it's fifteen years for you …"

After thinking for a moment, Sang-Ho continued, "I'll probably get about ten years."

Ji-Hyok wanted to ask him why he had not yet been tried even though he went down the mountain first, but he didn't.

"I heard about you," Ji-Hyok said.

But he did not mention what kind of benefit he got from the information that Sang-Ho had disclosed to the police about him.

"Dr. Yang Jae-Sung died."

Sang-Ho said this as if it were a cherished story.

"They say he got tuberculosis again, but perhaps he died of despair."

Sang-Ho then told Ji-Hyok about what had happened to Dr. Yang.

"What saved him from tuberculosis was hope, and his confidence in the revolution. Fascinated by the thoughts of Marx and Lenin, he imagined that he could participate as a revolutionary fighter in building a new ideal world. That was why he taught himself to be a doctor, he was making a new start in life. But after the dream collapsed, how could he sustain himself? How could he endure such a reality? In the end, the tuberculosis seized him again and he was beaten by it."

While talking about Dr. Yang, Sang-Ho was really talking about himself. Ji-Hyok was again reminded of the doctor's principled behavior and his fastidious perfectionism, which he had witnessed while pretending to be a hospital patient.

Sang-Ho continued: "What else can drive you crazy except for an uncertainty about yourself? One feels emptiest when all self-confidence is lost. As for me, I am afflicted with both uncertainty and insecurity about myself."

Ji-Hyok could not find any words of consolation or reassurance for him, for Ji-Hyok lived spontaneously and was not as logical as Sang-Ho. He did not want to think about his previous lifestyle.

After they found each other in the factory, Ji-Hyok and Sang-Ho had frequent conversations. Sang-Ho was suffering from extreme anxiety. Anyone under those circumstances would be nervous, looking up at the heavens as if praying for rain in a drought. Whenever anyone was summoned, Sang-Ho became tense. He would wait for the prisoner to return, often sleeping badly at night.

Eventually he received his sentence: ten years imprisonment, as he had expected. After that, he became more cheerful. But later he was again disturbed by a certain rumor that prisoners were being taken out on a ship and dumped in the middle of the sea. The inmates whispered that this method was devised as an efficient way to get rid of the dead bodies after the prisoners were shot, that trials were just a legal formality, and that they would all be killed in the end. They also whispered that the initial promise— that defection guaranteed one's life—was a lie. Another rumor was that, in order to avoid health problems, those who were ill would be executed first.

Whenever Sang-Ho heard such rumors, he lapsed into despair again. Under those circumstances, the inmates tried to suppress their apprehension.

One night, the inmates were called to assemble. The yard of the boat-building factory was empty, but policemen with guns openly came and went. The inmates who were sleeping woke up and rubbed the sleep out of their eyes. They had already guessed the situation by the rumors that had gone around the building. With hardened looks, they moved more nimbly than usual.

"At last, what we have been expecting has come," Sang-Ho whispered in a trembling voice as he approached Ji-Hyok.

"Let's face what we have to face to the end."

Ji-Hyok could not add, "How dare they throw us into the sea?"

People swarming into the factory yard looked bleached under the faint light of the guard lamps. The voices of those in command were also quiet. The sound of the guards' boots shook the night.

"We will now take you to the mainland. There, you will be assigned to different prisons where you will serve out your sentences. However, you will all be taken to Mokpo on board one ship. Keep this in mind so that you will maintain order during your voyage."

A man in his forties, carrying a gun, gave an order that the inmates barely heard. He then called out their names, organized them into groups of thirty, and ordered them to board the ship.

Those who were called first walked slowly, glancing back at the others in the yard.

Just beyond the factory yard was a dock. More than five hundred people were moving, and yet the sounds of footsteps could not be heard: the shoes that trod over that concrete road moved like ghosts in the night. And like thieves going over the walls of a rich man's house, people glanced around to try to read the expressions on each other's faces. Everyone was very cautious.

A six hundred ton cargo ship was filled with the prisoners. Barely able to sit on the floor that was covered with bags of straws, people huddled together, staring up at the ceiling of the ship.

"The ship is leaving."

The announcement came from nowhere, and people began to tremble as the ship moved. Their faces stiffened as a chill spread across the floor of the cabin. All were quiet, drooping their heads low, just as they had done when they left the dismal yard of the boat-building factory. It seemed as though they were saying goodbye to the island.

Ji-Hyok felt free and light as he left the gloomy factory that had been seared by the smoke of coals. He was also relieved by the thought that in completing this one step he was making a new beginning. He was not at all interested in the stories and rumors that provoked suspicion and doubt in people's minds. He just wanted to sleep at ease. While thinking about the fifteen-year sentence that he had received, he felt no concrete sense of time.

Someone shook him and he awoke. He did not know how long he had slept.

"How could you sleep?" Sang-Ho said as he moved closer to Ji-Hyok.

"You've got to sleep as much as you can," Ji-Hyok replied.

It was not just an empty statement. In fact, sleeping was the most enjoyable thing to do for Ji-Hyok.

Once he thought about how he would be happy if he died in his sleep. He wished to have a good sleep even amid the panic-causing rumors in this unresolved situation. He felt relief on board the ship. So, after a brief and childish thought about his stay in K city, he laid his head back and tried to sleep.

"We seem to be out of the Jeju Sea."

Two hours might have passed. With his butt still on the floor, Sang-Ho moved toward Ji-Hyok once again. He talked as if something might happen before the ship passed through this sea.

"I am nervous," Sang-Ho said. "They say that we all will be thrown into the sea, and those who can swim will be shot to death."

"Don't believe it. It's just a rumor."

"How could you be so carefree? Wouldn't it be more honorable to drown yourself in the sea than to be thrown into the sea and shot?"

Sang Ho said this quietly, biting his lips as he spoke.

"It's just because you are nervous. Let's have some faith in human nature."

Ji-Hyok spoke these words even though they could not console him.

"As everything else has betrayed us, how could we believe in human beings?"

Sang-Ho wanted to add something more, but he rose and staggered off.

The next morning, Sang-Ho could not be seen anywhere, though nothing had happened during the night. Rustling about and still intoxicated from a light sleep, people gazed with interest on a ray of light that was coming through a small hole in the wall. One by one they awoke from dreamlike states and came to realize that they were still alive.

It was noon when they disembarked from the cargo ship. Sang-Ho was still nowhere to be seen. A rumor soon spread and reached Ji-Hyok's ears that Sang-Ho had committed suicide during the night by jumping into the sea

*

"Let's get off first," the young man said as he approached Ji-Hyok.

"Why don't we get off last?" Ji-Hyok replied.

On the cargo ship, Ji-Hyok had looked, one after another, at the berth, the boat-building factory, the small city crowded with tin-roof houses, and Mount Halla, which dominated his view. The young man, smiling at this behavior, made eye contact with Ji-Hyok, who in turn felt a sort of intimacy between them. Ji-Hyok had at least that much freedom. People were bustling, striving to be among the first to get off, jumping up and down as if to shake off their annoyance with the boat ride.

After most of the passengers had disembarked, Ji-Hyok followed the young man off the boat. Standing on dry land, he wanted to embrace the broad harbor. He stood there, expressionless, for some time.

"I suppose you never thought that you would return to this harbor?"

The young man's question shook Ji-Hyok's heart. The dismal moment now came back to him, the moment when he left this quay with gun muzzles aimed at him Yet now he felt happy, standing there on his own feet. The two men walked slowly toward the harbor police station.

A three-quarter ton truck raised dry dust from the road as it stopped at the police station. Two policemen with M-1 rifles got out of the truck, and Ji-Hyok got in. After watching Ji-Hyok get in the truck, the young man sat in the driver's seat and started the engine.

Ji-Hyok turned his face toward the boat-building factory as they drove by it. He saw the chimneys, the building, the round storage tanks, and the desolate watchtowers that were used as guard posts at that time.

*　*　*

"You have done such great work."

Looking at Ji-Hyok with sharp and lucid eyes, a man in his forties, with vivid traces of shaving on his face, said this in an excited voice.

"Your choice will be a model for all people who are fighting for a free democracy, and will be remembered for a long time. Your determination deserves to be recorded in history."

The man was carried away with emotion, but Ji-Hyok could not feel any excitement.

"Let's tell all the people of Jeju about this courageous deed of yours."

As soon as he finished speaking, a young man who had been with them quickly left.

The next day, stories and photos of Ji-Hyok filled the front three pages of the local newspapers. It was good news to the people who had been anxious about the war. The communists had invaded South Korea, opened the prison gates, and praised the released political offenders as heroes, but Ji-Hyok renounced the hero's crown and returned home. Such a story was scandalous on the island. His past, in which he had succumbed to leftist ideology and had fought as a guerrilla on Mount Halla, was presented with a bit of exaggeration.

The news about him was read to students at school, something that depressed Ji-Hyok. He felt that people were gossiping and joking about the difficult choices he had made in life and the risks he had taken. He felt that they were ignoring his integrity.

* * *

As the gate of the prison opened, a red flag was raised and men in prisoner's uniforms shouted as they rushed out into the prison yard. They were all combatants for the revolution.

Ji-Hyok was surprised; he had no idea what was going on. A strange mood had pervaded the prison cells the previous night, but Ji-Hyok had paid no attention to it. During his incarceration in a narrow cell of that red brick building, he had gradually recovered a serenity of mind. Looking back on the past, he sometimes thought of Sang-Ho, who died by jumping into the sea from the cargo ship. It was Ji-Hyok who had led Sang-Ho to communism by talking about Marx and Lenin with such great enthusiasm. So he wondered why he had been unable to give Sang-Ho the courage to overcome his suicide on the cargo ship that night—why he had been unable to say anything, even though he had indoctrinated Sang-Ho with an ideology to save the world. Whenever he thought of Sang-Ho, he suffered from nightmares of shame. Strangely, Sang-Ho never appeared in his dreams, but Ji-Hyok wanted to apologize to him, if only he could meet him in a dream.

A communist faction in the prison had already spread news of the Korean War. However, because of the uncertainty of the situation, the political offenders were more cautious in their behavior. The mood in the prison became tense with the fear that if they were not cautious, there might be some actions taken against them. Yet the situation progressed too easily and rapidly. On the twenty-seventh day of that month the prison gate was opened, and the red flag was hoisted. Amid the noisy crowd drunk with joy, Ji-Hyok worried that something else, something independent of his own will, might happen.

A feast was held in the auditorium of the prison for the eighty inmates of the 4.3 Incident on Jeju and about sixty political offenders who carried out communist activities in other regions in South Korea. It was a luxurious feast served by beautiful women. A sumptuous meal and pretty women were enough to satisfy the prisoners who had fought bravely, overcoming mountain ranges of peril, one after another.

When the People's Committee in Seoul, who had prepared for this occasion, and the high-ranking members of the underground Communist Party in South Korea entered the auditorium, the room fell into confusion. Clapping, shouts, and cries shook the auditorium. All present were intoxicated with frantic joy. Someone from the People's Committee gave a welcoming address, which was immediately followed by a speech by another man, someone quite familiar to Ji-Hyok.

"... your great struggles will remain glorious in the history of the proletariat revolution in this country, and I have no doubts that, thanks to your blood, sweat, and tears, an everlasting heaven will be established for the workers in this country. The liberation of our fatherland is close at hand. Honor and glory are ready to be given to the comrades of the revolution in the name of the people. Let's take the lead in bringing about this revolution and make our best effort to carry out the task that has not yet been finished. I pay my respect to your heroic struggles in the name of the people and all members of the Party."

After his speech, there was an eruption of cheers and shouting. Casually listening to the speech that did not move him at all, Ji-Hyok came to his senses with the shouting. Now he could identify the man who was returning to his seat: it was Song Gwang-Chul. On second glance, he found that Mr. Song had not changed all that much, even though he had struggled underground. However, it was strange that he could not recall him sooner. Even if all the people in the world disappeared from Ji-Hyok's memory, he had always thought that he would never forget Mr. Song Gwang-Chul. Yet it had only been three years since they parted and, strangely, Ji-Hyok had actually forgotten about him for a moment.

The scene in the auditorium then turned chaotic. The ideals of the revolution and of the Party suddenly had no meaning for those who, having been imprisoned in a red brick building, were hungry for food, liquor, and women. Eating, drinking, dancing, shouting, flirting with women, and paying no attention to the fact that the high-ranking members of the Party were present, the prisoners went wild with pleasure. The high-ranking members, who were sympathetic with the prisoners, were also swept away with the festivities.

Watching from a distance, Ji-Hyok drank alone in silence. It was strange to him. He wondered why he felt no passion in his heart, now that the prison gate had been opened and the liberation of his fatherland was close at hand.

"Why," he asked himself, "do I have no desire to satisfy my hunger?"

A woman, having narrowly escaped the grasp of a mischievous man, came up to Ji-Hyok and smiled at him. Ji-Hyok glanced at her and emptied his drinking cup. Taking a bottle quickly, she refilled Ji-Hyok's cup.

"Are you not happy?" she asked.

"Are you happy?" he responded.

Perplexed by this unexpected question, she smiled awkwardly.

"Where are you from?" Ji-Hyok asked.

Her eyes widened.

"You are not supposed to ask such a question."

"Then, do you know what communism is?"

She stared at him.

"Baek Ji-Hyok!"

Song Gwang-Chul suddenly approached Ji-Hyok from behind.

"Ah, teacher!"

The title "teacher" came out of Ji-Hyok's mouth spontaneously.

"Good to see you. I knew that you were here."

Ji-Hyok could not say a word. Just as he had forgotten the teacher's face, he had also forgotten what he should say to him.

"Why are you drinking alone when other people are overwhelmed with joy?"

Song had been watching him closely as he drank alone.

"I do not have anything to be happy about," Ji-Hyok replied.

He wanted to say that it was an empty feeling to have been released from prison without any effort on his part, but he didn't. Song was trying to fill Ji-Hyok's cup.

"I've had enough. This is my first time drinking beer."

There was cynicism in Ji-Hyok's words.

"These are the spoils. Is there anything wrong with drinking what the imperialists drank and enjoyed?"

Song already perceived the confusion in Ji-Hyok's mind.

"It's good to see you. Let's talk later. We have to restart our mission."

He clicked his tongue, looking around at the frantic mood of the feast.

"Come with me after the party. You have to work with me from tonight on."

Finishing the conversation, he went back to his seat. Ji-Hyok then filled his cup with beer and thought to himself,

"Why was he so sober after his meeting with Song Gwang-Chul? Why was he numb to the exciting fact that liberation was near?"

Suddenly he recalled Sang-Ho's death.

"If Sang-Ho were present at this wild party, what would he be thinking about? Fighting for the liberation of the island, shivering with cold and hunger in mountain caves in the winter, and being exhausted with fear and the inability to predict anything in the dismal building seared by the smoke from chimneys—were these all done just for the sake of an invitation to this party?"

* * *

"Is this house also part of the spoils?" Ji-Hyok asked Mr. Song, as he glanced around at the expensive furniture in the living room of a luxurious Western-style house.

Song quickly read the cynicism in Ji-Hyok's eyes.

"Why are you discontent? This kind of reward is not a big thing compared to our struggles."

Mr. Song was already drunk. They had drunk together after the party, and then Mr. Song brought Ji-Hyok to this house.

It was the private house of a congressman of the South Korean National Assembly, and the Party had allowed Song to use it as his office from the day that they were freed. He had been placed in charge of assigning tasks to the comrades who had been active in South Korea based on an understanding of their unique character and dispositions.

"They're all rotten," Mr. Song said. "After a year of imprisonment, how can they be entrusted with another task? As they have only desires, how can they accomplish anything?"

He deplored the hungry state of the people in the feast. Ji-Hyok's thought was different. On hearing such criticism from Mr. Song, Ji-Hyok said,

"Sir, isn't it their nature as human beings? Who can blame those who want to satisfy their hunger?"

Mr. Song's complexion changed.

"That's also a bourgeois idea, or an expression of slavish nature," he said.

Ji-Hyok laughed inwardly.

"What I have learned is that those very things are the most precious things in life," Ji-Hyok replied.

Mr. Song fixed his stinging stare on Ji-Hyok's face.

"Then why did you not mingle with them?" Song asked.

"… because of a comrade who died."

Ji-Hyok talked about the death of Ko Sang-Ho. He admitted that he abetted his death by filling him with revolutionary ideas. And he added that he blamed himself for the incident.

"That's sentimentalism," Song asserted. "You will be more firmly strengthened through such events. You have the necessary qualities to be a revolutionary fighter."

Mr. Song accepted Ji-Hyok's words in a self-critical manner, for he himself had fallen into bourgeois sentimentalism.

"Now we have important tasks piled up in front of us," Song continued. "You have to work with me. Today I was so disappointed at the party. They're all wretches; they're only interested in the booty of liberation."

Mr. Song earnestly needed Ji-Hyok. It was not until the party that he could see a new side to Ji-Hyok.

"Sir, please do not try to bind me to you."

Ji-Hyok did not say anything further. He could not forsake his affection for this man whom he hadn't seen in such a long time.

"What do you mean by that?" Song asked, as he put down his drinking cup on the table with a thump.

"I want to go back home," Ji-Hyok replied.

Mr. Song understood Ji-Hyok's words in his own way: he thought that Ji-Hyok wanted a task that he could undertake at home. Ji-Hyok also wondered why Mr. Song did not react with surprise.

"I would like to examine myself for the time being. I seem to be neglecting things more urgent than the revolution. What is more important to me is to solve my own problems."

After speaking his mind, Ji-Hyok felt at ease.

"Don't talk about such things. Soon liberation will be achieved and we will have a lot of things to take care of."

Mr. Song was angry.

"Indeed, I do not have the strength to achieve those tasks. It would be absurd for me to try to carry them out. Far from being a revolutionist, I am not even worthy of being an ordinary member of society."

Silence flowed between the two of them for a moment.

"What are you going to do?" Song asked.

"I am going back."

"Where?"

"Home."

At that moment, Ji-Hyok uttered the word "home" too easily. By going back home, Ji-Hyok imagined that he could reclaim control of his own life.

"Think about some place else. That place is dangerous. You'd better choose the North or go to Russia and get more of an education. You may have such an opportunity, and so for the time being let's work together."

Still, Mr. Song gently tried to persuade him.

Ji-Hyok closed his mouth. His heart was beating violently. If he didn't stand on his own feet now, he would never again have control over his life.

The two of them drank through the whole night, but the next day Song did not try to prevent Ji-Hyok from returning home. All he said was,

"Someday, you will work with us. Take good care of yourself."

At dawn the next day, Mr. Song did not forget to give advice to Ji-Hyok as he took him across the Han River in Seoul on a military ferryboat. Ji-Hyok was grateful to Mr. Song for helping him return home. Thinking of how his teacher must have felt about this betrayal by his former student, he went toward Jeju anticipating that his teacher would let all of those emotions go someday. He felt the early morning air dash against his body; the air seemed to be no colder than his own body temperature.

6

Everything was buried, without a trace, in the darkness. Light breezes from nowhere swiftly drove steamy heat into the night. The infinite gloom was hardened with a still, heavy silence. Shaking that silence, the dull sound of truck engines was heard through the darkness. As the trucks staggered along, the night shook, and the sparse outline of the land appeared and disappeared sporadically.

The inside of the covered trucks was steaming hot. All around was darkness. The people being loaded like corpses into the trucks did not make a sound. They were quiet because they could not see each other in the dark. The moment of anxiety, even terror, had already passed.

Before and following the procession of trucks were cars with armed policemen. Inside the trucks, the armed guards swayed with the motion of the vehicles. The five trucks pushed along a country road in the darkness and mist.

Whenever the truck hit a bump in the in the darkness, Ji-Hyok began to think

"We decided to intern you in a separate camp. This is to protect you. I want you to arrive at the destination safely."

The inmates had been gathered in the middle of the night and loaded onto the trucks. Their hands had been tied behind their backs, and they were then tied together in groups of ten, with ropes strapped around their torsos. Ji-Hyok had given up thinking about his own survival, considering the dismal news of the Korean War. He thought that he was lucky to be alive in such circumstances.

He touched elbows with the person who was bound to him, causing the man to react nervously.

"Where do you think we're going?" the man whispered into Ji-Hyok's ear.

"I don't know. We've been driving for more than a couple of hours."

"Toward the sea or toward Mount Halla?"

Ji-Hyok did not answer. He tried to move his body and found that, despite being bound by the rope and having his hands tied behind his back, he could move a little bit. Shaking the upper part of his body several times, he slowly moved his arms. As the tightly bound rope loosened a little bit, he could feel some space.

"What will become of us?"

"There are escort cars in front of us and behind us ..." Ji-Hyok replied.

"Then, what about us?" the other man sighed.

Suddenly Ji-Hyok remembered the death of Ko Sang-Ho. He thought to himself,

"The sense of relief that he'd felt with the sentence of ten years' imprisonment had probably turned into despair at the bottom of that cargo ship floating on the sea. He must have thought that the only escape was to commit suicide in the middle of the infinite sea."

Then Ji-Hyok recalled his meeting with Mr. Song in Seoul, although he did not regret leaving Seoul. That was the only opportunity he had to exercise his free will. But he wondered how he could now respond to the fact that he would no longer be able to choose. There were no longer any alternatives.

News about the war was ominous. The feeling of ease, like that of taking a nap under a cotton quilt that has been warmed in the sun, did not last long. In the middle of the night a man from the police substation had visited him. Walking through the rainy night was all the more annoying due to the muggy heat. Arriving at the police substation, he found several people gathered there. No one talked about the reason for the gathering. The head of the police substation, with whom Ji-Hyok had met frequently, left word that they had been summoned by an urgent message and would learn more about it after arriving at some undisclosed location. He then disappeared.

Upon arriving at the police station, Ji-Hyok found even more people gathered there.

"We are going to protect you in a special place in preparation for an unexpected situation. Who knows? Maybe the enemy has already penetrated the island …"

The police captain said nothing more to the people gathered there. They were then bound together with ropes and placed on the trucks in the middle of the night.

As the truck shook, Ji-Hyok suddenly felt he was approaching his death, step by step. It seemed to him that when the shaking finally stopped, his heart would stop too, and everything would come to an end. He twisted his body and felt that the person in front of him was looking back. He stretched his neck and put his mouth to the person's back. His heart beat quickly as he felt the rough rope on his lips.

He pushed his nose and mouth into the back of the man in front of him and began to bite the rope with his teeth. The man stood still, though he seemed to be aware of what Ji-Hyok was doing. As the iron-hardness of the rope on his teeth gradually softened, he felt the misty dawn in that dark space.

"This is the end. This is the end!"

Panting for breath, with his mouth and nose on this other man's back, Ji-Hyok kept biting at the rope. Sticky blood soon began to gather in his mouth. The rain became heavier, and the truck labored as it slowly made its way up a slope. The vibrating movements of the truck grew stronger. Ji-Hyok was breathing rapidly as heavy rain pounded down on the roof of the truck. His sharp, bladelike teeth continued to gnaw on the tough rope.

Grandfather

1

It was yesterday evening when grandfather began acting strangely.

He had always been an energetic man; even at the age of eighty-five he dutifully took care of petty household chores. Although my father was no longer alive to support the family, it was not really necessary for grandfather to work. But from time to time, he would go to the field and watch over the workers. One morning, a few days ago, he took me with him to a tangerine orchard and a field where the grain was just beginning to ripen. On returning home, he became ill. At first we thought that he was just exhausted, but after he had been in bed for two days without any sign of recovering, relatives began gathering at the house, and some of them whispered that he might pass away this time. We prepared a vehicle, a motorized cultivator, to take him to a hospital in town, but he refused to listen to us. Nor would he take any medicine or food, not even a spoonful of thin rice gruel. Within three days, all family members and relatives, including my granduncle (*jongjobu*), had gathered at the house, thinking that he would soon pass away.

Early yesterday evening, most of my relatives who had gathered at the house in the afternoon went back to their homes for dinner, saying that they would return immediately. Only granduncle and a few other people remained, chatting on the living room floor. The door of grandfather's room had been left open so that people could watch over him from the living room. My mother and my wife were preparing dinner in the kitchen.

"Hee-Bin!" granduncle shouted.

I was standing in the yard when I heard my name called. Immediately I ran into the living room. Grandfather, who had been in bed all this time, was now standing, staring at the people sitting on the floor. This startled everyone, and no one moved out of fear of what would happen next. Everyone seemed to think that this was the behavior of a dying man in the final moments of his life; no one could have imagined what was to happen next. The expression in grandfather's eyes began to change when he saw me enter the room; his eyes became transparent, and his complexion turned sanguine when he spoke to me.

"You are Hee-Bin, and I am your father."

At first I took his remark as a sign of senility, but something incredible happened after that.

Grandfather said, "Uncle, how have you been?" as he turned toward granduncle and took a deep bow.

"Brother," granduncle cried, while trying to help grandfather straighten up.

I thought of how sad it is to become senile in one's old age, but then I realized that this behavior might be more than just senility, for it seemed as though I could see my father's face in grandfather's. I had never actually seen my father, but I imagined his face based on a photograph and stories about him that I'd heard from other people.

Grandfather, who was looking at granduncle, suddenly stood up straight, went to the narrow porch, put on his rubber shoes, which had been placed there neatly, and walked out into the yard. He looked around the house and cast his gaze over the fence toward the tangerine orchard, which was densely packed with tangerine trees. He looked at the orchard for a long time and then stretched with hands toward the sky.

"Honey!" he shouted, calling for my mother.

Hearing that word, everyone in the house looked at each other curiously. Mother was so shocked that she came out to the yard, shaking water from her wet hands. She heard her husband's voice, the voice she had often heard in her dreams.

Grandfather said, "Oh, darling, how long it has been! You must have undergone a lot of hardship."

With a warm smile on his face he took a step closer to mother. Everyone was dumbfounded.

"I wandered from place to place for a long time after I left home. And now I have finally returned. Please bring me some water, dear. I need to wash my face."

It was definitely the voice of my father in his younger days—not only his voice, but also his face. Grandfather looked young and healthy, just as my father would have looked in his twenties. All my relatives were bewildered to hear grandfather calling his daughter-in-law "Honey."

Granduncle looked around the house cautiously and was a bit relieved to see that there were no outsiders. He gestured to mother to bring some water. I could see a strange expression on mother's face, one that I'd never seen before. From the time she had become a widow in her youth until now, in her fifties, mother had been full of sorrow. But that sorrow suddenly disappeared from her face as she blushed. At the sight of this absurd, stunning incident, everything went black for me. I was worried that mother might begin to behave strangely, like grandfather. I had heard before that when a person is possessed by a dead man's spirit, he resembles the dead man, but I had thought that that was just superstition. Now I began to see the truth of that idea in grandfather's face. I wondered what would happen if mother began to mistake grandfather for her husband. It was unthinkable.

Mother went to the kitchen slowly and returned with water in a big plastic washbowl. Grandfather rolled up his sleeves and put his hands in the bowl, one after the other. A few moments later, he took them out and started to wash his hands. Mother and granduncle were watching him with blank expressions on their faces.

* * *

Thirty years ago my father was the vice-commander of the Civil Defense Corps in our village. One day, he was accused of conspiring with communist guerrillas and was killed with eight other youths on a grassy knoll in the front of the village. This incident was triggered by the death of the village chief, who was murdered by communist guerillas. At that time, mother was pregnant with me and would soon give birth. For my grandfather, who was the first son of his family, the death of his only son was an unbearable shock. Three months later, I was born. As a posthumous child, I didn't know anything about my father except what I had gleaned from other people's stories, including my mother's. My mother, who cherished my father, endured her pain and loneliness only by keeping the memory of my father alive.

* * *

Grandfather shook the water from his hands, and when he noticed mother standing beside him with a towel, he smiled.

"Please bring me my clothes. I haven't changed in such a long time …" Slurring his words, he went into his room without taking the towel from mother. I thought that his voice and demeanor must have been those of my father. After a quick look at granduncle, mother went to another room at the back of the house.

After a while, she returned to grandfather's room with some of his clothes. Receiving the clothes, grandfather said,

"Darling, are you sure these are mine? They look like father's."

Trying hard to conceal his strong displeasure, he refused to take the clothes. So mother took them and came back into the living room.

With a concerned look on his face, granduncle said to my mother, "Do you have your husband's clothes?"

He asked the question even though he was sure that no one would keep the clothes of a man who had died thirty years earlier. However, mother answered "Yes," as if she had been waiting for that question, and then disappeared into the room at the back of the house. A short time later, she returned with some traditional Korean clothes made of silk—they were father's clothes. She had kept them all these years either because she couldn't accept my father's death or because she believed that someday he might miraculously come back to her. Or perhaps she just wanted to hold onto her memory of him.

After receiving the clothes, grandfather said, "Thank you, dear, for keeping the clothes so well." He was so grateful that he would have held her hands if she had been next to him. "I'd like to sleep now," he said.

He spoke loudly so that everyone would hear him, and then fell down on the thin sleeping mat in his room. Everyone who had been watching this event suddenly heaved a deep sigh of relief. Mother then gazed at grandfather, who was already snoring. After covering him with a blanket, she stood up. Granduncle came into the room and looked at grandfather in his sleep.

"He looks just like Shin-Gyu," my granduncle said. He then returned to the living room, where he lit a cigarette and announced, "It's not senility. My brother is possessed by the spirit of Shin-Gyu."

Shin-Gyu is the name of my dead father. So even granduncle believed that my grandfather was possessed by the spirit of my father.

2

Grandfather slept for twenty hours; it was as if he were dead. After a while, people came to think that he would never wake up. That, in fact, is what my family hoped for. Granduncle told me to prepare for a funeral. On hearing this news, relatives began visiting the house continuously. However, nobody talked about the incident that had taken place the day before. Those who talked about grandfather's condition just said that he was showing signs of senility.

When the day broke, mother went to the tangerine orchard, which was separated from the house by a fence, and stayed there all day long, even though there was not much work to do. Using a short hoe, she vigorously pulled weeds out of the ground next to a tangerine tree loaded with yellow tangerines. This work was unnecessary. The weeds were going to die anyway, for there was no sunshine under those tangerine trees. But she didn't really want to pull the weeds. She hoed relentlessly because she wanted to vent the sorrows buried in her heart. Looking at her from behind, she seemed to be digging the earth with her fingers rather than with a hoe. It was as if she were scratching the wounds in her heart so that blood would flow forth from them. It was always like that when mother worked the earth. Though she had lost her husband in the 4.3 Incident, she could not live the typical life of a widow, grieving the loss of her husband. That was a time when you could not predict what would happen from one day to the next. Since her husband had been killed by the police on charges of conspiring with communist guerrillas to murder the village chief, no one would be willing to help her if she got into trouble.

* * *

After the confusion of the 4.3 Incident subsided somewhat, hunger became the most serious problem since the villagers hadn't farmed the fields in several years. Without even a proper burial ceremony for my father, mother walked sixteen kilometers to her family's house, with me, a two-year-old, on her back.

When he saw us, my uncle said, "A dead man is a dead man. Living souls should find a way to live on."

He then gave us some young tangerine plants. My uncle, who took care of a greenhouse, had prescient ideas about farming tangerines: he thought that someday tangerine trees would bring wealth. Mother left me in the care of her family and returned home, walking sixteen kilometers with the young tangerine trees on her back. She then planted the trees in a vegetable field. From that time on, whenever she was not feeling well, mother would go out to the field and work hard. While engaged in that work, she came to accept my uncle's advice—that living souls should find a way to live on.

* * *

While I was looking from the middle of the yard at the room where grandfather was sleeping, thoughts of my mother aimlessly digging the earth suddenly came to my mind. I began to feel extremely confused.

I thought, "What if mother thinks that grandfather, who is behaving like father, really is my father?"

It was dreadful even to think about, but it seemed increasingly possible. Considering the unresolved grief and sorrow in my mother's heart, it wasn't too difficult to imagine that happening.

There was some stir among the people in the living room and then granduncle gestured for me to come to him. Suddenly the door of grandfather's room opened with a bang.

"Hee-Bin!" grandfather shouted, while coming out to the narrow porch. It was not the face of a man who had slept for such a long time. The voice was loud and energetic and his eyes were shining with vigor. A picture of my father, taken while he was in his twenties, suddenly came to my mind.

"Where is your mother?" he asked.

Mother came into the yard at that moment, looking toward the ground and walking with an unsteady gait. Grandfather stared at mother blankly, as if he were in a dream and said,

"I want to wash my hands. Please bring me some water."

People began to look at one another without daring to open their mouths. Mother brought water and put it in front of grandfather. Just like yesterday, he washed his hands and got rid of the sleep in his eyes.

"Hee-Bin, I want you to come with me," he said.

After washing his hands, he led me away from the house.

"Brother, where are you going?" my granduncle asked, as he came running out of the house, trying to stop us from leaving. He feared that people in the village would think that grandfather had gone crazy.

"Uncle, I am going to visit the house of Mr. Yang, the village chief," grandfather said.

"Mr. Yang, the village chief?"

"You don't know Mr. Yang? He was the head of Nulbunduru village."

Grandfather was referring to Mr. Yang, who was the village chief when my father was killed. It was his death that had led to the death of my father.

"I want to see his son and prove that I didn't murder his father."

All of the people gathered at the house turned pale with surprise. They began to wonder about what grandfather hoped to achieve by bringing up this forgotten incident after thirty years had passed. I was not even born when the incident occurred, and now I am older than my father was when he was killed.

I thought to myself: "Why should we talk about it now? Even though he was possessed by the spirit of my father, could grandfather remember exactly what happened at that time?"

Grandfather walked out of the house slowly, leaving people standing there with blank looks of amazement. Vague thoughts about my father returned to me, thoughts that I had forgotten long ago—or, rather, thoughts that I had tried to forget long ago. But it seemed as though I could finally meet my father through my grandfather, possessed as he was by my father's spirit. So I followed him outside. With broad shoulders, long legs, and a swift walk, grandfather was once again a young man in his twenties. It was difficult for me to keep up with his pace.

Grandfather walked toward the old house where the former village chief, Mr. Yang, used to live. Yang's son, who is now in his sixties, is about the same age that my father would have been. Mr. Yang, if he were still alive, would have been about the same age as my grandfather.

* * *

It was in the spring of 1948 that the situation on Jeju Island became unstable. In the fall of that year, it deteriorated even further. The people in the villages located between the seashore and Mount Halla, in the middle of the island, were evacuated to the seashore villages, where there were police stations. Throughout the island, fighting had broken out between the police and the communist guerrillas, and the island was thrown into great confusion. Our village, however, was peaceful. Even though it is located twenty kilometers in the direction of Mount Halla from the main street of Jeju City, none of the people from our village went to the mountain to join the communist guerrillas. Also, the village youths had formed a Civil Defense Corps to maintain law and order since there was no police station in our village.

One morning in late fall a serious incident took place: the village chief was kidnapped by a group of communist guerillas. All the villagers were summoned to search for the village chief. When his dead body was finally found next to the stream that runs through the village, it was confirmed that he had been brutally murdered. He was found naked, with his arms and legs tied to a pine tree. He had been stabbed with spears and hit with stones. It was the first incident of its kind in the history of our village.

After seeing the dead body, some of the villagers began to behave unusually. The first of those to manifest such strange behavior were the son and other family members of the village chief, who ran down to the police station and said that the communists who had murdered their father were from this village. With this false accusation, my father and eight other young men were rounded up and killed. I was dimly aware of the incident, but I didn't try to learn more about it. Grandfather and mother behaved similarly. No one was really interested in whether or not father had actually murdered the village chief. They just accepted the fact that such a thing could have happened, especially during those troubled times, and that the best way to cure the pain was to forget about it.

* * *

Gil-Sam, the son of Mr. Yang, was sitting on a narrow porch when we arrived at his house. He had just returned home from work for a short break, but it seemed as if he had been waiting for us. He stood up instantly when he saw my grandfather coming into the yard. The color of his face changed when he saw my granduncle and the others who were following us.

"Gil-Sam, it's been a long time," my grandfather said.

Gil-Sam was standing uneasily, hesitating about whether or not he should bow. My grandfather took his hands and shook them joyfully. Suddenly the expression on Gil-Sam's face changed. Grandfather was old, but his voice sounded like that of a young man, someone who was very close to Gil-Sam. Furthermore, Gil-Sam was surprised by grandfather's changed appearance.

"Don't you recognize me? It's me, Shin-Gyu."

Gil-Sam was surprised again when he heard my father's name. Grandfather had now become my father. Gil-Sam lost all the color in his face. He tried to move his lips to say something to me, but he couldn't. I could not tell Gil-Sam about grandfather's condition, for what would I have said—that grandfather is crazy, senile, or possessed by the spirit of my father?

"Gil-Sam, I didn't kill your father. You know that, don't you?"

It seemed to me as though the words came from deep within my grandfather's heart. There was a crying, pleading sound in his voice, like that of a spirit or a wind that shakes the branches of trees in the middle of a winter night. The words caused the people in the yard to tremble.

The wrinkles on the face of Gil-Sam quivered with fright. Because he could not talk, he just stood there staring. Then granduncle came forward and tried to hold my grandfather back.

"Uncle, I didn't kill the village chief," grandfather pleaded, as he looked around at the people who had gathered in the yard. His was the face of a man who was pleading his innocence in a court of law. With no evidence for his innocence, and only his plea, there was no way for him to escape the trap of the perfect crime, the false accusation. The only thing he could count on was his actual innocence. While looking at the pleading eyes of grandfather, I was overcome by shock. I now firmly believed that my grandfather was possessed by the spirit of my father, and I thought that what he was saying might be true.

With fear in his eyes, granduncle approached grandfather and said, "Brother, pull yourself together! What are you saying? Why are you bringing up things that have long been forgotten?"

After looking at granduncle for some time, grandfather turned to Gil-Sam and said, "Gil-Sam, didn't we work together to make the village peaceful, whatever the cost? And then, suddenly, the unexpected occurred."

Grandfather repeatedly swallowed his saliva as if he were thirsty. Standing beside him, I noticed the sinewy, twitching tendons on his wrinkled neck. But with his erect posture, he didn't look feeble. He opened his mouth again and said, in standard Korean dialect, "Listen to me attentively." His story then flowed forth, as if he had been preparing it for some time.

"That night we played cards at Jung's house in the upper village. It was an informal meeting. After eating some buckwheat noodles, we started to gamble at cards. Beginning with a chicken bet, the wagers grew larger and larger. Almost all the members of the Civil Defense Corps, excluding those on duty, gathered at Jung's. Some of us participated in the rounds of cards, while others just watched. While we were completely absorbed in the game, your wife ran to us and said that your father, the village chief, had been kidnapped by communist guerrillas. The people at Jung's were shocked by the word 'guerrillas,' and they scattered about fearfully. Immediately I ran to the office of the Civil Defense Corps and found the soldiers snoring, with their iron spears put aside. A state of emergency was soon declared and all the members of the Defense Corps were summoned. But they would not come readily. They must have dreaded the idea of fighting guerrillas armed with guns. Nevertheless, several members gathered at the office near dawn and went to your house. Only your mother, little brother, and your sisters remained at home; they were all seized with terror. We looked for you and were told that you had gone to the police station. At that moment I realized that we had forgotten to report the incident to the police. After daybreak, the police officers came to us in the office. Together, we searched for your father everywhere in the village. Two days later, we found his body—he had been brutally murdered. I didn't know what to say to you about his tragic death. It was a couple of days after your father's funeral when the policemen came in a big truck and gathered all the members of the Civil Defense Corps. We assembled there, thinking that we were going to be deployed in the punitive unit ordered to arrest the guerrillas. Twenty members gathered there. Following the orders of the police, we boarded the truck bound for the police station. When we arrived at the station, the police changed their attitude toward us and began treating us like communist guerrillas. They said that they intended to arrest the members of the Defense Corps who were involved in the kidnapping of the village chief. At first we shook our heads at the outrageous idea. But then calamity struck when we equivocated in answering the question as to where we were on the night of the accident. Because we felt uneasy about the gambling, most of us who had been at Jung's answered that we had parted immediately after dinner, concealing the fact that we had gambled after the meal. A couple of days later, finding out that the answer turned out to be to our disadvantage, we told the truth, but it was too late. To make matters worse, the police questioned why the commander and the vice-commander of the Corps had delayed the search until the next morning in spite of the urgency of the situation. They also suspected that the members of the Corps had, on the pretext of having eaten together, neglected their duty of guarding the village. We had nothing to say. However, we did not worry too much because we were not involved in the kidnapping or the killing of the village chief. We also believed that you were with us on that night and thus everything would be fine. We needed your testimony, and the interrogator decided to hear it. Everything would have been fine if you had said just one thing—that we were all at Jung's playing cards when your wife ran to the house with the news of the accident. But our expectations were dashed."

Grandfather then paused and cast a reproachful glance at Gil-Sam. Gradually the eyes of the people who were surrounding grandfather brightened strangely. These people all looked nervous, as if they were anticipating a serious situation. They sensed that this old man in his eighties and the other in his sixties would make an embarrassing scene.

Granduncle became impatient. He too was afraid that this senile man would cause trouble, but he was even more concerned about some unexpected event due to grandfather's statement. All of those gathered there had the same idea.

"We thought that you would resolve the whole problem. Your one word would clear us of suspicion. But we were suddenly frightened by the grotesque desire for blood in your eyes. Until that time, we were not particularly scared of the interrogator."

Tears and sighs were mingled in grandfather's voice.

Gil-Sam then said, "Since Jung's house had so many visitors that night, I cannot clearly remember who was with me at that house when my wife arrived. And if someone was with me at that time, it does not mean that he was not involved in the kidnapping of my father ..."

Grandfather responded, "You walked out after spitting out those words. The only thread of our hope was cut off. Your statement turned to our disadvantage. The interrogator claimed that everything was premeditated, insisting that the dinner and game of cards were designed to camouflage the kidnapping of the village chief."

No one, except the interrogator and Gil-Sam, had ever heard those details of the incident. All the men accused of the murder were now dead. Even Gil-Sam might not remember the details of what happened thirty years ago. However, grandfather remembered everything about it, though the spectators were not particularly interested in what he was saying.

Grandfather then said, "Gil-Sam, you can tell the truth now. Wasn't I with you that night, from the beginning until the end?"

Gil-Sam's face turned pale and the margins of his lips began to quiver. Grandfather suddenly approached him and grasped him by the right arm. In an instant, Gil-Sam lost his balance.

"Let's go to Jung's old house. I will tell you in detail what happened on that night long ago."

Seizing Gil-Sam by the arm, grandfather pushed through the people in the yard and dashed away. It all happened in the blink of a moment. A man around the age of sixty was being dragged by an old man over eighty years old. Bewildered, my granduncle and the crowd followed them. I followed them too, worrying that I might lose sight of grandfather.

Grandfather and Gil-Sam came to Jung's house at the entrance to the village. It was a tumbledown cottage. Because of the approaching people, a dog sitting on the terrace stones scurried away to a fenced-in lot at the back of the house without barking at all. The gate had been left open, but no one could be seen in the house.

Walking into the yard, grandfather released Gil-Sam and looked around the house.

"That's the room," grandfather said, as he pointed at an inner room of the cottage.

At that moment, the villagers who had been following them came into the yard.

3

"I remember every detail of what happened that night."

Holding Gil-Sam by the hand, grandfather went to the backyard. Fenced and shielded by densely planted camellias, the backyard was a little dark but otherwise cozy. A small room of the cottage was facing the backyard, and its door was so small that a person could barely go through it.

"Some were playing *yut* on the living room floor, and we were playing cards in this room. You were sitting here, I was next to you, and the leader of the Civil Defense Corps next to me."

Gil-Sam sat by the door, near the shelf in the wall, and grandfather was seated next to him. Grandfather explained that the leader of the Civil

Defense Corps sat in the center of the room on that evening long ago. He then began to reenact the card game. The villagers who had gathered there watched this strange scene with curious smiles and gestures.

"You lost all the money. I still remember how nervous you looked when you lost your money."

As he became slightly more relaxed, grandfather smiled at Gil-Sam, who just closed his mouth firmly and gazed at my grandfather.

"After losing your money, you went out to borrow more and then came back. A moment later, your wife came in. On hearing the news, you stood up, threw down your cards, and took a quick look around. I realized later that you were looking for a friend who was willing to go with you. But we were so shocked by the word 'guerrillas' that we could neither sympathize with you nor understand your situation. We just ran away. Our behavior could have hurt your feelings, but isn't it undeniably true that I was with you on that night? Those eight men who were executed were the ones whose faces you saw when you threw down your cards and looked around at us. Isn't it the truth? Answer me, Gil-Sam. Why are you not speaking?"

Keeping his hold on Gil-Sam, grandfather pleaded with him for an answer. Then he looked for me.

"Hee-Bin! You heard that I was here in this room …"

I was seized with fear and a sudden heartache. A chill crept over me when I realized that I was talking with my father who had passed away thirty years ago and that I might go insane. However, I was determined to listen to this story to the end without losing my mind.

"I was not a guerrilla. Nor did I kill the village chief," grandfather asserted.

He continued to press Gil-Sam for an answer, but Gil-Sam kept his mouth firmly shut, trembling while his face turned white.

"Hee-Bin, you believe me, since you heard my testimony. I am telling you that I was not a guerrilla."

Hearing no answer from Gil-Sam, grandfather glared at me, as if to assure me of his innocence. Then, suddenly, he ran out of the room.

Gil-Sam continued to stare into the empty air, while the villagers began talking among themselves.

"The old man is utterly insane."

"He is senile."

"The spirit of the son has transmigrated into the father. His voice and gait—he is so much like his son."

Paying no attention to these remarks, I struggled to repress the feelings coming from deep inside me. I ran after grandfather with all my strength.

"Hurry up. What on earth is he doing?"

Granduncle's anxious voice could be heard from behind me.

Grandfather returned home and searched for mother, who was digging with a hoe in the tangerine orchard across from the house. It looked as though she were trying to exhume the bones of my father's corpse that had been buried ignominiously so long ago. Her digging seemed to be a painful yet joyful action. She plunged into the earth with grief in order to overcome it. She resented the fact that grandfather had reminded her of a memory almost forgotten, but her vigorous digging suggested that she was also happy to have been reminded of that memory.

Grandfather washed his hands for a long time, like he always did, with the water that mother had brought. He said he was hungry and asked mother for something to eat, so she quickly prepared a meal for him. He smelled it and tried to spoon it up, but he barely ate a morsel of it before asking mother to clear the table and bring him some water. Soon after drinking the water, he went to bed and immediately began snoring.

When night came, my relatives gathered at the house.

"He will not survive tonight so we must be prepared."

Granduncle, the eldest of my relatives, asked the other relatives to take care of all the arrangements for the funeral.

Although I was not at all happy with what was going on, there was nothing I could do. None of my family members said anything about what had happened during the last two days. I secretly suspected that granduncle was consciously avoiding any comment on grandfather's behavior. That is the reason why he was hastily speaking of funeral arrangements.

I approached granduncle because I wanted to clarify something. He was the only one who had knowledge of my father's death.

"Is what grandfather said totally absurd?" I asked him.

I was about to bring up my father's death, but I was interrupted by granduncle.

"It is a thing of the past. What is the use of bringing up what has been forgotten? You shouldn't be concerned about such a trivial thing while an important duty is at hand. You are going to be the chief mourner at the funeral."

I was discouraged, but I did not want to disregard the matter of father's death. As I tried to raise the issue again, granduncle took no account at all of my intention.

"Sometimes ignorance is bliss. What if you come to know more about the incident? And what makes things worse is that this is all coming from a senile man."

He then insisted that the man sleeping in the room was my grandfather even though he appeared to be possessed by the spirit of my father.

I took a close look at each of my relatives gathered in the living room. They all looked somewhat anxious. They were more worried about grandfather regaining consciousness than they were about him dying. They were worried that some hidden truths might soon be revealed.

4

Grandfather slept soundly through the night. Day broke, and the sun moved toward the center of the sky. There was still no stir in grandfather's room, though he had surely survived the night. People were afraid that when he awoke, he might cause some trouble.

"Perhaps he will not make it through the day."

"He has had a long life, and that is enough."

"He has gone through many difficulties in his life, but he was blessed enough to have had a great grandson …"

My relatives exchanged such comments with each other. Granduncle asked a couple of stout young men to stay close to the house in case of an emergency.

Around 11:00 in the morning, grandfather finally got up.

"Hee-Bin!" he shouted.

Grandfather frowned at the relatives sitting on the living room floor and came out to the yard, looking for me. I came forward immediately.

"What is all this noise in the house? No one has greeted me, even though they have not seen me for so long."

Again, he cast an unpleasant look at those in the room and called on my mother to bring some water for washing up. While he was washing his hands, granduncle approached grandfather and asked,

"What do you want? Do you want an exorcism to console your sorrowful spirit?"

Some relatives had recently advised granduncle that grandfather had borne so many sorrows in his life that he needed an exorcism in order to have a peaceful death.

"Why are you talking about an exorcism? I just want to let the people know that I am not guilty of the murder of the village chief. I am innocent. I never was a communist guerrilla."

Grandfather spoke to granduncle reproachfully, looking straight at him. My mother sobbed and wiped some tears from her nose with the edge of her long skirt.

Grandfather then said, "Hee-Bin, let's climb up the hill. Uncle, send Gil-Sam to the hill, too. I must have one final word with him."

He grabbed me by the right arm, and walked out of the house at a rapid pace. He was so strong that my right wrist became stiff and numb.

We arrived at the grassy knoll in front of the village. It was a place for people to gather and talk. It was also the place where the eight young men and my father had been executed.

Clasping his hands behind his back, grandfather stared at the village from the center of the knoll. One by one, people began to gather.

"Hee-Bin, go over there," grandfather said.

He drove me away with hand gestures, as if he were expecting some trouble. Looking at all those gathered around him, he recognized Gil-Sam.

"Gil-Sam, come over here," he said.

Gil-Sam wedged his way through the crowd and approached grandfather. People were watching the two men, worried that something bad might happen. I was observing the scene at a distance from the crowd. My eyelids were quivering, and I felt as though I were suffocating.

"Gil-Sam, we were taken to this place, because we were alleged to have been the guerrillas who kidnapped your father. We were pronounced guilty in front of the villagers."

People were holding their breath, staring at grandfather and Gil-Sam. Perhaps they were waiting for the moment when grandfather would take a knife out of his pocket and stab Gil-Sam.

"Nevertheless, we did not give up hope. We were expecting that you would tell the truth right before our death."

Grandfather began to speak in a calm yet serious tone, and Gil-Sam nervously stepped back in an effort to protect himself.

"However, as soon as we got off the truck, bound up with rope, we heard your mother cursing at us. At the same time people began to throw stones at us. I saw you among them. You were shouting at us with bloodshot eyes. I felt all our hope fading away. Still, thinking that I would not die guilty …"

Grandfather kept speaking, looking reproachfully at Gil-Sam. Sensing that there would be no trouble between the two men, people became somewhat disappointed and began to stir slightly. At that moment, thrusting Gil-Sam aside, grandfather ran down the hill. I ran after him but soon stopped following him. Grandfather then ran down into the center of the village.

"Good god!"

Villagers gaped at this unexpected sight.

"What are you doing? Go quickly …"

Granduncle shouted at some young men to chase after grandfather.

While looking at grandfather, who was running for his life, and the young men who were chasing him, I began to think of the last moments of my father's life. I was told that he had loosened the rope around himself and run away just before his execution, but he was quickly overtaken by the police and executed. From grandfather's behavior, I could vividly imagine my father's state of mind when he tried to escape his execution.

Shouting, "My God! Why?" the villagers focused on the narrowing distance between the young men and grandfather. I knew that just as it was a tragedy for my father to be caught while trying to escape, so too was my grandfather's predicament tragic. Nevertheless, I could do nothing other than to feel pity for him.

I wondered, "Why were the young men chasing grandfather? Will he be treated as an insane old man? Will his story end as an absurd one?"

When the young men finally caught him, grandfather struggled to break free. On seeing this, I could not even raise my head because of the deep despair that had overcome me. After a little while, I opened my eyes at my father's calling.

"Hee-Bin!"

The villagers now surrounded him. His eyes were extraordinarily bright. When I forced my way through the crowd to move closer to him, he moved his lips slightly. He was trying to say something, but then he fell to the ground. People began to make noises, and granduncle ran to him, calling his name.

Soon after he was taken to the house, grandfather passed away. My relatives quietly arranged his funeral. They said that it was fortunate that the senility before his death had not been too serious. Nobody mourned over my father's death nor talked about what had happened during the last couple of days. It was as if they had agreed to keep silent about it.

Fever

1

"Is it true that the deceased, Kim Man-Ho, will receive some award?"

My father's cousin suddenly raised the question while we were chatting over a few drinks, after a memorial service for our ancestors. We were at the house of the head family, which was the final stop for the memorial service. My father's cousin was visiting his hometown after having lived in Japan for a long time. His question erased the effects of the few drinks I had already had.

The head family's eldest son, who is like a nephew to me, replied, "That's right. It's the Pioneering Citizen's Award, given by the Hangook Newspaper Company. Only those who have already passed away are eligible to receive it since one's entire life cannot be judged accurately until it is over."

Another family member who had recently retired from a long career as the headmaster of a school, a man who is like a grandfather to me, then explained the achievements of the deceased.

"Kim Man-Ho really did great service for the community even during the difficult times of the Japanese Occupation. And during the chaotic period following Liberation, he contributed a great deal as one of the leaders of the local community. Among other things, he built a junior high school, which enabled young people in the community to receive an education. That wasn't an easy thing to do—even today it would be an outstanding achievement."

After he finished his remarks, other people began to talk about Kim Man-Ho.

"Well, yes, he did do a lot for the community, but he does not deserve the award," said my father's cousin, after listening to the others.

Everyone in the room then turned their eyes toward him.

"What are you talking about?" the headmaster said. "How dare you say such a thing after having lived away from the hometown for so long?"

Angered by his remark, the headmaster railed at my father's cousin in front of the others gathered there, but my father's cousin did not retreat. Instead, he tried to persuade the headmaster.

"Uncle, don't get me wrong, but I did know him well. During the Japanese Occupation I watched him more closely than anyone else could have. Of course, he did do the things that you mentioned, but that does not mean that he deserves the award."

The headmaster promptly interjected in a loud voice. "What are you talking about? He did many things for the community, but he does not deserve an award? I cannot understand you."

My father's cousin then blushed and fell silent after this public rebuke by the headmaster.

After a brief moment of silence, the first son of the head family tried to end the discussion by saying, "It is true that he served the community. And isn't it an honor for all of us if a person from our hometown receives a national award?"

No one immediately responded, and it seemed as though the discussion would end in this way. While some faces revealed interest in what my father's cousin had said, no one expressed any support for him. And because it seemed that the opinion of the headmaster would prevail, no one was willing to continue the discussion.

But just then, my father's cousin spoke up again.

"Uncle, we have to think about this matter more seriously. I think that if the Occupation had continued for another ten years, Kim would have become a Japanese citizen. People say that he served the community well, but can't you see that he always associated with those in power? That's why he can't be a person of justice. I cannot tell my children to emulate Kim Man-Ho and live as he did. As a role model, Reverend Kang Sung-Su is much more admirable."

After Reverend Kang was mentioned in the conversation, and contrasted with Kim Man-Ho, the atmosphere in the room suddenly changed. Everyone looked at my father's cousin.

With a confused look in his face, the headmaster yelled at my father's cousin once again.

"Are you out of your mind? Why are you mentioning him, a man who was killed for being a communist in those chaotic times? I understand that you do not know the situation here very well, since you have been away from the hometown for so long, but you should know better than that. How can you compare the honorable Kim Man-Ho with Kang Sung-Su?"

But my father's cousin did not back down. He refused to yield to the headmaster.

"Don't talk about ideology. I knew Reverend Kang very well. I can guarantee that he was not a communist. Jang Sung-Hwan or Bak Jong-Ku in Japan, both of whom are still alive, can also testify to that. Reverend Kang fought against the Japanese while Kim worked as a town mayor under the Japanese government, and Kang did not change his family name or his given name. Wasn't he the man who closed his own church because he would rather live as a mute than give his sermons in Japanese? Who else in our town fought against the Japanese at that time as fiercely as he did?"

"But at that time," the headmaster replied, "it was impossible to speak out against Japan. Everyone knows that Reverend Kang died because of his ideology. I don't understand why you suddenly mention him now."

"Uncle, we do not have many years left to live. Now is the time for us to reflect upon our lives. We need to verify what Kim Man-Ho really did. In the past, we ignored history and merely struggled to survive, but shouldn't the future be different?"

The atmosphere was now tense, as neither elder seemed willing to yield to the other, and no one else wanted to get involved in the discussion.

Turning his face toward me, my father's cousin said, "What you do think? Since you are an educated man, and also a newspaper reporter, you should understand these things better than we do."

Though I had come to the memorial service only by chance, I was excited to hear the views of the two elders. But I could not add anything to the discussion since I knew little of the people they were talking about. Besides, I had an assignment from the newspaper to do a story on Kim Man-Ho.

One day earlier, while I was busy preparing a special feature for the New Year's Day edition of the paper, my boss unexpectedly asked to see me.

"Something strange has happened," the boss said, as I entered his office. "Do you remember the man named Kim Man-Ho, the one who was chosen to receive the Pioneering Citizen's Award from our newspaper? He's from your hometown, isn't he? We've received a strange petition about him. Well, can I call it a petition? Anyway, in a word, it says that he does not deserve the award. It says that he worked for the Japanese during the Occupation, and that he was always on the side of power, even until he died. The petition acknowledges that Kim served the local community to a certain extent, but insists that his community service was not enough to atone for the other things he did. So, I'm afraid that we may have handled the selection process too carelessly. We did check the record of his achievements and consider the opinion of those in the community, but who would say something negative about a person who was already selected for the award? Nevertheless, no matter what sort of excuse I might make, I have a bad feeling that we may have made a mistake."

The boss talked about things that I could not fully understand, and he looked at me a few times while speaking in order to see my response. This did not seem to be a simple assignment. Because I had left my hometown on Jeju such a long time ago, I did not know the circumstances on the island very well. But I did know that Kim Man-Ho was the sort of person who could not be ignored easily. He had built a school and was a person of influence in the community. When I heard the news that he would receive an award, I was glad that a person from my hometown was being honored.

"Mr. Choi, don't allow this assignment to become too burdensome. Just inquire about him when you visit your hometown for the New Year's holiday. There may be a hidden story here that people don't know about."

The expression on the boss's face indicated that he was uncomfortable speaking about this, though he tried to treat it as a trivial matter.

"Pro-Japanese activity is a very delicate issue," he said. "If we give the award to a Japanese sympathizer, people will raise questions about the political inclinations of this newspaper. Well, maybe I should transfer you to some position where you can have some free time to work on this matter."

I left the boss's office without giving too much thought to his request. As he suggested, I thought that I would inquire about Kim Man-Ho during my visit home on New Year's Day. Only after being transferred to the editorial office did I realize how serious this matter was. That the decision regarding the award might be reversed made the thought of my visit an unpleasant one, especially since the whole thing was related to my own hometown.

It was in this state of mind that I returned home. Just by chance, I heard stories about Kim Man-Ho while I was at the head family's house. I also heard stories of Reverend Kang Sung-Su, whom I did not know about before. These things made me nervous.

2

Reluctant to get involved in the discussion between my father's cousin and the headmaster, the other people gathered at the head family's house remained silent. No one wanted to ruin the atmosphere on New Year's Day with a story of some unrelated person. Also, it was obvious that a discussion of this kind would never reach a conclusion and would only make people uncomfortable. Nevertheless, everyone looked somewhat unsatisfied that the issue was not discussed further.

* * *

An empty feeling crept into my hollow heart as I stood aimlessly on the central roundabout in my hometown, a town that had recently been transformed into a city. After leaving the head family's house, I roamed around this small city to find the familiar places of my old hometown: the police station, the elementary school, the vocational school, the Japanese shrine, the hospital, the port, and the post office. While searching for these places I got lost, but with some effort I finally found the roundabout. In front of the dried-up fountain, I stared at the dark sky. It seemed like it was about to snow. Suddenly, a church came into sight. I remembered that an old church with a tin roof once stood at that very site. In those days, the church marked the outer limits of the town. The sharp wooden cross on the top of that church used to be visible from any point in the town. One day the cross was removed and the church door was nailed shut with two big planks of wood that crossed each other. I once noticed that the planks of wood nailed to the church door formed the shape of a cross. This realization occurred when I was very young, probably around the age of five or six. The children in those days avoided walking in front of the church just as they avoided walking in front of a house in which someone had recently died. Now, on that same spot, stood a modern church, reaching high toward the sky.

"You are here."

I turned to see who had said this and found my father's cousin standing behind me. I was really glad to see him again—it seemed as if I had been waiting here for him. We went to a nearby coffee shop.

After ordering some coffee, I briefly told him about my assignment regarding Kim Man-Ho.

"He was my senior by three years. He graduated from the same agricultural school as I did. I know every detail about him, from the top of his head to the tip of his toes."

With these words, he began to talk. Unlike a typical seventy-year-old, he remembered things in detail. He talked without hesitation, as if he had prepared all of this in advance.

Kim's family had been well-off, but his grandfather lost the family fortune when he became immersed in *Sundo*. From that point on he wasted his time searching for propitious gravesites for his ancestors. After losing the family fortune, his grandfather barely managed to survive. He collected tuition from the local primary school students, to whom he taught the Chinese script. Since there was no land to till, his father lived like a bum, working as a laborer at neighbors' houses and frequenting gambling shops during the winter. Things changed, however, when the Japanese Occupation began. A new port was built, and the Japanese army was stationed right next to the port. Since Kim's father spoke some Japanese, he became close to them. His father was a rather worthless man but quite intelligent, and his ability to speak Japanese suddenly became very useful. After graduating from elementary school, Kim entered an agricultural school, the only junior high school in town. During vacations he would return to his home village and gather young children, those who were just hanging around with nothing to do after having finished elementary school, and teach them Japanese.

He said to the children, "The world has changed and we can no longer waste our time just trying to survive. We should learn new things as soon as possible and go live in a bigger world." Kim knew that the ability to speak Japanese would be very advantageous, even if only to work as a laborer in Japan. That's why he taught the children the Japanese language and farming, and advised them to go and live in a bigger world.

"I must admit that Kim Man-Ho was an extraordinary person. He started something similar to the New Village Movement that we began in the 1970s. However, his educational movement ultimately destroyed the spirit of the people. Around that time, some other people were busy teaching

Korean, but Kim taught Japanese. Reverend Kang Sung-Su was different from him."

My father's cousin seemed to have stronger feelings for Reverend Kang than for Kim Man-Ho, so I became interested in learning more about Kang.

"Both of them attended the same elementary school and agricultural school, and they were widely known in this area as brilliant students ..."

My father's cousin paused a little before continuing.

"After graduating from agricultural school, Kang got a teaching job at the elementary school here. He also taught classes at an evening school for children who could not afford the day school. I helped him out on vacations or on Saturdays when I returned home from school."

During those years, Kang Sang-Su and Kim Man-Ho quarreled with each other frequently. Kang was not happy with the fact that Kim was teaching the children Japanese, and Kim thought that Kang was arrogant and out of touch with the changing world. During those years, the situation worsened, the school for Korean language was closed, and Kang had to leave his hometown.

"You know, it was Kim Man-Ho that closed the Korean language school. He secretly informed the police, who then punished us. As a result, I could not finish school, and I went to Japan because bad things kept happening to me here."

My father's cousin talked about the past as if it were only yesterday.

"Not only that, Kim did many other terrible things. However, when I returned after the end of the Japanese Occupation, I was surprised to find him behaving like a big man around town. I couldn't bear to see it, so I returned to Japan."

My father's cousin had a strange look on his face.

After working for three years at the agricultural co-op, Kim Man-Ho became the town mayor at a very young age—he was younger than thirty—but my father's cousin thought that Kim must have been the worst mayor in history. What he could not forgive or forget is the fact that Kim outwardly pretended to be doing things for the people of the hometown, but in truth, he was always acting in his own interests. There were thirteen town mayors on Jeju Island at that time, and Kim Man-Ho was the only one of them to have the confidence of the governor.

While talking about the past, the tone of my father's cousin became coarser. He said that even in the twilight of his life, at a time when one can usually understand and forgive everything, he could not forgive Kim Man-Ho.

"Think about it," he said. "How can you give such a person the Pioneering Citizen's Award? It would make sense if the award were coming from the Japanese government, since he worked like a pioneer for the Japanese. But this is not just an issue about one individual, Kim Man-Ho.

The recipient of this award should be a model citizen, someone for others to follow. Shall other people be encouraged to live like him? No, never."

He spoke loudly, as if he were talking directly to Kim Man-Ho, and that made everyone around us turn and stare.

After we left the coffee shop and parted ways, I felt like meeting the headmaster. Of course, he would say something totally different from what I had just heard from my father's cousin, but he might provide me with some new information.

* * *

"I knew that you would come to see me."

The headmaster, who was dressed in *hanbok* and sitting on the floor, surrounded by a ten-fold screen, arose to welcome me. The words on the screen, words that he himself had inscribed, were from some Buddhist scriptures, the *Prajna Paramitasutra*. He was a happy old man, the kind of man that grows old gracefully. He spent his whole life of sixty-odd years working for the education of children. He retired some years ago, although he was still treated as a teacher by the people around here. On top of the stationery chest in the corner of the room, there was a Korean plant, a *cymbidium kanran*, whose beauty seemed to match the headmaster's graceful character. The cushions that were scattered about the room indicated that visitors had recently come to pay their respects to the headmaster on New Year's Day.

He knew why I had come to see him.

After telling him about my assignment with the newspaper, I said, "I've heard that you had a long friendship with Kim Man-Ho. Since you would have known him better than anyone else, I would like you to tell me all that you know about him, including some personal things."

However, I did not feel entirely comfortable with this request since I did not have a clear standard for judging a man's life under the Japanese Occupation.

"It is true that he worked as an official and even served as the mayor of our town during the Occupation. But even in those times, someone had to work as mayor, so we cannot judge his character by that fact alone. I also worked as a teacher for more than ten years, teaching the doctrines of Japanese colonization, so I am not in a position to talk about what is right or wrong regarding his behavior. The reason why I raised my voice at the head family's house some hours ago has to do with your father's cousin. I was angry at him because he spoke as if he knew the situation here well, even though he has lived in Japan for so long. And how could he have lived there without collaborating with the Japanese people in one way or another? It is impossible. Perhaps he flattered the powerful Japanese more than anybody else. Don't you agree that those who have lived outside the hometown for so long do not have the right to judge the people who suffered here?"

"I've heard," I said, "that the dispute between Kim Man-Ho and Kang Sung-Su started when they both volunteered to teach at a night school during the Occupation. Is that true? And didn't someone secretly inform the police that subversive activities were being carried out at the night school, that people were being encouraged to resist the rule of the Japanese government?"

I asked these questions because I wanted to know whether the story that I had heard from my father's cousin was true—that it was Kim Man-Ho who had told the police about Reverend Kang.

"There was indeed such an incident. Kang Sung-Su wanted to impress a certain ideology upon the young children, who had no ability to think for themselves, and he did so while pretending to be teaching the Korean language. Outwardly, he said that he was participating in a movement for the Korean people, but inside he had his mind on something else."

The headmaster emphasized that Reverend Kang was a socialist, while avoiding my question about Kim and the Korean night class.

"How can a pastor be a socialist?" I asked.

The headmaster responded sharply: "Is there any law that says a pastor cannot be a communist?"

The tone of his response betrayed a nervous temperament.

At that moment I understood why the headmaster had gotten so upset at the head family's house by the remarks of my father's cousin. I began to feel uncomfortable and realized how funny words can be. However, I decided to subdue my anger, thinking that I might yet be able to hear some stories that others do not know. I thought that I should be ready to fight with anyone if I want to get to the heart of this matter. I took a deep breath and straightened myself to listen carefully to the headmaster.

"I've heard," I said, "that Kim Man-Ho worked for adolescents before becoming town mayor. Do you remember anything related to that?"

I already knew about these things roughly, through the report on Kim's achievements, but I wanted to know how this retired teacher interpreted these accomplishments.

"Well, everyone knows about them. One of the things that we still regard as a wonder is that he started revolutionary movements such as demolishing superstitions and old evil customs. Even today, these are difficult tasks. He led those movements, which we now consider to be consciousness-raising activities."

The headmaster continued to talk about the movements for adolescents that Kim Man-Ho led before he became mayor. Through these stories I learned some interesting facts, such as that he distinguished himself by demolishing a village shrine and by cutting off the topknot from his own grandfather's hair.

The governor of Jeju Island, the chief administrator, had many problems in carrying out policies on Jeju due to the many village shrines for gods and the prevalence of traditional superstitions. Thus, he ordered villagers to voluntarily demolish the shrines and eradicate traditional superstitions. However, it was not easy to carry out his orders. In each village, the town office or the police station mobilized the local youths to demolish the shrines. However, because of resistance coming mostly from women, many unfortunate incidents occurred. Also, beliefs in the traditional gods were rooted so deeply in the hearts of the people that few were willing to participate in the destruction of the shrines. However, the district of Namdo, where Kim Man-Ho took the lead, was an exception. In recognition of his success in demolishing all the shrines, he received an award.

"What a new way of looking at things, don't you think? Because he succeeded in carrying out a task that was difficult in those days, and would be difficult even today, he was considered to be a man of foresight. In fact, even though I was an educator in those days, I wouldn't dare to think of doing such a thing."

As the headmaster continued to speak, it seemed that I was talking to a new person, someone unfamiliar.

"After that, he became the mayor of our town at the young age of twenty-eight. In that position he faced many challenges. All of the previous mayors regarded the post as an honorary position and were interested only in exercising their power over others. Kim Man-Ho was different: he was a modest and ordinary citizen, and he devoted himself to improving the town for everyone. First he widened the streets. Even though a new port was built and the town was expanding, the streets had remained in the same condition as in the old days. The government office wanted to widen the streets, but they couldn't because landowners refused to give up their land. No previous mayor wanted to become an enemy of the townspeople, so nothing was done about the narrow streets. We had to suffer in that condition, but ..."

The headmaster paused briefly, and then went on to tell the following story.

After Kim Man-Ho became mayor, he solved the problem simply and quickly. First, he gave up his own land and had it surveyed to build a road through the middle of it. After that, he visited all the other landowners around his field and asked them to give up their land. While he was persuading his neighbors, an airport was being built in a large field behind the town. This made it easy to persuade the others of the need to widen the streets. Who could object to building a wider road that would connect the port and the airport for military purposes? Once it was decided that a road would be built, Kim decided to make it bigger than was originally planned. After the road was built, big cherry trees were planted along both sides. Some years later, the grown cherry trees blossomed and the town became a popular spot for sightseeing. Many Japanese came to live in our town, and thereafter the town took on the appearance of a new city.

Among the many things that he did, the removal of the topknots was his greatest achievement. It showed a new aspect of his character.

Our town, Namdo, was inhabited by many so-called scholars who had received some sort of education at a Confucian school. In those days, because of the complaints of these scholars, even an official could not easily command the people in this town. Even during the Japanese Occupation, these people did not change their attitude at all. Therefore, officials had problems in carrying out orders in this area. When Kim became mayor, those old scholars were still wearing topknots on their heads. They kept them even though most of the people on Jeju Island had removed theirs. With their topknots intact, they continued to think in their old-fashioned ways.

One day, Kim Man-Ho invited the elders of the town, those who had kept their topknots, to the auditorium of an elementary school. He said, "As the mayor, and an unworthy son of this town, I am responsible for the livelihood of the people. Please have sympathy toward me and help me do a good job."

He then bowed politely and treated the elders to lunch. The elders were quite pleased, since this was the first time for them to be treated to lunch by a mayor.

"The world is changing," he said, "but our town is still living in the old world, practicing evil customs. Should we be content with being big fish in a small pond? Should we pass on our poverty to our sons and daughters? No, we should pull ourselves together. The first thing we should abandon is the topknot of hair that taints our minds. Even King Ko-Jong cut off his own topknot and abandoned those old customs. That was so long ago!"

While saying this, Kim Man-Ho studied the elders' faces. Suddenly he moved closer to where the elders were sitting and, with one clean stroke, cut the topknot off his own grandfather's hair, who was listening carefully to his darling grandson's impassioned speech. It happened in the blink of an eye.

Kim's grandfather was at a loss with this impudent act of his grandson, but he stood up and said, "It is my shame that my own topknot was cut by my grandson, and not by myself. But you, you can cut your topknots by yourselves. Let me tell you, I had no idea that I would feel this refreshed with my topknot gone."

Kim's grandfather shouted with joy, as if the whole event had been rehearsed. And those who had been gathered and brought to the auditorium—employees in the town office, some schoolteachers, and the members of a youth group and a women's group—applauded loudly. The elders who were sitting there suddenly started to feel uncomfortable with their itchy topknots. They also felt ashamed.

The problem of the elders' topknots was thus solved. Not one of the elders at that auditorium returned home on that day with his topknot intact.

"What an accomplishment!" the headmaster said. "With the topknots gone, our village was able to develop about twenty years faster than it otherwise would have. The topknots themselves were not retarding development; the problem was the mindset of keeping the topknots. From that time on, more young people went to Japan, earned money, and studied there. Everything is owed to Kim Man-Ho. He looked ahead into the future and got things done."

The headmaster then closed his eyes softly as he continued to speak of those events that were suddenly revived in his mind.

"Of course, he also received many criticisms during his long years as town mayor, but no one can deny the fact that everything he did was done for the people in the community. What's the meaning of patriotism and nationalism if people in the country cannot make a living while working so hard? Did any other official in any period ever donate even one bowl of rice to feed the hungry? No, never! Rather, they deprived the poor people. But Kim Man-Ho worked for those people. Though he served as an official during the Japanese Occupation, he served better than any of the officials in the old days under the Korean kings. He made sure that the fruits of all labor were returned to the townspeople. Some say that Kim helped to sell the country to the Japanese, but they are the minority. Think about it. He served as mayor for more than ten years during the Occupation, but no one threw a stone at him after Liberation."

With these words the headmaster concluded what he wanted to say, indicating that it was the absolute truth. He then looked at me, as if he were asking whether I could throw a stone at Kim Man-Ho. But even if I could not criticize him, could I say that his way of life was desirable? The more that I thought about it, the more confused I was. I could neither blame nor praise him. I was embarrassed by my inability to make up my own mind on these matters. The faces of the people gathered at the head family's house a few hours earlier flashed across my mind, and I even admired the first son of the head family for being able to present his own opinion without any reservation.

After leaving the headmaster's house, these thoughts weighed on my mind, making me more depressed.

3

During the first few days of the New Year, my thoughts became more confused from my visits with the headmaster and my father's cousin. So for the next several days after that I didn't meet anyone. I could not pull my thoughts together.

"Why," I wondered, "did my father's cousin think of Kim Man-Ho in such a negative way? Are Kim's pro-Japanese activities really so objectionable? Was Reverend Kang Sung-Su a communist?"

I kept pondering these questions. In order to answer them objectively, I resolved to investigate some of the events that had taken place in this town immediately after Liberation from the Japanese Occupation. I met some people who had lived in the hometown around that time, but I did not hear anything new from them. The headmaster and my father's cousin are related to each other by nine degrees of kinship. They attended, at slightly different times, the same elementary school and agricultural school, which was the only junior high school in town. (However, my father's cousin did not graduate from the agricultural school.) The headmaster was known as a typical scholar around this area, so it was not likely that he was a prejudicial man. That made my investigation of Kim Man-Ho more difficult. I thought that I could get additional details by contacting more people, but I was wrong. Therefore, I just wanted to file the facts that I had gathered up until that point and be finished with my assignment. In fact, it was much too difficult for me to examine accurately the lives of Kim Man-Ho and Kang Sung-Su; I just wanted to report the situation to the chief editor and get this assignment off my hands.

I made a reservation to fly to Seoul the following day. But then, just by chance, I happened to see a book entitled *The People Who Made Our Town Famous* on the desk of my female cousin, an elementary school teacher. The editor was the headmaster. The book was published by the provincial Department of Education and distributed to the schools as educational material. It included a three-page article on Kim Man-Ho. I read it and found that it was very similar to what I had heard from the headmaster. The article described Kim as a pioneer, but I felt that the content was seriously exaggerated.

A strange thought occurred to me while reading the article. Through this material, Kim Man-Ho had been described to students as a pioneer and a person who served the community well. And while he was being presented to the students as a pioneering citizen, I had been wandering around painstakingly trying to uncover the truth about him. How interesting! If the headmaster wrote that article, and if it was accepted as an established fact, certainly there was nothing new I would find out about Kim from the headmaster. Suddenly I wanted to know more about that educational material. I was curious about the responses of the students and the teachers to this material so I decided to visit a friend who was vice-headmaster of the elementary school from which I had graduated.

On my way to visit him, my father's cousin gave me a call and said that he wanted to meet me. I told him that I would see him after meeting my friend and went straight to the elementary school. My friend was waiting there for me. It had been a long time since we had last seen each other, so we chatted about our lives for a while. Then I asked him about the headmaster, pretending that the question had just come to my mind. Since the headmaster had taught both of us, it was natural for me to ask about him.

"He still has a lot of things to do. That's why he's still healthy. I've heard that he is writing something these days."

"What's he writing?" I asked.

"Ah, you wouldn't know about it. He edited a regional educational booklet entitled *The People Who Made Our Town Famous*, which has been well received. As a result of that booklet, every educational institution in the nation started to make such material. His original intention was to find role models and leaders among the people around us and to introduce them far and wide. He thought that we needed more tangible role models, local people from the present, rather than foreigners or people from the remote past. In his opinion, there are many such people. Soon there will be a new, revised and enlarged edition. He might include stories of devoted children, chaste women, loyal subjects, or those of humble birth who lived honestly. I heard that he has almost finished collecting the stories and that he's currently writing about them."

My friend had just told me the story I wanted to hear without my asking. I became interested in the fact that the headmaster was writing more articles for the revised edition.

"What were the responses of the schoolteachers to the book?" I asked.

"At first, no one was really interested in the book, but after it received a positive evaluation from an official in the Ministry of Education who was visiting Jeju Island, many people changed their minds. Besides, one of the figures in the book, Kim Man-Ho, was chosen as the winner of a Pioneering Citizen's Award. So I can say that the book has fulfilled its purpose."

Through my friend's words, I was beginning to see the truth.

"What was the relationship between Kim Man-Ho and the headmaster?" I asked.

This is the question in which I was most interested. I wondered if there was a reason why the headmaster was so fond of Kim Man-Ho, something that others might not know about. Their relationship might have also affected the relationship between Reverend Kang Sung-Su and the headmaster.

"You cannot say that they had a special relationship. Yes, they were very close to each other. They attended the same school, though the headmaster graduated a few years after Kim did, but that is not the reason why they were close. Rather, both of them were influential people in the community, and that might have drawn them close to each other. You know, the headmaster worked at the elementary school all of his life. If he had been transferred to a junior high or a high school, he might have been promoted to the rank of superintendent of educational affairs. He spent his whole life as an educator, without concern for a higher social position."

My friend added that the headmaster has a great deal of influence in this community.

"When do you think the revised edition of the book will come out?" I asked.

"Well, it might come out soon since it is the beginning of year."

Thinking that he might be able to tell me something about Reverend Kang, I mentioned the name Kang Sung-Su, but he shook his head—he didn't know anything about him. I stood up feeling somewhat unsatisfied.

While we were walking toward the front gate, a strange stone monument standing just inside the gate attracted my attention. It was a large granite monument covered with white stone mushrooms. As I approached it, I saw that there were no words etched in it; it was just a big stone. I thought that the inscription might have been worn away with time so I cleared the surface of the monument in an effort to discern any faded words.

"Why doesn't this stone monument have an inscription on it?" I asked, as I turned my eyes toward my friend.

He was behind me, smiling. I then walked around the stone monument and found a plaque about thirty by thirty centimeters on the left side, indicating that the monument was erected "To encourage academic pursuits." The plaque said: "A rich person, who deplored his own ignorance, erected this stone monument with no words on it to encourage children to study hard."

"I've not seen this kind of monument before. It wasn't here when we were students, was it?"

My friend then explained the history of the monument to me.

"The headmaster found it somewhere in the village and moved it to this place."

"But what about the history of the monument? Is there some kind of legend to it?"

"Well, I don't know," he replied. "But doesn't it look suitable in a school yard? The words on the plaque were written by the headmaster himself, and people said that it seemed fitting."

We then parted, promising to meet again for a drink sometime. But the expression "seemed fitting" bothered me.

* * *

My father's cousin was waiting for me when I arrived at our designated meeting place.

He began by saying "The reason I wanted to see you ..." but then paused and stared into my face for some time. I was going to mention the educational material and the monument that I had just seen, but then he continued.

"To tell you the truth, I was the one who sent the petition to the newspaper to reconsider the award for Kim Man-Ho."

He said it without changing the look on his face at all. The fact that he could say it without any emotion surprised me. Suddenly he seemed dangerous—not because he objected to the award going to Kim Man-Ho, but because of the boldness with which he told me the news. Jeju is a small island and everyone is related to everyone else, directly or indirectly, so this was the sort of secret that couldn't be revealed easily. I thought that there must be a good reason for him to say this, but I was afraid to know about it, lest I too might become involved in his scheme.

"Don't be so surprised. When people come to know that I am doing this, they will say that I've started to behave like a dotard since I don't have many more years to live. But isn't it right for me to tell you the truth since you are trying hard to discover it? It is not a pleasant thing to speak ill of someone, especially since I am an old person. But wouldn't it be terrible if the truth is forever concealed or distorted? That's why all of this started. Anyway, I think I am doing the right thing, but I'm sorry if it causes problems or makes you suffer. I find that it is really difficult to change entrenched ideas."

He said these things slowly and calmly, but I heard them with breathless anxiety. After listening to him, I thought I understood his intentions to a certain extent.

"Have you seen this?" I asked, as I passed him the educational material.

"Yes, I have. It was written by the headmaster himself."

We remained silent for sometime, and then he said,

"The headmaster was a scholar, you know. That makes me wonder why he does this kind of thing. On that New Year's Day too, there must have been some reason why he raised his voice against me. He was the one who did all the reporting on Kim Man-Ho's achievements and secretly recommended him as a candidate for the award. He himself may have been just like Kim."

Though my father's cousin was not at all pleased with what the headmaster had done, he referred to him as "uncle" or "headmaster." He was upset by the fact that while he and the headmaster were closely related members of an extended family, they were now opposed to each other because of someone unrelated to them. But I wondered what my father's cousin meant by saying that the headmaster may have been just like Kim Man-Ho. What relationship did the two of them have?

"Do you mean that Kim Man-Ho and the headmaster are in some special relationship?" I asked.

"No, not a special relationship. They were just close to each other because they were raised in the same hometown. The headmaster did things for Kim Man-Ho because they had been in similar situations. The headmaster had been a teacher for more than ten years during the Japanese Occupation, advocating the doctrines of Japanese colonization. Given his character, he must have done it with all of his heart. Now, as he nears the end of his life, he wants to find an exit from his past by endowing it with a special meaning. Think about it: if Kim Man-Ho falls down, then so too does the headmaster."

"If Kim Man-Ho falls down, then so too does the headmaster?" I couldn't understand what he meant.

"Everyone has a tendency to rationalize one's own behavior, even if one has to fabricate the past to do so. Well, if I were in that situation, I might have behaved the same way. Outwardly, he looks like a philosopher who is not concerned with worldly affairs, but really he is trying to conceal the truth."

The thoughts of my father's cousin were very firm.

I then broached the topic of the stone monument. "Have you ever heard about that monument before, the one in the school yard?" I asked.

When he heard me, the edges of his mouth quivered.

"You mean that monument is now standing inside the school?"

After giving the matter some serious thought, he stood up and announced, "I have to go and see it myself."

* * *

He stood in front of the stone monument and stared at it for a long time before turning to me to speak.

"This is fraudulent! How could this happen? A monument 'To encourage academic pursuits'? What a beautiful description! A monument that is erected by an illiterate person—what a story! This is the arrogance of the elite. How can he deceive those innocent children?"

His face became red with anger, and then he seemed puzzled.

"You mean you know about this monument?" I asked.

"Of course I do. How can I forget such a significant thing? What a racketeer! He is the greatest thief in the world—one who steals history."

His anger then compelled him to recount the story of the stone monument.

One day Kang Sung-Su, who had left our hometown after the night school incident, suddenly returned. It had been five years since he left. At that time, Kim Man-Ho was the town mayor. Kang had looked somewhat defeated; his appearance was shabby and his manner timid. The townspeople thus talked about him in whispers, looking at him suspiciously.

Some time after he returned, he began to work as an evangelist. Together with a young woman around twenty years old, who had come to the town with him, he went around spreading the teachings of the gospels. The people whispered that he was out of his mind, but he was not crazy; he was perfectly normal. After he left his hometown, he had wandered around and finally entered a missionary school in Pyongyang. Later, he graduated from a theological seminary, was ordained as a pastor, and then returned to his hometown.

The study room in Kang's house, where the church service first began, came to be filled with followers in less than a year. And after some time, a church was built on the field that Reverend Kang owned. That church could be seen from anywhere in the town, and it became increasingly prosperous as time went by. The church was open every day, not just on Sundays and Wednesdays, and children and teenagers went in and out of the church as if it were their own house.

As the church prospered, the police station began to interfere in its affairs. However, the number of followers was so large that even the police had to be cautious in their dealings with the church. Reverend Kang was also careful not to irritate the police in his sermons, lest the church that he had established be shut down by force. He advised the church congregation not to cause any problems with government authorities. And he resolved to endure humiliation until the church was fully established. However, there was a limit to his perseverance.

One day the police superintendent came to the church and announced that "upon orders from the superior office, the Japanese language must be used when you preach from the podium."

At that time, Japanese was the official language in Korea. Korean newspapers were discontinued and classes in schools were taught in Japanese.

"How can I preach in Japanese? The church members do not know Japanese," Reverend Kang responded. He knew that the incident he feared had finally happened.

"If you continue to preach in Korean, the church will be shut down. If the church members do not know Japanese, you, the pastor, should first teach them how to speak Japanese, then you can preach," the policeman sneered, leaving Kang with only two options.

"How can I teach Japanese? I myself am not fluent enough to preach in Japanese!" Reverend Kang responded.

Kang recognized that this was all just an excuse to shut the church down. Nevertheless, he pleaded, trying to find a way out. He knew that the church would take a strong root in the community within a few years. He also knew that if the church were controlled by external forces, then the seed of the gospel would not bear fruit. That was why he behaved so carefully in his dealings with the police.

The police superintendent did not budge. He said to Kang, "First, study Japanese for several years, and then preach."

Reverend Kang begged leniency, asking for more time.

On the following Sunday, Reverend Kang preached as usual in Korean.

But the police superintendent threatened him once again: "Do you think that God does not know Japanese? Why don't you follow orders? Do you really want the church to be shut down?"

Looking at the back of the policeman as he walked away, Reverend Kang suppressed his anger. However, being angry did not solve the problem.

After agonizing over this for some time, Reverend Kang finally went to see his friend, Kim Man-Ho, the mayor.

"It looks like my church will go through a hard time. Is there any way to avoid it?" asked Reverend Kang.

Though Kang did not want to ask a favor of Kim, he felt desperate. Since not all of the churches in Korea preach in Japanese, Kang wanted to hear about a way out of this difficulty. But Kim was very callous.

"What else can be done? Times have changed. There are only two ways. If you want to save the church, you should follow the police orders. Or …"

Reverend Kang stormed out of the room without listening to the rest of Kim's advice. He then went straight to the police superintendent and asked for his permission to preach in Korean one more time on the following Sunday.

On that Sunday, Reverend Kang had so many things to say that the sermon did not flow smoothly.

"This is the last sermon I will give in Korean. Maybe we will not have any more chances to hear God's words in this church …"

The church members wept during his sermon. Reverend Kang preached for about two hours, which was not his plan. During his long sermon, the church members often repeated the word "Amen." Their faces were covered in tears.

The problem worsened on the following Sunday. Instead of preaching in Japanese, Reverend Kang stood at the podium, as he had on previous Sundays, but did not speak. During the speechless sermon, the church members bent their bodies, reading the Korean Bible silently or praying with their eyes closed. From time to time, the church members said "Amen," while praying in tears. Tears also flew from the eyes of Reverend Kang, who was standing in front of the congregation. The speechless sermon lasted an hour, and then the church members prayed by themselves until the end of the worship period.

They continued to do this for a month until another notice came from the police station stating that if the sermon were not given in Japanese, the church would be forced to close. Nonetheless, Reverend Kang continued his speechless sermon.

Then on one hot summer day while Reverend Kang was giving his speechless sermon with his face covered in sweat and tears, Japanese military police rushed into the church. The loud sound of the combat boots caused the church members, who had been praying quietly with their bodies bent forward, to lift their heads and look at the pastor. They saw Reverend Kang in his *hanbok* surrounded by policemen.

An old woman suddenly ran up to the policemen and said, "Take me instead."

The other church members then stood up and surrounded the police who were surrounding Reverend Kang. At that moment, other policemen who were watching over the scene fired blank shots into the sky.

"Please, stay calm. No one should be hurt," Reverend Kang pleaded.

But no one listened to him. The church members and the policemen struggled with each other until Kang finally succeeded in getting the congregation to cooperate. The police then arrested Kang and pressured him to accept the policies of Japan with the promise that the church would not be forced to shut down. They also asked him to respect the Japanese shrines and adopt a Japanese name. However, since he refused all of these requests, he was sent to trial.

Soon after, the church was shut down. The church members were not even allowed to gather and pray by themselves. The police had nailed shut all of the church doors.

One day, in fall of that year, the youths of the church came and nailed two logs crosswise on the church door. Even from a distance, the two logs, which had been nailed in the shape of a cross, could be seen clearly. It happened after the police had demolished the bell tower of the church and removed the bell and the wooden cross. A few months later, some young men of the church erected the stone monument with no inscription on it at the corner of the backyard of the church. It was erected in honor of Reverend Kang, who had been arrested while performing a speechless sermon, and to pay tribute to the church congregation, which preserved its faith even in that dire situation.

"Only those who were directly involved in erecting the stone monument knew the reason. After liberation from the Japanese Occupation, Reverend Kang was released from jail, but for some time after his release, Kang could not work on the church and the building was left deserted. When Kang was finally ready to rebuild the church and concentrate on his pastoral duties, the 4.3 Incident occurred and he was killed under false accusation. After that, everyone forgot about that stone monument, and those who were involved in erecting the monument all disappeared. Now that very same stone monument is in the school yard and has been transformed into a memorial 'To encourage academic pursuits!' How could such a thing happen?"

Whispering this, he stared gravely at the sky.

"The world has changed so much and people just live for the moment, having easily forgotten things of the past. The world is full of those who distort the truth to promote their own position …"

My father's cousin looked straight at me while he spoke in this serious manner. It seemed that he wanted some response from me.

Then I asked him, "Did you see the speechless sermon?"

I was tense from the story that I had just heard, but I wanted to know about those events in more detail.

"Yes, I saw it. I certainly saw it. It happened when I visited our hometown. I returned home at that time because I really wanted to settle down here, but after that incident, I left again."

Suddenly, I wanted to believe him.

4

A young man in his thirties, the son of Reverend Kang Sung-Su's cousin, came out of a tangerine storage house and reacted guardedly when he saw me. After hearing my explanation, he seemed to loosen up. Maybe he felt safe. Nevertheless, he insisted that he did not know anything about Reverend Kang.

"I heard of him when I was young, but I am not interested in someone who destroyed the family."

He said this in such a callous voice. I asked him whether Reverend Kang had any closer relatives, but he just shook his head.

"Do you attend church?" I asked.

Again he shook his head strongly. I asked him whether his father attended church while he was alive, and he replied bluntly that no one in his family went to church. I was surprised to hear that none of his family members had any clear memories of Reverend Kang. And this young man seemed determined to erase completely any lingering memories, good or bad, of the pastor.

I thought to myself: "Maybe Kang was a difficult person to accept. How strange it is, then, that he is alive only in the memory of my father's cousin, a man who lived for so long away from the hometown? Was it because no one in the town was open-minded enough to keep the memory of Reverend Kang alive?"

I went to the town church, hoping that I might be able to find something there.

After hearing why I was visiting the church, the pastor, a man in his mid-thirties, said that he didn't know the history of the church in detail since he had come to this post only recently, but he did know that the church had accomplished a great deal through its struggles and persecution. Looking somewhat embarrassed, he said that he would soon put the history of the church in order.

When I asked about Reverend Kang Sung-Su, the founder of the church, he spoke reluctantly.

"Yes, I've heard about him only in passing. I heard that he engaged in anti-Japanese activities and that he had some different ideology …"

"Do you think that he was a communist?" I asked, even though I felt that this question might seem too direct.

The pastor looked at me suspiciously. He did not answer.

"Did you hear that Reverend Kang gave speechless sermons during the Japanese Occupation?"

I wanted to confirm what I had heard from my father's cousin.

"Yes, I heard about it from the church elders in this area. Unfortunately, I could not confirm it with any church member who was alive at that time since none of them still come to this church."

I said, "I've heard that, after Reverend Kang was arrested, he was indicted and jailed. Is there any record of that?"

"Well, there should be some record of the trial."

The pastor answered reluctantly, showing no interest in the matter.

"By the way," he added, "I have a friend who studies the history of Korean churches. I've heard that nowadays he is collecting materials concerning the suppression of church services during the Japanese Occupation. Maybe he has some material on Reverend Kang Sung-Su."

This was a very equivocal answer. It seemed that he said it just to save face. While listening to his response, I was frustrated that people did not have any interest in the past. I thought, "If this man is not interested in the blood-tainted history of his own church, how can he plan the future of the church?" After realizing that this indifference to history was really indifference to the truth, I felt that it was a cruel and cold-hearted world indeed.

"I would like to meet someone who attended the church at that time. It doesn't matter whether they still attend church," I said.

After speaking to the deacon, an old man who took care of church affairs, the pastor said, "There is one such person, but she might not remember those events of so long ago. She is too old."

The pastor then asked the deacon to lead me to that old woman.

The woman, who was well over seventy, was lying in bed reading the Bible when I visited her. I explained the purpose of my visit, and she looked at me vacantly for some time, not saying anything. Her face was dark and covered with deep wrinkles, as if she had suffered from smallpox, but her eyes were twinkling. Since she hadn't yet said a word, I thought that she might be hard of hearing. I was about to shout when she said,

"Who are you?"

I understood why she was asking that question. I was going to introduce myself as a newspaper reporter, when the deacon introduced me, mentioning my grandfather's name.

"This is his grandson." The deacon added, "Since he has lived in Seoul for a long time, you would not recognize him."

Having the deacon there made her feel comfortable.

After these words were spoken, the old woman turned her gaze from me and fidgeted with the Bible.

"I must have lived long enough to have met a person who is interested in Reverend Kang."

She drew a long breath.

"Reverend Kang was two years younger than me. If you had heard his sermons, you surely would have become a Christian. Not only did he speak well, but he was also a man of character. His belief in God was like Paul's."

With her toothless mouth, she spoke imperfectly, but without a pause. After describing Reverend Kang's character, she talked about the founding of the church, Reverend Kang's arrest by the Japanese police, and the stone monument. She seemed excited as she spoke. Everything she said corresponded exactly to what my father's cousin had told me.

"I don't understand," she said. "Why did he become a communist? Our church could have been the most successful one on Jeju Island …"

The old woman finished the conversation with a deep sigh.

As I left the old woman's house, I too was somewhat excited. I was now more interested in Reverend Kang than in Kim Man-Ho. Maybe, as my father's cousin had said, Kang was not a communist. Maybe there was a special relationship between those two men.

When I returned to my uncle's house, I called up the main office of the newspaper company and asked for a few more days' leave. I wanted to uncover the truth about Reverend Kang, the truth that would otherwise be buried forever. I wanted to go to Jeju City and meet a person who would know about those events of the past.

As I was leaving for Jeju City, I got a call from someone. It was a young, insolent voice on the other end, and I could not put a name to it. He introduced himself as someone from my hometown, someone who knew me well. He said he wanted to meet me for a short time. I was not really inclined to meet him, but I agreed to do so.

The young man looked to be about twenty-seven years old and seemed rather rude. When we introduced ourselves, I came to know that he had graduated from the same junior high school that I had attended. He therefore called me *seonbae*, but his attitude showed that he didn't really regard me as a *seonbae* at all. He was praising me to my face, but doing so in a sarcastic tone of voice. He introduced himself by saying, "Nam-Song is my uncle."

Since I couldn't associate the name "Nam-Song" with anyone, I didn't answer right away. However, I sensed some hostility in his eyes.

"Why don't you know Nam-Song?" he said. "You seem unconcerned about the people of your hometown."

He jeered at me as he spoke.

Just then I realized that "Nam-Song" is the pseudonym for Kim Man-Ho, but I pretended not to be aware of this.

"Stop what you have been doing here for the last several days. Can't you think of anything better to do than to dig up some scandal in our hometown after having lived somewhere else for many years?"

He glared at me, plainly showing displeasure on his face.

"Whatever one says, my uncle Nam-Song is the spiritual backbone of this town. I am not saying this because I am his nephew. Go ask anyone. You will get the same answer. Why are you fretting so much not to be able to disgrace him? You should try to find more people who are not yet known to the world, and let the world know about them, rather than trying to disgrace someone without reason, someone whose accomplishments have already been acknowledged by people. I don't understand your purpose."

His tone of voice became tougher as he talked, and soon he sounded very threatening. Not only did he not treat me as his *seonbae*, it seemed that he was about to hit me. I tried my best to tolerate him—I didn't want to confront such a person—but just listening to him put me in such a rage. I felt as though I could see Kim Man-Ho in his nephew's behavior, and I felt the atmosphere of this town. Just as Kim had become successful by cutting the topknot off of his own grandfather, I could clearly see that this man too would do anything, good or evil, to achieve success.

After listening to him, I wanted to explain my position clearly.

"I am just doing what I was ordered to do as a journalist. The purpose of this visit is to discover the truth about Nam-Song, not to disgrace him. I am only doing my job."

I then regretted having said this.

"What is the truth? What Nam-Song did for the community is the truth. As I said, just ask anyone passing by in the street. That is the truth. Why are you trying to think differently? I am sorry to have to say this, but just report the generally accepted facts to the newspaper. As one lives a life, there are things that cannot be avoided. What is important is that his life should be evaluated as a whole—especially so in a country like ours, which suffered such historical events. Who could possibly be regarded as a person of integrity if the important things in his life are disregarded and the trivial things scrutinized?"

Suddenly he became rather polite and tried to persuade me. His change in attitude got on my nerves. The way he talked revealed that he was not, after all, a brute. The reason he spoke so aggressively at first was to scare me and dominate me.

Finally he said, "Think it over. I am glad that you are not the sort of person to make errors in judgment, but you never know what will happen in the future."

He finished the conversation with this ambiguous sentence and stood up, choosing to ignore anything else that I might have to say. After he left, I became angrier than I was before. I felt as if I had been hit on the back while walking along an unfamiliar street at night.

5

I drove to Jeju City, on the other side of Mount Halla, because I wanted to meet the director of the Jeju branch of the newspaper company for which I worked. It was about 9 P.M. when I left for the city, so I considered meeting him the next day, but I was so anxious that I took the liberty to call him that night. The director came to my motel room even though it was very late.

"I got a call from the main office. I will help you in anyway I can," the director said to me.

He looked to be in his mid-fifties and seemed to know about my situation. I told him about Kim Man-Ho and asked him to introduce me to someone who might clearly recall the situation on Jeju Island immediately after Liberation.

He thought about it for some time and then said, "There is a man who would probably know a lot. He was close to Kim during the Occupation."

The director then told me about a man who had been a detective in a police unit whose function was to monitor the political movements of Koreans during the Occupation. This man had also worked with the National Intelligence Agency after Liberation. Trying to make me feel at ease, the director said that he too had some knowledge of the events around that time. But before meeting that man, I wanted to hear a rough description of those events from the director himself.

Though it was quite late, the director was willing to talk. We went to a *sashimi* restaurant near the seashore. The tide was high and the waves were crashing against the shore.

Looking at the sea hidden in the darkness, I was overcome with feelings of loneliness. I felt as though I were alone in some distant place. I still had a lot of friends here and fond memories of this place, since I had attended elementary and high school here, but in the last several years I had visited very rarely. So the place now seemed totally unfamiliar to me.

A winter wind was blowing and the sky was hanging low over the land. The sea could be discerned only by the sounds of the water and the dim warning lights that outlined the seashore. The night sea is secretive indeed, but even in the middle of the day the sea is mostly hidden from us. People think only about what they can see; they don't think about what is in the sea. They regard that as the concern of divers and oceanographers. The sea occupies a great portion of this small planet on which we live, but because it is not something that we can step on, people are mostly uninterested in it. This indifference to the sea made me feel very lonely.

It's not that I want to blame people for their indifference toward the sea. It is natural for people to be interested in only those things that are somehow related to them. Indeed, that is why no one is interested in me. So it must seem strange to others that I am interested in someone else's life history, especially that of a man who is deceased. No one in this area is really interested in Kim Man-Ho, and they are even less interested in Kang Sung-Su. These people simply accept the established opinions about those men.

I felt strange while thinking about the sea, hidden in the darkness, asserting its existence only by the sounds it makes.

After a few drinks, I told the director about what had happened during the last several days and explained why I wanted to see him at that late hour. He listened while he drank, and then, looking at the dark sea, he began, "Mr. Choi, I was a reporter for over twenty years, a resident reporter."

After the system of resident reporters was abolished, he became the director of the branch.

"I realize how difficult and important it is to write an accurate story. I may feel this way because I cannot write any more. Nowadays I often think about the stories I did not write, those that I threw away. Reporters talk about the responsibility of telling the truth in the stories they write, but they seldom talk about the important stories they did not write, or could not write, because of external influences. If you think about it objectively, shouldn't the reporters feel more responsibility for those stories that were sacrificed? If you write a false story, it will be soon revealed that it is wrong and, thus, the story itself helps to uncover the truth. But if the story is intentionally buried, then the truth itself is also buried. That's why I realize these days, when I no longer write, how valuable it is to write. I now see how important, but also how difficult and painful, it is to write an accurate story. The easiest way to write is to tell the readers what they want to hear, but most of those stories are embellished or distorted and only mask the truth. So I understand what you feel right now."

He spoke at length, as if bewailing his own life story.

"Even if you hear from me what you want to hear and become convinced that it is true, you still would not be able to write everything about it. You would find that it is more difficult to write about the truth than it is to discover it. Wouldn't you feel more frustrated if that were to happen? That's why people usually do not want to discover the truth and why they avoid taking chances that might lead them to the truth. This is especially so for those who lack self-confidence. It does not apply only to writing."

The director pretended to talk about his own story, but in fact he was talking about me. It seemed as if he had prepared long ago to have this conversation with someone he knows well. However, it didn't make me feel awkward. Rather, in realizing that we had lived with the same thoughts, I began to regard him as someone I could talk to, a sort of brother. That's why

I told him about the incident with the young man who claimed to be a nephew of Kim Man-Ho.

"That's very likely. In fact, if anything unfavorable about Kim Man-Ho were to be exposed, those people would not remain silent. And it's not just because their ancestor would be disgraced. Those who admired and emulated Kim would also be disgraced. If you take a simple approach to evaluating Kim, you will find him to be a man who did a great service for the community. In particular, the fact that he built a junior high and a high school in this area is highly commendable, considering that the educational system here had deteriorated after Liberation. Nobody knows about this, but he owes that success to Reverend Kang Sung-Su. It was Reverend Kang who, not only suggested building the schools, but also developed the construction plans and took care of the affairs of the schools for a while after they were built. He did so to give Kim an opportunity to atone for what he had done during the Japanese Occupation. To tell you the truth, right after liberation, Kim received a great deal of help and protection from Reverend Kang. Thanks to Kang, Kim's wrongdoings during the Occupation were easily forgotten in the minds of the people."

I became increasingly tense as the director continued to tell me about the relationship between Reverend Kang and Kim Man-Ho.

After spending two years in jail, Reverend Kang returned home. Then the country was liberated. After the Japanese army had retreated, an army of youths was formed to maintain the peace in each village and town. Reverend Kang became the commander of the youth army. One day, Kim Man-Ho, who had disappeared after Liberation, visited Reverend Kang and asked for his protection, which he received. Kang also ensured that the youth army would not engage in any acts of retaliation. Because of his efforts, there were no disgraceful events committed by the army, and peace was maintained.

After Liberation, the American army stationed itself at Jeju and asked Reverend Kang to be an advisor to the military administration. He was a pastor, had the confidence of the people, had established peace and order in the chaos following Liberation, and spoke fluent English. However, he declined the offer courteously and recommended Kim Man-Ho instead as the best man for the administrative work. Kim had lots of experience as the town mayor and thus had administrative ability. He also knew the situation on Jeju Island during the Occupation, and he spoke English quite well, although no one knows where he learned the language. Anyway, authorities from the American military accepted his recommendation.

After the military administration was established, political issues on the mainland affected Jeju Island as well. Reverend Kang kept his distance from these political matters and concentrated only on rebuilding the church. However, one day he was assigned to a strange post, something like vice-chairman of The Committee for the Establishment of a New Country, which was under the leadership of Yeo Yun-Hyung, the communist who led the Korean independence movement. Later it was discovered that Kang was assigned to this post without his agreement. The whole thing was arranged by one of his friends, an influential person who also played an active role behind Yeo. Since the people on Jeju Island were not well informed about the political situation on the mainland, most of the influential islanders participated in that committee of which Kang was the nominal vice-chairman. They believed that it was the party that would unite the people of Korea and represent the new Korean government. But the political orientation of that committee was in fact quite different from what most islanders thought, and this later caused problems for those people.

Reverend Kang, however, kept his distance from politics and did not participate in any communist or anticommunist activities. He concentrated only on the affairs of the church and, for a short while, took on the responsibilities of the school that Kim Man-Ho had founded. His noninvolvement, however, caused some misunderstanding. At one time, there was a rumor that he was objecting to the foundation of the government of South Korea. Around the election of the first Constitutional Assembly, the 4.3 Incident occurred. One day, Reverend Kang was arrested. According to the information collected by the police, he was the vice-commander of the Jeju branch of the Labor Party, a communist party. He was interrogated intensely, but since he had never actually joined the Communist Party, he was released. Around that time, Kim Man-Ho became an official of the Korean Youth Organization and started to participate in communist witch-hunts.

Though Reverend Kang had been released by the police, he was under constant surveillance. So he confined himself to the church. In the winter of 1948, the situation on Jeju Island deteriorated and fighting between the communist and anticommunist forces began again. The communist guerillas often attacked the police stations or military buildings, and the unified forces of the police and the military began to eradicate the communist guerillas in fullscale. One day that winter, the Namdo region came under a full-scale attack from the communists. The powerful guerillas seized the village by mid-noon, burned all of the houses, except for some around the police station, and plundered food and livestock. Finally, the army arrived and was able to drive the guerillas back, but the village was completely devastated. On that day, Reverend Kang was found dead inside the church. Strangely, however, the church had not been burned.

"Even if he had not been killed in that incident, he would not have survived very long. He had nothing to do with the communists, but the situation in the village would not have left him untouched. The police probably knew that he had no connection with the communist party, but they still regarded him with suspicion. And even if the villagers would not have thrown a stone at him, the police or the army would have killed him."

The director sucked sharply on his cigarette and looked out at the dark sea for a long time. Then he continued.

"People believed that Reverend Kang was connected with the communists just because he was taken to the police station for questioning. And because the church was left intact when he was killed, people thought that he was killed by the anticommunist forces. There was a rumor that he welcomed the communist guerillas when they entered the church. The story was fabricated in someone's imagination, but as time went by, people came to believe it as a fact. It was probably because of prejudice. Isn't the world a dangerous place?"

Now I was beginning to understand the situation. But I thought to myself, "Was it really due to prejudice that Reverend Kang Sung-Su was mistaken for a communist? And if so, then why did he confine his attention to the affairs of the church and not take some measures to protect himself in those complex and turbulent times?" I could not understand him.

"Unlike Reverend Kang, Kim Man-Ho was a very different kind of person. He was always calculating exactly what would happen next."

With this remark, the director began his story about Kim Man-Ho.

After the 4.3 Incident, the Korean War broke out. Around this time, Kim moved to Jeju City and put all of his energy into social work. Under the first Korean government, he entered the local assembly and became the vicepresident. He also worked on the schools that he had founded, developing them into prestigious institutions. As time went by, he acquired political ambitions, became an influential person in the province, and won public support as a candidate for governor of the island. People thought that some day he would become a member of the National Assembly.

After the Revolt on April 19, 1960, student demonstrations in Seoul spread to other provinces. At one social gathering, attended by the heads of the local governments and the influential people of the province, Kim used harsh language against the demonstrating students. At that time, it was not clear whether or not the incumbent president would step down. Later, Kim's speech at that social gathering got him into some trouble, but other people praised him, claiming that only he could speak his mind in such a dangerous situation.

When the first Korean government collapsed, Kim faced other difficulties, including intense criticism from people around him, but he overcame them. Eventually he made some compromise with the forces in power and ran for the position of provincial governor. He lost the election, but it was a chance to show how much support he had among the people on Jeju Island, for he won more votes than were expected. After the military coup on May 16, 1961, Kim was prevented by law from becoming involved in political events. Later, he spent some years engaged in nonpolitical activities, such as cultural affairs and education. These nonpolitical activities made his position more secure. He formed a private organization with the graduates from the schools he had founded and was prepared to run for the National Assembly if he were to be nominated as a candidate for the party in power. However, no such luck was bestowed on him. Instead, he worked behind the scenes, helping someone else become a member of the National Assembly. Nevertheless, he was an influential person, acting as a godfather to a member of the National Assembly.

"Until the late 1960s, he maintained the dream of becoming a member of the National Assembly, but when the political situation in Korea worsened, he abandoned that dream completely and concentrated on his business. He really was a man who could understand the world clearly. Around that time, there were many people who fell into obscurity after leaving the National Assembly. However, Kim Man-Ho was different. As time went on, he consolidated his position and became even more influential. It was often said that, regardless of one's political orientation, if one wanted to become a member of the National Assembly, one had to pay a visit to Kim Man-Ho and greet him with a deep bow. He was, in a word, a shrewd man. And now that he has finally won this award posthumously, he is a man blessed with all the happiness in the world."

The director concluded his account of Kim Man-Ho by saying that he was a man who had lived very shrewdly. And that's exactly how I felt while listening to the director: Kim was a man who had lived according to a plan—his own plan.

After hearing so much about Kim Man-Ho and Kang Sung-Su, more than I expected to hear, I felt a little bit better than before. However, I was still curious as to why Reverend Kang was killed and why most villagers considered him to be a communist.

"Regarding the ideology of Reverend Kang, I'm sure that Jang Sung-Hwan is the person who knows best. Anyway, Kim Man-Ho and Kang Sung-Su were distinguished figures in this area after Liberation. By looking back on how they lived in those days, we can learn some lessons about how we should live at present. It's probably for that reason that our newspaper made the Pioneering Citizen's Award. Nowadays, we live without worrying about our meals and we have TVs, washing machines, and refrigerators. So now is the time for us to think about how to live with human dignity and integrity. Our society is poor in ethics. Don't you agree? We push our children to be great people, but when we come to the question of what a great person is, then we are short of answers. We mention loyalty and obedience to parents as the qualities of greatness, but they are too abstract. Children think that the great people are the presidents, doctors, generals, congressmen, pastors, or philanthropists. So when we push our children to be great people we are merely filling them with the desire to be promoted to higher social positions. Isn't it frustrating? If you cannot be one of those great men, you have to find a way to live happily by yourself. What's important is the consciousness of the middle-class people. In economic respects, the middle-class people are advanced, but with respect to ethics, they are not advanced at all. Therefore, the responsibilities of your generation are great."

As he spoke, the director, who was a bit intoxicated, occasionally smiled at me; at other times, he looked serious. But he always spoke earnestly. It seemed that he was telling me a story that he had never told anyone else. While listening to his story, I considered myself as someone who had once thought like the director, but who now lives ignoring those thoughts. I spend my days in anxiety, believing that there is no alternative than to swim with the ways of the world. I feel powerless and afraid that someone might expose my true identity. I myself have not yet developed my own standards of integrity.

The director then added, "Jang Sung-Hwan will be able to give you more details, since he was close to both Kim Man-Ho and Kang Sung-Su. He was close to Reverend Kang during the Japanese Occupation and later worked for a long time as an investigator with the National Intelligence Agency. So he would be quite an expert as far as the ideology of Kang Sung-Su is concerned. Besides, unlike others in that sort of position, he has class—he's not a man of prejudice. He could probably tell you an interesting story."

Several times the director mentioned the name, Jang Sung-Hwan, and it seemed that I had heard it somewhere before. After thinking about it for some time, I remembered where I had heard it: on New Year's Day, at the head family's house, my father's cousin had said to the headmaster that Jang Sung-Hwan and Bak Jong-Ku in Japan can both testify to the fact that Kang Sung-Su was not a communist.

The director and I finished drinking and went outside. It was almost midnight. The owners of the restaurants standing along the bulwark were hurrying to close their doors. The street lamps were shaking in the strong wind. The sound of the waves was getting louder. We strolled along the boardwalk, but our bodies were shaken by the wind. The director stood there for a long time, embracing the strong wind, and looked out on the sea hidden in the darkness. I suddenly thought that, in comparison with the enormous sea, human beings are so trivial: Both Kim Man-Ho and Kang Sung-Su are dead. The director and I will also soon die. My father's cousin said that he is determined to reveal the truth about these two people because he has not many years to live. I became envious of him for trying to do what he thought was right. At the same time, I felt powerless. The director continued to look down at the dark sea, which could only be identified as such by the sounds of the waves.

After we parted, I returned to my motel. Though I had drunk a lot while listening to the director, I was not completely inebriated. I went to bed, but could not sleep easily. People say that the life of a human being is short, but that it is difficult to live such a short life. And there are many people whose life history is not known accurately or is hidden completely. These thoughts drove the sleep away. While I was tossing and turning in bed, the telephone rang. I looked at the clock and it was almost 1 A.M. The only person who knew that I was staying in this motel was the director, so I was curious about who could be phoning me now. I answered the phone.

"Is Mr. Choi from the *Hangook Newspaper* there?"

The person on the other end spoke rather rudely.

I almost hung up the phone with a curse, but I suppressed my anger.

"Yes, this is Choi."

"Let me introduce myself. I am the president of the Alumni Association of Namdo High School. There is a rumor that you are attempting to disgrace our Kim Man-Ho. Stop now when I tell you nicely. That will be good for both of us. Both you and I are people with social status, so I don't want to talk with you in person; I might get angry and the situation could become awkward. That's why I called you at this late hour. Do a passing job on this and go home to Seoul. That will be good for you. This is advice from someone with sympathy. Sorry for calling so late."

He sounded drunk and wild. I became so angry I could hardly breathe, and I almost threw the phone aside. After I gained some composure, I said,

"Mister, how can you, the president of the Alumni Association of Namdo, be so impolite? Were you really a former student of Kim Man-Ho? If so, then Kim Man-Ho must not be a man of character. How can a person like you be the president of the Alumni Association?"

I could not yield to him, so I continued to snap.

"Let's talk tomorrow face to face. When you come, show your manners."

I hung up the phone, but it rang again immediately.

"Don't act like a person with manners," said the voice on the other end. "You don't have much time. This is advice for you. There are more than ten thousand graduates of my school who want to kill you, and I had a hard time holding them back. Don't let yourself be humiliated. Just follow my advice."

"Listen," I said. "Let's talk face to face tomorrow. It's one o'clock in the morning."

I hung up the receiver and asked the switchboard operator to disconnect my phone. I tried again to sleep, but that voice on the other end lingered in my ears. So I could not sleep. There is nothing more dangerous than an impertinent person. I thought it over and finally decided that I had no choice but to call the director. Upon hearing the news, he rushed to my motel to try to help me.

"Mr. Choi, contain yourself. That's the cultural level of this island. People do not know how to behave decently. There are some people here who think that they can ignore others because they have money. They may behave more rudely because they know that you are from this island. They tend to disrespect people of the same hometown more than people from other places. Just watch—if he calls here again, I'll give him a hard time."

While he was talking, the telephone rang, even though I had asked for it to be disconnected. The director answered the phone.

"Who is this calling at this hour? I am the director of the Jeju branch of *Hangook Newspaper*. Do you know what time it is now? Isn't it time to sleep? Mr. Choi here is doing his job under the orders of the newspaper company. Do you want to fight with our newspaper company? This is interference of our work. Are you intending to interfere with his news coverage for your personal benefits? Mr. Choi got so angry that he almost reported your call to the police station. That's why I came to calm him down. Have you no shame? You are disgracing our hometown."

The director yelled at the caller. After some pause, he said, "You can talk to him during the day. Think about dignity and your position."

He then hung up the phone.

"These people are vicious. They are like small fish, so you have to scare them away by weakening their courage."

The director apologized for this incident several times and suggested that we go some place to drink again, so we left the motel.

6

The place was unfamiliar, but it did not look like a motel. I was thirsty, I had a headache, and my shoulders were sore. I looked at my watch and it was past 9 A.M., so I quickly stood up and began putting on my clothes. Suddenly the director entered the room, smiling. I felt embarrassed but was relieved to see him.

"Did you get some sleep?" he asked. "I drank too much yesterday, so I had a hard time getting up. Let's go outside, get some fresh air, and eat some food to get rid of the hangover."

I looked around the room and it seemed like a house. It was probably the director's house, but I could not remember what happened the night before. I rarely sleep in other people's homes, so I felt very uncomfortable. I was also nervous that I might see someone on my way out.

The director knew what was bothering me, and he tried to make me comfortable. He said, "What's the matter? This is my house. My house is your house, you know."

A sharp, dry wind was blowing outside. For the last several days, there had been clouds but no snow. It looked like today would be the same. I laid down on the back seat of the car that the director was driving. I was numb with a headache and could not think straight, but I tried to recall what happened the previous night.

The director said, "We drank until four o'clock in the morning. You sure can drink! When I was young, I drank as well as you do, but now at my age, I can't keep up with you."

He was driving the car to the seashore, to the same place we had met the day before.

I said, "I hope I did not say anything stupid or bother you too much."

I was worried, since I know how I behave when I am drunk. If I drink when I feel bad, I drink until I lose my mind, and then I do all sorts of crazy things. I thought that I must have acted the same way the previous night.

"Nothing special happened," the director said. "I'm just glad that you followed me to my house and got some sleep."

"Did I cause any problems?"

"Well, you made a totally reasonable demand. You insisted that you had to see the president of the Alumni Association of Namdo High School in order to put an end to a quarrel right away. You kept saying that he had been impertinent and that you wanted to meet him right then and there. I had a hard time calming you down."

While we were talking, I felt like sinking into the ground with shame. I couldn't look him in the eye.

I thought that the director might look down on me, thinking that I am brave only when I drink. To be honest, I was angry when I got that call at the motel, but at the same time I felt fear. I was worried that they, the Namdo alumni, might rush into my room while I was sleeping or strike me on the head while I was walking along the street at night. I was lucky that the director came and yelled at them. Otherwise, they would have bothered me all night long. Those thoughts made me feel indebted to the director.

After getting out of the car and embracing the sea wind, we entered the *sashimi* restaurant that we went to the previous night. In a loud voice, the director ordered some *jeonbokjuk*. An old gentleman in a gym suit then entered the restaurant carrying a tennis racket.

"Hello, you are as punctual as ever," said the director, as he stood up to shake the man's hand. "Let me introduce you to each other. Mr. Choi, this is Jang Sung-Hwan, the man I talked about before."

I was quite surprised that this gentleman was Jang Sung-Hwan. I would never have suspected that he was a police detective who monitored the political movements of Koreans during the Occupation or an investigator for the National Intelligence Agency after Liberation. He looked like a gentle and broadminded person. I was afraid to speak to him in my present condition.

I said, "I've heard a lot about you from the director. It's a pleasure to meet you."

I looked closely at his face as I greeted him. He seemed somewhat familiar; I must have seen him in my high school days. This island is so small that it often seems that everyone knows everyone else.

We ate *jeonbokjuk* for breakfast and then had another drink to kill the hangover. Jang did not drink alcohol and had only a small amount of food. He said with a smile that he did not feel good these days, so he had to drink less.

"Do you exercise?" I asked.

"Well, you cannot call it 'exercise.' I am carrying this tennis racket as a habit. Without it, I feel that something is missing. But as time passes, even carrying a tennis racket is getting difficult."

He spoke very calmly. There seemed to be a difference of more than twenty years between us. He probably knows me. If he doesn't know me, he surely knows at least someone in my family. However, his face didn't betray any such knowledge. He treated me courteously. Thinking that his behavior comes from his cultivated manners, I guessed that it might be difficult to hear what I wanted to hear.

"You look pretty healthy," the director said.

Jang just smiled back at him. His smile was so impressive that I stared at his face again. It was obvious that he was very sick.

I was wondering how I would start the conversation when he suddenly said,

"I've heard a brief account of what you are up to from the director. But I'm afraid that I do not have many things to tell you. Both Kim Man-Ho and Kang Sung-Su graduated from the same school as I did, a few years earlier. I was close to both of them when I was young. However, I am not in a position to talk about them. I used to work as a detective, and while it's been more than ten years since I left that job, I still take my responsibilities seriously. That's why I cannot talk about it."

Though I was about his son's age, he spoke to me courteously.

"I understand," I said. "I'm sorry to have imposed on you. I know that what I want to hear is not something pleasant. It is something that ought to be forgotten, along with the shameful history of Korea. Since my question is likely to dig up something shameful and painful, it is unpleasant even to me. But I thought that there was a story that needed to be told and that's why I wanted to hear it from you."

I really was sorry that I had put it so bluntly, so I was not terribly disappointed when he said that he didn't want to talk about it.

"You probably heard this from the director," I said. "While I was doing some background research on Kim Man-Ho, the name Kang Sung-Su kept coming up. I heard that he was killed during the 4.3 Incident because of his communist ideology, but I was not satisfied with the given explanation of his death. Also, the question of whether he really was a communist arose in my mind. That period was so chaotic, and it seems that many people who were not communists were killed on suspicion that they were communists. What disappoints me most is that people still think that Reverend Kang was a communist. I can tell you for sure that I am not simply lamenting the death of a communist out of sympathy. What I want to know is the truth. I wanted to meet you because you might know something that we don't know."

I spoke at length, thinking that I had to explain what I was doing, even if he could not speak about it. He listened to me very attentively and then responded.

"It is true that people think that Reverend Kang was a communist. I have nothing further to add to it. However, the truth will be revealed sooner or later. In that respect, a reporter should have some beliefs, such as that the truth will be revealed someday and that history can be trusted. If everyone had these beliefs, it would be good for the community. Then political corruption, illegal economic affairs, and social crimes would diminish. Now, as I have little time left to live, that's what I have come to believe. To tell you the truth, my life is full of shame. I happened to have worked as a detective during the Japanese Occupation. And after Liberation I worked in a special unit of the National Intelligence Agency, one that targeted the communists. Sometimes, I worked to maintain the power of those in control by investigating political opponents. Now I have come to believe that the shame of my life should end in this generation and never be repeated. That's why I am writing a memoir, which is a sort of confession. But that will be the end of it. I am writing it just to redeem myself through writing, and not for any other purposes. I am quite happy that I can be introspective and examine the history of our country through writing. It is truly painful, I should confess, but since I haven't experienced it before, it is also somewhat pleasurable. Meeting you today is a very important event for me. Who knows, you might be the one who publishes my memoir later."

He smiled at me. Each word of his permeated my skin and bones and is now etched in my mind.

"People in the past left either novels or autobiographies whenever possible. I am envious of those people who have managed to write, even if they only wrote about their own achievements. Through writing, they were able to be introspective and through that introspection, they must have learned to fear, but also to trust, history. Mr. Choi, I once wanted to become a reporter. I also wanted to write a novel."

He smiled sadly as he said this.

The director then spoke.

"You were arrested and tortured by the Japanese because of the reading club incident. After being released, I wondered how you became a detective during the Japanese Occupation. But since you now have the chance to leave a memoir that could serve as a witness of history, I wonder whether God may have predetermined your life in this way."

"I am now earnestly attending a Christian church, and I was baptized last fall."

His gentle smile and the wrinkles around his eyes made him look like a philosopher as he spoke.

I wanted to hear some stories about Kang Sung-Su, but I became tongue-tied. What struck me as the truth at that moment was that Reverend Kang was not a communist. However, that was just a gut feeling.

"Then I have to wait for your memoir," I said, as I looked him in the eye.

He turned his face away and said, "My trivial memoir might trouble you."

He smiled sadly.

Though nothing was gained from the meeting with Jang Sung-Hwan, I realized that I was not the only one who was interested in the events surrounding Kim Man-Ho and Kang Sung-Su. I also realized that there are difficulties in investigating the truth. I felt that it was time for me to wrap things up, but I did not know how to conclude my assignment. Nevertheless, it seemed that nothing would be gained by staying here any longer.

* * *

I told my father's cousin what I had heard from the director and Jang Sung-Hwan.

He said, "Reverend Kang is the one who made Kim Man-Ho a great man. The rumor that Reverend Kang was killed because of his communist ideology was probably spread by Kim Man-Ho on purpose. You know, as long as Reverend Kang was around, Kim could not wield his power as he wanted to. Now, people consider Kim Man-Ho a great man, but at that time right after Liberation, Kim was like a cat beside a tiger. My guess is that Reverend Kang was like a godfather to Kim."

He also said that he was sorry to hear that Jang had failed to provide me with more substantial information.

"The truth will be known gradually. Everything will be out in the open if Bak Jong-Gu in Japan opens his mouth. The truth must be revealed someday."

After hearing this from my father's cousin, I was sorry that I didn't hear about Bak Jong-Gu when I spoke to Jang the previous day.

Anyway, I had to wrap up my investigation of Kim Man-Ho. I felt that I wouldn't hear anything negative from the people here. Though I could theorize about some possible problems in Kim's background based on what I had heard from the director and Jang Sung-Hwan, reporting that would be too subjective. Had I not heard their stories on Kim Man-Ho, writing a report would have been easy. But after having heard their stories, I couldn't disregard them.

While I was thinking about this, I got a call from the chief editor in Seoul.

"Mr. Choi, why are you making problems down there? The boss is really upset. He asked why you are not doing your job properly—why you are causing problems by doing things unrelated to your job. We've heard that you are working to redeem the honor of a dead person who was accused of being a communist. Mr. Choi, how old are you? How could you be so naïve? Stop this assignment immediately and return to Seoul. Just forget about Kim Man-Ho."

The chief editor then hung up the phone without listening to me.

I was devastated. I thought that I might have to resign from the newspaper. I got so angry, but there was nothing I could do about it. I felt so helpless I couldn't move. Still, I just couldn't stay in the hotel room.

I began drinking in the early evening. From a nearby bar, I tried several times to phone the boss directly, but every time I dialed the first three or four digits, I immediately hung up. After returning to the hotel, I fell onto the bed and slept. All night long, I was troubled by evil dreams. In my dreams I was naked and shamefully wandering around among people. I climbed up a big ladder, but on my way up, the ladder began to give way. I was scared by the dream, but right after it ended, another dream began. It happened like this again and again. All night long, I was troubled by dreams, and then finally the day broke.

I told my father's cousin that I should go back to Seoul the next day, and he said, with determination in his face, that he would do his best to clear the dishonor of Kang Sung-Su. He said that Jang Sung-Hwan would open his mouth someday and that Bak Jong-Gu, who had switched from the pro-Pyongyang federation of Korean residents in Japan to another pro-Seoul group, would also surely tell the truth one day. He said that he would find the record on Reverend Kang that would show that he had vigorously protested against the Japanese Occupation. He also indicated that he would recommend Kang for an honorary award.

"Think about it," he said. "I have done nothing for the world. And now, as I approach my death, I feel that I have to accomplish this one thing at least. While I am alive, I want to do something that others won't do and ensure that history cannot be manipulated. If I succeed, people will begin to fear history, won't they?"

I was envious of him for speaking with resolution. He is so honorable in comparison to me. I'm the sort of person who returns to Seoul with just one curt word from the editor, throwing everything else aside. I felt miserable about myself. I had done nothing more than to drink in rage and to entertain bad dreams.

7

The boss did not greet me when I entered his office; he just glanced at me and then took a drag on his cigarette. So I decided to stand there without saying anything.

"Mr. Choi, you were sent to cover a story for the newspaper. You should have concentrated on your assignment. Why were you wandering around creating problems?"

His face was stiff; he was obviously suppressing his anger. Usually he did not get angry in front of his employees, especially the reporters. This time there must have been a good reason to get upset, so I decided not to talk about the things I really wanted to say. He looked as if he had had many things in mind, but he just said,

"If you have anything to say, talk to the chief editor."

With these words, I walked out of his office in disgrace.

The chief editor stood from his chair and beckoned me. It seemed that he had been waiting for me.

"How did you make such a big mistake? The president got really upset. The National Intelligence Agency thought that your interest in Kang Sung-Su was encouraged by our newspaper. Anyway, someone must have informed the Agency. It is very likely that those involved in your investigation spoke ill of you. Besides, since the director of the Jeju branch of the newspaper and Jang Sung-Hwan, a former national intelligence officer, appear in your news coverage, those in the intelligence agency must have felt nervous. They probably thought it quite strange for the newspaper to cover stories it was not interested in before. And besides, those close to Kim Man-Ho probably saw this as a good opportunity to attack you, since you were finding faults with Kim and showing favorable interest in Kang Sung-Su. The National Intelligence Agency did not have any problems with this at first, but those around Kim Man-Ho could not accept what you were doing. How could you be so foolish? Anyway, if you just stop digging for dirt about Kim Man-Ho, this whole thing will end. Don't worry about it."

The chief editor was trying to explain what had gone on here while I was away, but I couldn't understand exactly what he was saying.

While studying my face, he said, "This is part of the procedure. Just write it and do not think about it too seriously."

I didn't know what he was talking about. I just stood there, looking at him blankly.

"I mean a written explanation. This is part of the procedure. Just write it."

"What do you mean by a 'written explanation'?" I asked, losing my temper.

"If you don't want to call it a written explanation, let's call it a written account of what went on."

I glared at the chief editor as he continued to speak.

"What a senseless man you are! Don't you think we need to show something to the Intelligence Agency? Just do it, and consider it a part of the procedure."

"I can't," I said, stubbornly. "Who should write a written explanation for this kind of activity? Aren't you the one who ordered me to dig into Kim Man-Ho?"

"What an obstinate man!" the chief editor replied, with his characteristic grin. "If you don't want to write one, then I'll do it. All the responsibilities are on me anyway, since I'm the chief editor."

He turned to me again and gave me a wry look.

On that night, I followed the chief editor to the bar for a few rounds. While we were drinking, I heard about what had gone on while I was at Jeju Island. The Intelligence Agency raised questions about my investigation into Kang Sung-Su, saying that the investigation of a man who was killed as a communist is not a trivial matter. They demanded an account. The president of the newspaper company tried to control the issue since he was quite sensitive to the anticommunist laws. The newspaper executives held a meeting to find a way of settling this situation and also to show that they considered it to be a serious matter. The Intelligence Agency demanded my resignation, but the boss decided that a month's suspension from the office would be enough. Luckily, an executive director at the newspaper knew someone in the Agency and used that personal relationship to my advantage. In the end, they agreed to end this incident with "a written explanation." According to the chief editor, in giving me this light reprimand, the president showed a lot of consideration for me.

So I asked the editor, "What kind of work did I do to be considered such an important figure?"

"Don't you know what kind of a country Korea is? Do you want to live like those demonstrating students who are filled only with righteousness? Do you think that other reporters don't write about the kind of story you are interested in because they don't have a pen?"

The chief editor suddenly lost his temper. He was criticizing me for having acted indiscreetly.

"Of course, you can be interested in that kind of story as an individual. However, it becomes a big problem when your research is carried out in the name of the newspaper. We still have to follow anticommunist laws, and the laws say that we must not say or do anything that might benefit the enemy. The laws of the world are not always fair. We cannot dig out all the truth in the world. That's why one needs to study history and literature. Don't you agree? There will be people who will do that kind of work later in the future. We are busy now. We cannot even finish what we are supposed to do …"

I then responded to the chief editor's admonishment.

"Yes, there is some truth in what you're saying. But I've realized something very important this time—that there are many facts from which we turn our faces, that those hidden facts become distorted, and that people are ultimately misled by those distorted facts. With time, these facts become shrouded in mystery. Therefore, we have to dig into the facts to reveal the truth. Otherwise those who have been associated with some dark events under false accusations have no way to be cleared from that disgrace. A society in which truth is clearly revealed without being distorted or hidden is … well … a just society. I've realized that a just society is not something special. It is simply a society in which no one is falsely accused. You know, I just wanted to discover the truth about someone who had sacrificed his life for society and for justice, but who was known to others incorrectly. How can justice exist in a society where false accusations are accepted as truth? That is a sick society. Even in the old days, those who were killed with false accusations appeared as ghosts and appealed to people to dig into the truth. If their appeals are not accepted and resolved, the ghosts will avenge those who refused to listen to them. A society in which right and wrong are clearly revealed is a good society, one in which no evil can be hidden. In the old days, smart officials took care of the appeals of the ghosts who were falsely accused and killed. But nowadays, I think that writers, especially reporters like us, should take care of those appeals. That's all I wanted to do. And you now ask me to write 'a written explanation'? Aren't you a reporter yourself? A reporter forever? How can you ask me to write 'a written explanation' when I, as a reporter, acted like a reporter? How is it possible?"

"That's why this affair can be settled with just a written explanation—because everyone acknowledged your integrity as a reporter. If you cannot accept this, start up your own newspaper company and write whatever you want to write. Mr. Choi, you sound like you have to repeat the internship again in order to learn the system. Why don't you understand this after having worked so many years as a reporter?"

We continued to talk, in a depressed manner, under the influence of liquor.

Since I was now a member of the editorial staff, a job that is not very demanding, I began coming to work late, leaving earlier than others, drinking a lot, and imagining what thoughts were hidden behind the chief editor's smile. From time to time, I thought about the dark sea that surrounds Jeju Island at night and the director of the newspaper branch, himself a former reporter. I pictured his back as he stood in front of me looking at the dark sea from the bulwark. I thought about the gentleman who worked as a national investigator, but who had had a dream of being a newspaper reporter or a novelist. I also thought about my father's cousin, a man in his seventies who wanted to reveal the truth about Reverend Kang Sung-Su before he dies. I felt depressed because of the incident of the written explanation. So I painfully wasted my time doing nothing but drinking, blaming the president, and criticizing the powerlessness of the chief editor.

Around that time, very strange news came to me—a statue of Kim Man-Ho was to be built by the graduates of the school that Kim had founded. The thought of the students in that school looking up to the statue of Kim and emulating him sent a chill to the marrow of my bones. After I heard that news, I started to drink more heavily, and my life became a mess.

I spent that winter steeped in liquor. I went to drink either alone or with friends who didn't work at the newspaper. The newspaper work became less important to me as time went on. The president, who had encouraged me to do research on Kim Man-Ho, and who had transferred me to the editorial department for that purpose, said nothing about my report when I submitted it. He just wanted to forget about the whole incident. This was due partly to the protests from supporters of Kim Man-Ho. They said that they did not want the award to begin with, but that after having attracted people's attention by selecting him as the recipient of the award, the newspaper would disgrace him if it didn't give him the award. I drank as if I had been betrayed, and I started to think that this might be the right time for me to quit this job before I got too old.

But time heals all wounds. With spring, the weather became warm, and the trees along the street shook of the winter's dust and turned green again. These changes soothed my mind to a certain extent. After I was given a new assignment, I began to forget about the incident of the written explanation, and the things that had made me depressed earlier no longer bothered me much. I got over it and was ready to live just like others.

That's when my father's cousin came see me. Saying that he had come directly from the airport, he handed me a business envelope.

"This is the memoir of Bak Jong-Gu, who was the vice-commander of the communist organization on Jeju Island during the 4.3. Incident. He swung to the pro-Seoul Federation of Korean Residents in Japan last year and still works hard for it."

I pulled the manuscript out of the large envelope. It had been written in fountain pen and was entitled "The Memoir of a Convert."

"I talked to him about Reverend Kang, and he said that before he dies he should write about it. That's how this was written. It clearly says that Reverend Kang was not involved in communist activities. It also states that Reverend Kang was killed by communist guerillas during their attack on the village of Namdo. It shows that they had a plan to kill him even before the attack since he was uncooperative with them. With this record, the spirit of Reverend Kang, a man who was falsely accused, will be consoled."

My father's cousin spoke energetically. I was afraid that someone might overhear what he was saying, so I ushered him outside.

He continued, "This would be enough to clear Reverend Kang from the false charge. After it is revealed that Reverend Kang was not involved in communist activities, I'll collect evidence of his activities against the Japanese Occupation and petition the government. With signatures from people in our hometown, I am planning to recommend him as a hero who fought for national independence. Since you are a reporter, you should help me."

Listening to him, I felt as if there was nothing I could do for him.

"You should publish his manuscript in your newspaper," he said. "After I received it, I had put everything else aside and came up to Seoul to see you. You can make stylistic changes to it if necessary."

He handed me the manuscript, but I didn't tell him that I could publish it. He smiled while looking at my face, probably thinking that I would publish it. I felt more and more disheartened, and suddenly I came to fear my father's cousin for being so actively involved in somebody else's affairs while in his seventies. I started to think of him as an alien, and I felt uncomfortable being around him.

"Don't overexert yourself. Take your age into account. If you are too concerned with something, it will hurt your health."

I spoke as if I were worried about his health.

"Think about it," he said. "How many more years do I have? I can even see for myself that I am getting weaker and weaker these days. It seems that there is no one but me who would do this job and that makes me feel anxious. Keep this in mind. Just in case something happens to me, you should be responsible for making sure that this job is completed."

He looked at me closely for a long time, waiting for an indication that I would publish it. Then he stood up, saying that he needed to meet a friend, a pastor, who studies the history of churches in Korea.

After the meeting with my father's cousin, I felt frustrated. He called me several times after returning home, asking when the memoir would be published in the newspaper, but I had not even shown the manuscript to anyone. That kind of memoir could be published in a monthly magazine run by our editorial department, but I was no longer interested in Reverend Kang.

After a month, my father's cousin came to see me again; this time he wanted me to sign a petition. It said that Reverend Kang was not a communist, that he had fought against the Japanese Occupation, and that he was a patriot who should be honored for his struggle for Independence. It also described the details of his fight against the Japanese.

"Strangely," he said, "people are reluctant to sign their names to this. But I don't understand their hesitation since this is an honorable thing to do. If it had something to do with money, people would flock to sign their names to it."

He grumbled while handing me the petition. The signatures filled less than three pages. Most of those signatures were those of retired pastors who had been students of the same theological seminary that Kang attended. Only a few were people from the same hometown.

I wrote my name, my address, my social security number, and signed it. While I was signing, I felt confused. My throat was filled with lumps of anger, as I thought about my father's cousin, at his advanced age, visiting others who were not interested in this matter. He must have looked like a beggar.

"I will now try to collect more signatures from people in the town, including the church members. It should be easy to get at least a thousand signatures. When Kim Man-Ho was recommended for an award, several thousands of people in the hometown signed, but now ... I don't understand what people are thinking. By the way, about that manuscript, why isn't it published yet? If it were published in the newspaper, it would be much easier to get the signatures. You are not saying that even the newspaper wants to ignore this, are you?"

My father's cousin was angry when he asked this question.

"It will be published soon," I said.

I told him something that was impossible.

"I will go to home then, with full confidence in you," he replied.

He left with a bright smile on his face.

After that, he didn't contact me for a while. I spent my time immersed in other work at the newspaper, but from time to time I thought about him. And whenever I did, I became tense.

8

One afternoon in late May I got a call from the chief editor to attend, in lieu of the president, a ceremony for the unveiling of the statue of Kim Man-Ho. I grumbled, thinking that this was strange.

"Why do you want me to attend?" I asked the chief editor bluntly.

"Ask the boss. He asked you to attend to show his special concern for you."

"Special concern?"

"Can't you read what he has in mind? It shows that he is not angry with you anymore. Anyway, it was you who had the most trouble because of Kim Man-Ho. Don't you think that it is best for you to finish this matter?"

I could not win at this, so I gave in with a feeling of self-abandonment.

* * *

I arrived at Jeju airport the day before the ceremony. The director of the Jeju branch of newspaper and some of the surviving members of Kim Man-Ho's family were there to greet me. I was embarrassed. I was now suddenly included in the group of Kim Man-Ho supporters.

"What a surprise! We thought that the president himself was coming."

The director smiled as he shook my hands, but Kim's relatives looked at me with suspicion.

"Mr. Choi, you must have the president's confidence! The chief editor or many others could have come in his stead."

The director, who seemed to know why I had come, spoke loudly, as if he wanted Kim's relatives to hear him.

Then he suddenly changed the subject and put a cigarette between his teeth.

"Welcome to Jeju. If you had not come, I would have gone to Seoul. Jang Sung-Hwan has died. We held a funeral yesterday."

"What?"

The news of Jang's death shook me from the apathetic state I was in.

"There was some manuscript he wanted me to deliver to you," the director whispered in my ear, keeping a sharp lookout for the surviving family members of Kim Man-Ho.

"Manuscript?" I asked.

"Don't you remember the manuscript he talked about last winter? He said that he was writing a memoir …"

Then I remembered what the director was talking about.

"He died too early," I said.

I was saddened by the news of his death.

"No, not really. When you saw him, he was already pronounced incurable. He was in the final stages of liver cancer. He survived as long as he did only because of his strong will."

"He looked quite healthy at that time," I said. But then I remembered the sickness in his face when I met him.

"He said that he would survive the cancer. After meeting you, he probably became more tired finishing up his memoir. What mental anguish it must have been for him to write! Especially so since it is not a story that one can be proud of."

Jang's graceful features flashed across my mind. Why did I have such a good impression of him? It must have been because he accepted his fate of living with an unfortunate history and in unfortunate circumstances, and because he was keenly aware of his own misery. What did he think while writing his own shameful story at the threshold of his death? The man who admitted, without reservation, his beautiful dream of wanting to be a novelist must have had an admiration for writing and the strength of character that is required to write. He must have finished his memoir with the attitude of writing his last will.

After settling me in a motel, the director invited me out for a walk. I told him that I wanted to read the manuscript, pressing him to hand it over to me. Looking it over, I could see that it was well written. So I read it right there in its entirety. The stories of being expelled because of the "reading club" incident, his wanderings in Japan, becoming a detective, the relationship between Kim Man-Ho and Kang Sung-Su in the final stages of the Japanese Occupation, Kim's pro-Japanese activities, how Kim plotted behind the scene to close Reverend Kang's church, how Kang protected Kim in the unstable period after Liberation, and several stories during the 4.3 Incident—all were written in an interesting and provocative manner. The story about Reverend Kang's ideology was the same as that in the manuscript that was written by Bak Jong-Gu, the converter.

The memoir said that Kang Sung-Su was not the vice-commander of the Communist Party in South Korea, and that the claim was fabricated by the communists to have the police get rid of him when the communists failed to win him over to their side. When he was released, after having been arrested by the police, the communists plotted to kidnap and kill him. When they attacked the village of Namdo, they murdered him. However, they left the church building intact so that people would think that the police had killed him. According to the memoir, these facts were confirmed by a communist guerrilla who had defected. There was some complex reason for making the public believe that Reverend Kang was the vice-commander of the South Korean Communist Party. Kim Man-Ho was one of the people involved in that story. The memoir also plainly described Jang's mental suffering when the investigative team for which he worked became involved in political affairs. And the memoir detailed the history of people who lived as nonconformists.

While reading the manuscript, I suddenly remembered things about Reverend Kang that I had forgotten until that moment. I wanted to publish this manuscript either in the newspapers or in a journal. I thought that this would not only shed light on the history of Korea after Liberation, but would also be interesting and educational reading material for anyone. It would show people how objective writing can be.

The ceremony for the unveiling of the statue was splendid. The playground was filled with more than five thousand students, about two hundred graduates, the heads of some government institutes, and other important people in the province. Since I was attending the ceremony in place of the president of the newspaper company, I was treated as one of the important guests. Kim Man-Ho's nephew, who once had a quarrel with me, was busy taking care of things for the ceremony. I saw the headmaster and exchanged nods with him.

During the ceremony, the headmaster described the history of Kim Man-Ho's life. He mentioned and praised the accomplishments of Kim. Listening to his words with my eyes closed, I blushed and became uncomfortable being there. The statue of Kim Man-Ho, an exemplary citizen and wise man, was finally unveiled in the bright light of May. There was thunderous applause. The sound of the band resonated magnificently. The bronze statue that was located about two meters away from the school gate towered over the students gathered in the large playground. Now students would look up to it and aspire to be like Kim. From time to time, teachers, including the principal, would talk about Kim in class, in the playground, and outside the school. These thoughts tormented me, and I realized how absurd this world is.

After the ceremony, I greeted the surviving family members of Kim Man-Ho. Since I was attending in lieu of the president, I should have said something nice, even if I didn't mean it, but I couldn't. Even at the tea party, I merely followed other people, looking stern. Everywhere people were talking about Kim Man-Ho.

The headmaster accompanied me on my way downtown.

"Thanks for your troubles. You were a great help in publicizing the life of Kim Man-Ho."

The headmaster looked happy while saying this, but I worked hard to suppress my anger since I knew what he had in mind. He said this in order to make me give up the idea of working on this case any further.

I tried hard to think of something that I could use to get back at him, and I found something.

I said, "Did you meet my father's cousin when he came back from Japan?"

This remark caused a change in the headmaster's complexion. However, he tried hard not to show it.

"He seemed to show senility," the headmaster said. "How dare he ask me to sign my name to recommend Kang Sung-Su, a man who was killed because of his communist ideology, as a hero in the struggle for Independence? You didn't know about that?"

It seemed that he was asking me this question in order to pump some information out of me.

"Did he get many signatures?" I asked, feigning ignorance.

"Who would sign that? Think about it. Who, other than crazy people, would sign their name to that? Would you do it?"

My heart stood still when I heard him. I thought, "Doesn't he know what I have in my mind? Or does he want to make fun of me until the end?"

I almost told him that I did, but I suppressed my impulse to answer.

"But it seems that there is enough material supporting the fact that he was not a communist," I said.

I then looked closely into the face of the headmaster. His complexion changed again. He finally realized what I had in my mind. While saying this, I searched for another line of attack.

I said, "I've heard that Jang Sung-Hwan died."

He looked at me directly with suspicious eyes.

"Do you know Jang?"

"Yes, I met him several times. He knew a lot about the situation on Jeju after Liberation."

The headmaster's face stiffened. I laughed inside.

"While he was dying, he left his memoir to me as if it were his will. His memoir described the situation on Jeju very clearly. Since he was a detective during the Japanese Occupation, he knew about the relationship between Kim Man-Ho and Kang Sung-Su very well. After Liberation, he investigated communists. He certainly knew a lot about the ideological problems on Jeju."

I talked as if the memoir contained some big secret in it.

"Can I take a look at it?" he asked, emitting a dry cough.

"It will soon be published in the newspaper. You can read it then."

I answered him calmly. He smiled at my answer.

"Will it really be published? Your father's cousin kept saying that Bak Jong-Gu's memoir would be published in the newspapers, but I couldn't find it anywhere. Where was it published?"

He said this to himself, looking outside the window. Then he turned his face toward mine. The sneer at the edges of his mouth pierced into my heart. His remarks made me feel so powerless that I couldn't move my body. He already knew that I was on Kang's side, not Kim's. He just wanted to confirm my position through several questions.

"The memoir of Jang Sung-Hwan will be published in the newspapers. Wait and see."

I wanted to yell this at him, but the sounds were spinning around within my mouth. He smiled at me complacently.

* * *

The visit to my hometown made me tired. After parting with the headmaster, I visited the grave of Jang Sung-Hwan with the director of the Jeju branch of the newspaper. I drank until the following dawn and came back to Seoul on the morning flight.

When I showed up at work in the afternoon, the chief editor told me to write a story on the ceremony for the unveiling of Kim Man-Ho's statue. He told me that I should summarize what Kim had done for the community and offer readers the chance to reflect on civic values through the comments of the Jeju people on Kim Man-Ho. He added that this was by request of the president, and said that it was natural for our newspaper to publicize the man to whom we had given an award.

"I will try to write the story as you said, but I have a request as well. On my visit to Jeju I obtained some valuable material. I have a memoir that was written by a person who served as a detective during the Japanese Occupation and after Liberation …"

I explained Jang Sung-Hwan's memoir and said that I wanted to have it published in the newspaper.

"I already know about it. The president also knows that you have that memoir."

The chief director stood up and looked down at me, rolling his eyes.

"Don't you have another manuscript?" he asked. "That of Bak Jong-Gu, the converter? Why didn't you talk about that manuscript? Look. If both of those stories came out in the newspaper, what would happen to Kim Man-Ho, the man who was selected by our paper as a 'pioneering citizen'? When you work, you should be prudent. What should I do with you! Maybe after ten years, or when you have your own newspaper company, you can publish those manuscripts. Even at that time, it won't be easy since you will have been the one who wrote the article on the ceremony for Kim Man-Ho's statue. How can the same person write two contradictory stories? This is the real world. Now just go and write the article on the unveiling ceremony."

I stood there dumbfounded.

* * *

My article on the unveiling ceremony was published as a feature story in the newspaper. That afternoon, I was sitting at my desk with the newspaper in my hand, feeling very lonely, when a messenger handed me a telegram stating that my father's cousin had died. I dropped the newspaper onto the floor and stood up.

I went outside, but there was no place to go. I looked up at the sky, but the pollution in the air made the world before my eyes turn gray. I closed my eyes and stood still. I could hear the voice of my father's cousin. The faces of Jang Sung-Hwan, Bak Jong-Gu, and the director of the Jeju branch of the newspaper flashed across my mind. The stone monument without any inscription on it haunted me. The thought that I should inscribe the truth on that moss-covered monument came to my mind, making my body itch. I opened my eyes and saw a glimmer of light shining through the polluted sky. My body became as hot as a fireball, and I started to tremble.

The Homecoming

"Leaving Osaka by air on the 18th—Father"

It was a brief international telegram but, after reading it, those few words were forever etched in my mind. That my father would return home was a fact, but I did not want to accept it as such.

Ten days ago, one of my father's cousins journeyed to our house before daybreak. Though it takes only a couple of hours by car, I rarely visit my hometown anymore—maybe just once or twice a year. I usually visit around the first day of August in the lunar calendar just to cut the weeds around the graveyard. In my place, my mother goes there frequently to attend all the family events. My relatives often complain that I contribute neither time nor money to these events even though I am in a better position than they are to do so. I turn a deaf ear to these remarks. I am around forty years old, but my bitter feelings toward my hometown are revived whenever I go there, even if only by chance. For days afterward, I moan and groan as if suffering from a fever, and this, in turn, breaks my mother's heart, which only makes matters worse.

My father's cousin, who is ten years older than I am, opened the door of our house with a bewildered look on his face. Without acknowledging my family's greetings he indicated that he wanted to be alone with me, saying that he had something urgent to tell me. Since he is my closest relative, he is the one with whom I discuss family matters if there are any. He had graduated from a junior high school in our hometown and then lived there as a farmer, but he was always dignified, and I always addressed him with respect. So on that day, when that proud man looked at me with an uneasy face, it worried me. We quickly entered my room and sat down.

"Well ... did you hear any news?"

I didn't immediately understand what he had in mind, so I looked at him with a confused expression.

"I almost rented a taxi to come here last night."

He was fidgeting with something in his pocket and then he pulled out a letter.

"I received it last night."

With this remark, he handed me the letter and then turned his face toward the window.

The letter had come from Japan. When I looked at the back of the envelope and saw the sender's name, I felt dizzy. A moment later, my heart began to pound and gradually my whole body started to tremble.

The name written on the envelope, "Park Sung-Bin," was my father's name.

"The handwriting is certainly your father's."

The man facing the window said this with conviction, but his voice was trembling. The fact that he even remembered my father's handwriting after more than thirty years of separation touched me deeply. The calligraphy on the surface of the white envelope was elegantly written, even to my untrained eyes. The letter, which had not yet been opened, was addressed to me.

"This is unusual. I have a bad feeling about this."

His face stiffened, as if it were frozen.

"How many years have passed! I could not sleep at all last night."

It was exactly thirty-four years ago that my father left our hometown. My father's cousin's deep concern over this letter from my father, who had never contacted us before, was therefore not surprising. Besides, the rumors concerning my father's activities in Japan warranted concern. Ten years ago, we confirmed that he was still alive, a fact that deeply disturbed my family. After that, no one dared speak of my father again. So when I saw that letter, I felt that something was about to disturb our uncomfortable silence.

No one had ever talked to me about my father in detail. But as I was growing up, I discovered and confirmed things about him by myself. Like the moisture that surrounds my house in the hot and humid Korean summer, sorrow has surrounded me all my life. The more that I have tried to escape from it, the more inescapable it seems to be. Though I do remember the happy moments I shared with my father long ago—memories such as picking up flower petals under cherry trees on a bright spring day—the dominant memories are dark and dismal.

Even the first memory I have of my father is a depressing one. It was on a gray evening late in the fall. It had been raining for some days. Since I was only four years old at that time, I do not clearly remember things the way they happened. But people around me later talked about it many times, and that's how it has remained in my mind ever since.

On that wet and windy day late in the fall, a dense thicket of tall trees near the fence was rustling in the loud wind. After dinner, my entire family sat on the living room floor, and talked about the weather. Everyone was worried about the hay that had been cut but not yet gathered. Suddenly, a dark figure that resembled a person burst into our front yard, carelessly walking over the loose hay that had been spread on the ground. I was so frightened that I ran toward the living room, calling for my grandfather. Why had I been so frightened? We had many guests in those days so it was not unusual for someone to visit our house at dusk. Even as an adult, I have often wondered why I felt such fear on that day.

Suddenly, it became silent in the living room. A young man, that dark figure that I saw in the yard a moment earlier, ran up to the narrow porch, soaking wet, saying "Father, I've returned." Everyone stood up in surprise. Shouts of joy erupted when that man stepped into the house, filling it with all kinds of emotion. After changing his clothes, the man came back into the living room. My grandmother then lifted me off her lap, and said to me,

"This is your dad. Bow to him."

That was the first time I heard the word "dad." At that moment, I turned my face toward my mother who was standing silently behind my grandmother. My mother was smiling at me and that smile reminded me of my aunt's face when she first returned to our house after marriage and met my grandmother and uncle. For a brief moment, father and I stared at each other. He then lifted me high up to the ceiling, and rubbed his hairy face on mine. Because he was still a stranger to me, I remained silent while being held in my father's arms.

From that evening on, I slept with my grandmother. My mother smiled at me bashfully each morning after having slept with my father. For several days, the house was filled with excitement, but gradually the atmosphere became subdued. Soon my father started riding a horse, the horse that my grandfather prized the most. Once he placed me, just a four-year old, on that horse, held the horse by the bridle, and said, "This is the horse your father rode." My grandfather would also brush the horse's mane and stroke its back and hips, making its glossy hair more lustrous. The horse enjoyed it whenever my grandfather did that, and my mother would stare at this scene blankly while doing the dishes.

On the first day that my father started to ride the horse again, the entire family came out to the yard and watched; it was as if everyone had gathered to say farewell to my father before he embarked on a long journey. When my father got on the horse and whipped its back, saying "Let's go!" the horse ran swiftly to the front gate. Everyone was happy to see the horse running again. After I grew up and learned about the history of our family from my mother, I understood why father had started riding.

* * *

My great great-grandfather moved to this village, a large prairie village next to Mount Halla, with his brothers. Together they made a fortune, primarily from raising cattle. But his son, that is, my great-grandfather, squandered away most of this fortune, leaving the family in poverty. My great-grandfather, who knew how to enjoy life, was better at spending money than at collecting it, but the main reason for the downfall of the family was *Sundo*. My great-grandfather lost his head to *Sundo* and spent his life searching for propitious burial sites for his ancestors. Believing that the end of the world was near, he considered it to be his goal in life to find the best burial site for his father, who had passed away as a middle-aged man. My great-grandfather exhumed his father's body five times, each time transferring it to what was supposedly a better site. He did this with the help of a *pungsusa* who lived at my house. Whenever he found a new *pungsusa*, he would also change his father's burial site. By the time my grandfather was married and had a child of his own, the family was already quite poor; they were at the point of having to worry about where their next meal would come from.

Grandfather and grandmother had asked great-grandfather to take care of their son during their absence and they went to Japan to earn money. They did whatever it took to make money and returned to Jeju Island after having worked for ten years in Japan. With the money they had earned, they bought back the land that the family had once owned. Since the country was quite poor at that time, it was relatively easy to purchase the property my great-grandfather had previously owned. The next thing they concentrated on was planning the best education for their son, my father. They sent him to a junior high school in a city for a couple of years, and later sent him to Seoul for a better education. My grandfather's dream was for his son to attend Gyungsung Imperial University, one of the best universities in Korea at that time, and his dream was finally fulfilled. Just as my great-grandfather directed all of his attention toward securing a propitious burial site, so my grandfather put all his effort into his son's education. He was such a dedicated father that if he heard that his son was returning home for vacation, he would ride a horse, taking another one for his son, from my hometown south of Mount Halla, across the prairie up to Sanji Port in Jeju City to greet his son. Father and son would then return home together, crossing over the mountains on horseback. When they appeared in our hometown, people would come out of their houses waving their hands. For these people, there was no doubt that my father would become an important person in the future.

* * *

"Do you know how loudly my heart was pounding when I saw your father wearing the fancy garments of a university student and riding a horse?"

My mother, who was left alone at home when my father went off to war, said this to me several times, and whenever she did, she would blush.

My father married my mother three days before he went off to fight in World War II as a student soldier. Since my mother had no formal education beyond elementary school, my parents seemed rather mismatched. However, the marriage was a difficult decision for my mother too. She must have had great strength and determination to marry a man who would soon leave for war. And like a posthumous child, I was born while my father was away at war.

During the next two months, my father rode his horse often and, together with my grandfather, inspected the family's various fields and ranches on the mountain. Grandfather showed his fortune to his son and pledged in front of him to never let the family fall into poverty again.

After spending the rest of that year in the village, my family moved to the city the following spring. My father was to teach at a junior high school in the city, the same school that my uncle was attending as a student.

Disregarding my grandfather's plea to continue studying in Seoul, my father decided to work as an English teacher in a junior high school. The school's residence, where Japanese teachers used to live, was covered with cherry blossoms in the spring. The tall students, who could be seen over the fence, looked awesome to me. I was only five years old at that time, but that memory is still clear in my mind. My mother was so happy to send my father off to school in the morning and welcome him back at night. She looked uncomfortable, though, as if she were not accustomed to this kind of happy life.

In the fall of that year, people often visited my house at night. Most of them were students and young men. Many times, my father's room was brightly lit until dawn, and my mother would knit, silently but anxiously. Sometimes, if he awoke late in the morning, my father would not go to school. The school also began having more days off, and from time to time, I could see groups of students fighting with each other, sometimes with clubs. Amid this confusion, spring came again. As more and more troubles occurred at school, my grandfather took my uncle away to our hometown, but my father remained in the city, unconcerned about the problems at the school.

One night I awoke to some whispering. I did not open my eyes; instead, I concentrated on listening to what was going on next to me. When I heard my mother's feeble sobs, I opened my eyes slightly. I saw my father standing in the middle of the room and my mother packing things into the trunk. The clothes my father was wearing looked like those of someone who was about to embark on a journey.

"Take care of yourself," he said.

With these words, he turned swiftly toward the door. Mother followed him with a large trunk in her hands.

"Don't worry too much. I will come back when the new world comes."

My father said this calmly as he took the trunk from mother. I was quite relieved to hear that he would return, but mother didn't say anything. My father left just like that, as if he would return shortly.

But things did not end there. Early in the morning, there was some commotion. Policemen descended on our house while it was still dark. A couple of them were standing outside watching over the area. Some of the others came into the house and turned it upside down. They took some of my father's belongings and escorted my mother to the police station. I was left all alone. I spent the night at a neighbor's house, and the next day my grandfather and uncle came to get me. After hearing the news of my father's disappearance and the policemen taking my mother away, grandfather became silent. He left me again in the care of a neighbor, and went away with my uncle. Several days later, my mother came back with my grandfather. Holding me tightly, she shed tears, and from time to time, she gazed directly into my face.

We then returned to our hometown with my grandfather. The image of my father entering the house on that wet evening in the fall and the image of him leaving on that night seem unreal to me even now, but they were deeply engraved in my mind. As I was growing up I often wished that I had been born as a posthumous child, and I was not the only one with that thought—all of my family members wished it at one time or another because of the suffering caused by my father's disappearance. Such was the bitterness that my family felt toward my father.

That is why the news of my father's imminent return was so troubling. My father's cousin was just as anxious as I was. We wondered what would happen this time. Above all else, I was afraid because of a shocking event that had taken place ten years earlier.

* * *

After graduating from university, I prepared to study abroad. It was during that time that I came to know that my father was still alive. Before then, I had completely forgotten about my father—a fact that was a blessing for my family. My grandfather, my mother—a widow from an early age—and the cousin of my father, the closest relative to my family, all were trying to forget my father through their expectations regarding my future.

After my father's disappearance, my uncle joined the army as a young student soldier to fight in the Korean War, in which he was killed. My grandmother was murdered by communist guerillas, and my baby sister, who was born after my father disappeared, died just two days after she was born. My mother, my grandfather, and I lived discreetly, carefully watching over each other's expressions. All of us felt that my father was responsible for the deaths in our family, but we never expressed our opinions openly because we believed that father himself was dead. After my father left the school's residence that day, there was no more news from him, and we interpreted the absence of any news as a sign that he was dead. We therefore hoped that he would be forgotten from people's minds forever. On the assumption that he was dead, we were able to recover gradually from the pain that he had caused.

My grandfather accused my father of being selfish since he disregarded the wishes of his parents, who had lived such harsh lives, and decided instead to become an activist to fight for his progressive ideas. Grandfather spoke of his son as an indiscreet fool who does not understand life. This sort of criticism of my father was, at the same time, an admonition for me. Grandfather gradually turned his dashed expectations for my father toward me. As I grew older, I came to realize the extent of these expectations.

After the 4.3 Incident and the Korean War armistice, my family moved back to our hometown from the seashore village to which we had been evacuated. I finished elementary school in our hometown and then went to a junior high school in the city. Despite our family's poor financial situation, my grandfather wanted to send me to a good school. The war was over, but my family was still in bad shape. My father's disappearance had caused a great deal of hardship for my grandfather and mother, and most of the family's fortune was lost—all of our cattle had been given away to poor people during the 4. 3 Incident, and we had to sell most of our fields to make a living. More than the physical damage though, the deaths in the family left the surviving family members in severe pain. More than half of the extended family had died during this period.

After graduating from junior high school, I went to Seoul to attend high school and then university. During those years, hatred toward my father's legacy dominated my life. To overcome this, I tried hard to conform, to swim with the ways of the world. I could not afford to ride a horse, crossing the huge fields on the gentle slopes of Mount Halla in the garments of a university student, but even if I could have afforded it, I would have spit at the very idea of this petty-heroism. I tried hard, while I was studying in Seoul, to rid myself of any traces of my father that might remain in my body. For that reason I chose science and engineering as my major at the university. After getting my degree, I worked like a slave in a university laboratory, assisting one of my professors. My loyalty to that professor was later rewarded when I was offered a scholarship to study in West Germany. That was good news, not only for me, but also for the whole family, which hadn't experienced happiness in such a long time. With the news of my scholarship, our dark and desperate family home was suddenly filled with hope and joy.

To prepare for my departure to Germany, I left my job at the laboratory and returned to my hometown. For the first time in my life, I came to understand what it could be like to live in happiness with my grandfather and mother. During this period, my mother, a widow from youth who was now in her fifties, and my grandfather were able to forget the bitterness in their hearts.

A month or so after I returned home, I received a telegram from my professor requesting that I come to Seoul. When I arrived in Seoul I was told that I was not eligible for a passport. What upset me most was the reason: I was disqualified because of my father, who was still alive. He had secretly entered Japan, gotten married, and had become an important figure in the North Korean movement in Japan. I couldn't help but think that this whole event had been planned by some evil spirit who had died in bitterness and now wandered about this world seeking revenge.

"Wretch!"

After hearing the news, my grandfather shouted this one word and nothing more. How could anybody understand the feelings of a father who curses his own living son, a son thought to be dead! He was bitter, not so much because his grandson could not go abroad to study, but mainly because of what his son had done—he had risked his life to go to Japan, not contacted the family in more than twenty years, and devoted himself to realizing his communist ideals. The family had already been devastated by my father's behavior, but just as it was beginning to overcome that bitter disappointment, the evil spirit reappeared.

"He was possessed by the evil spirit of communism. We should either perform an exorcism or transfer the bodies of our ancestors to new graves."

My father's cousin said this to my dumbstruck grandfather in a cold voice. The cousin, a fastidious man, was the son of my granduncle. When my granduncle saw his father wasting money, he asked my great-grandfather to give him his share of the family fortune even before he got married. After receiving his fortune, he moved out, worked hard, and got married. His son too was a frugal man and did not like the idea of spending money on studying. Therefore, his attitude toward my father was negative from the beginning.

"He is not my son anymore."

Without informing my family, my grandfather went to the chief of the police in town and said only those words. Upon returning home, he became ill. My grandfather was more frustrated than I was, even though I was the one who could not travel abroad. For an old person with not many years to live, it was too much pain to suffer this kind of hardship again. His heart was torn apart by the second betrayal of his son.

He passed away after four days of illness. It was a sort of suicide. He refused to eat anything during those final four days, and no one could persuade him to do so. He was a man of strong will, and he manifested his willfulness even to the very end, when he deliberately chose death. Before he died, he passed me an envelope and said,

"When I die, follow the instructions in this letter and then bury me."

With these words, he passed away. His final moment was so solemn that I couldn't even feel the sadness. Within the envelope, there were all the necessary documents to officially declare my father's death and to eliminate his name from the census register. They were complicated documents that requested official acknowledgment of my father's death on the grounds that he had left home twenty-three years ago and there was no evidence that he was still alive. I submitted the papers to the township office immediately and, a week later, I reported a second death: the death of my grandfather. By the time of my grandfather's death, my father had killed four people.

* * *

When my mother and I moved back to our hometown from the city, where my father had worked as a teacher, my grandfather started to put the matters concerning the family in order. In September of that year, I entered an elementary school, located about two kilometers away. It was a small, rural elementary school with only four or five classrooms. Gradually the village fell into disorder. Every night there were signal fires on the small hills around the village, and policemen and soldiers frequently entered the village. Rumors spread of people being arrested or even killed. After sunset, we would lock up the house and not leave until daybreak. As fall set in, my grandfather hurried the harvest and rounded up the cattle and horses. Two barns were thus filled with fat cattle. One day, while feeding fodder to the cattle at the entrance to the barn, I saw my grandfather's eyes sparkled strangely as he scratched the back of a calf born in the spring. Many years later, I came to realize that his eyes had been sparkling with tears.

On that evening, my grandfather had invited the chief of the village and my granduncle to the house and talked with them well into the night. After a few days, we started to pack up all of our things. Grandfather distributed most of his cattle and horses to the villagers; he kept only my father's horse and two cows that were strong enough to pull a carriage. In addition to the cattle and horses, he also gave away all of our household furniture and food.

He said to the poor people in the village, "I am not giving away the cattle. When things become peaceful again, you should return them to me. But you can keep for free any calves that are born. Also, take as much fodder as you want from the barn."

In this way he gave away about twenty cattle to the villagers, cattle that he had been raising his entire life. My grandfather did not intend ever to reclaim those cattle, even while saying that he would. Rather, he said this to console himself since it was so painful to give them away. And of course nobody returned the cattle years later.

At dawn the next day, we prepared to evacuate the village. We were to walk six kilometers to a seashore village that had a police station and a government office. About fifty people were to be evacuated, including the families of my granduncle and some public officials. After loading furniture and food onto a carriage, grandfather nailed shut all the doors of the house. The dull sound of a wood-hammer reverberated into the pine tree fields behind the house and further into the sky.

As a waxing crescent moon faded on the western horizon, we left the house, following a loaded wagon. Grandmother wiped her nose several times with the long bow of her *hanbok*, and mother followed her like a shadow. Grandfather put me on my father's horse and ordered my uncle to lead it. When we arrived at the entrance to our village, the previously agreed point of departure, all of the people who had promised to go together were already gathered there. Some policemen and members of the Civil Defense Corps were also in the group. We left the village without saying anything. The only sounds that could be heard were those from the wagons, sounds that reverberated in the moonlit night.

When we left our village and arrived at the border of the neighboring village, the policemen and members of the Civil Defense Corps who were walking ahead of us gestured to us to hide. The wagons came to a stop because the roads were blocked with stone barriers. We didn't know what to do, and then we heard gunshots in the trees near the street. People began screaming, and the cattle that were pulling the wagons started kicking madly.

My father's horse was also raging wildly and threw me off. Later I heard that I had fallen into my grandfather's arms and that the horse that ran away after bucking me was shot. By dawn on that day, we arrived at the seashore village with no belongings—we had abandoned them during the commotion. Two members of our group had died there.

After narrowly escaping death, we rented a house in the seashore village and obtained some furniture. Grandfather's generosity over the years enabled us to make a living in this village. However, an unforeseen event happened two months after we arrived. Communist guerillas invaded the village and turned it into a blazing inferno. They murdered about a hundred people and burned down most of the public buildings and private homes, including our rented house. They also stabbed my grandmother to death with spears. After that incident, everyone in the village changed and began to act abnormally. From that day on, the villagers' hatred of the communist guerillas turned toward us, the people who had been evacuated from the villages between the seashore and Mount Halla. Grandfather and mother were frequently taken to the police station. They were pressured to confess whether or not they were secretly communicating with my father. My family suddenly became a family of communists. However, my grandmother's death helped us escape that hatred to a certain extent. If it hadn't been for her death, our family members would have suffered more severely.

My grandfather had enormous hatred toward the communist guerillas—partly because of my grandmother's death, but more so because of his endless love for his son. My grandfather blamed the communist guerillas for the fact that my father had become a communist, and his inability to restore the family to the position it once had made this hatred even more intense. However, the villagers never fully acknowledged my grandfather's bitter feelings toward the communists. The distribution of cattle, furniture, and food to poor neighbors in my hometown before we left also became a seed of trouble. They claimed that it was the way of the communists. They turned on us as if they were going to stone us. My uncle and I lived under the constant intimidation of our peers, since I was the son of a communist guerilla and my uncle was his brother. Because we could not afford to go to schools in the city, I attended a school in the village and my uncle went to the local junior high school. There, we had to endure the disdain of the other students.

Sometime later, my uncle was selected to receive military training every day and to participate in subduing and punishing captured guerillas. Not all the junior high school students joined in punitive attacks against the guerillas, but there was enough reason for my uncle to do so.

People like us who had been evacuated from the villages between the seashore and Mount Halla built a long makeshift house in the open area in front of the police station, divided it into several cubicles, and lived in it. Those from the seashore village, who lost their houses in attacks from the communist guerillas, built stone huts and lived there as well. However, the area they lived in was different from ours. There was a big open field in between those two areas that was used sometimes as a children's playground, sometimes as a gathering place for the punitive forces, and sometimes as a place to kill communist guerillas who had been arrested.

On my way home from school one day, I heard children shouting loudly in the center of that field. So I ran over there and pushed my head through the ring of the children standing there. There was my uncle, fighting with someone—they were rolling over each other and throwing punches. I simply watched, stamping my feet. After some time, my uncle gained the upper hand, mounted his enemy, and was about to strike him with a blow, when a loud voice was heard.

"You're a communist, a wretched communist."

Someone from the crowd shouted it out. In an instant, my uncle glared angrily in the direction of the place where those words had come from.

"Who's the bastard? Who said 'communist'?"

After saying this, my uncle stood up and prepared to fight with that person too.

"It's me. And aren't you a communist?"

A junior high school student, who was far shorter than my uncle, stepped forward and made the announcement, raising his eyes.

"You bastard!"

My uncle dashed at him and almost hit him when he heard the people around him hissing and hooting.

"Look at the communist!"

Hearing this, my uncle just stopped right there. He did not move.

"How can I be a communist? My mother was killed by one of the guerillas."

With this, he fell on his knees and started hitting the ground with his clenched fists. I choked, realizing that my uncle was directing his anger away from the crowd and toward the ground. I wanted to run to him, shouting "uncle," and cry and hit the ground together with him, but I was afraid of being ridiculed by the others. Suddenly, the boy who had been fighting with my uncle stood up and rushed to my uncle to tackle him. My uncle did not respond; he just sat there and allowed himself to be hit.

Several days later, my uncle volunteered to fight against the communist guerillas, and my grandfather did not stop him. Even when an arrested communist guerilla was being killed, my uncle was there.

One day, I saw a guerilla being killed by the family members of a victim of communist aggression and some other young people.

"Aren't you afraid?" I asked my uncle.

"Not really. At first, I could not eat and sleep well, but not any more. When they are in front of me, I feel as if they are going to stab my mother with a spear. Then I lose my mind. If I do not kill them, they will kill my mother."

His words seemed to make sense to me. My uncle had progressed from childhood to manhood in such a short time. Though my family was worried about my father's well-being, we were filled with stronger feelings—intense hatred—toward the communists who had stabbed my grandmother more than five times with spears and left her covered in blood. On that day when the communist guerillas attacked, my grandfather and grandmother ran away from those who came rushing into the front yard; they ran through the back door into the backyard. As he was climbing over the fence, grandfather tried to help my weak grandmother up, but the guerillas followed them and savagely stabbed her with spears while she was hanging on the fence. Grandfather repeatedly told us about that incident afterward.

I do not want to speak of it any more since it is too painful. After my grandmother's death, we had to face my uncle's death. Between these two deaths, my baby sister was born, but she died soon after the birth, without even being named.

When the Korean War broke out, my uncle, who had already received training in fighting the communists, volunteered to join the army even though he was only sixteen years old. He was a senior in junior high school at the time.

* * *

Just before the Korean War, my family was slowly recovering from the pains it had suffered. As the communist guerillas around Mount Halla lost some of their power, villagers became less hateful toward them, and we gradually began to overcome the double tragedy of my grandmother's death and the stigma of being the family of a communist guerila. Mother tried to contact those who had defected to the seashore village, hoping to hear any news about my father, but my grandfather forced her not to reveal her thoughts to others.

One night, while sleeping, I heard my grandfather scolding my mother for visiting a communist defector from the mountain and secretly inquiring about my father's condition.

"Forget everything. Consider him as having died in action in World War II. My son is dead. Do you remember the day when we evacuated our hometown to come to this village? His horse was shot and killed, and I decided then and there to believe that my son was killed at the same time."

My grandfather's voice sounded stiff and formal, but it was full of conviction. Though it was absurd to relate the death of my father's horse to that of my father, it sounded convincing at the time. Those words convinced us all of my father's death. Maybe that was what we wanted.

The story about my father's death was told again and again from that evening on. From our neighbors next door to their neighbors, and so on, the rumor spread; soon everyone believed that my father was dead. That news finally returned to my own house, and the person who brought the news to my family said, "It is a great loss." He even offered his sincere condolences to my grandfather.

Things like this relieved our burden. However, when the Korean War broke out and the recruitment of soldiers began, my uncle was the first to volunteer.

"Dad, I will join the army to kill the communist guerillas," he said.

One day, when my uncle came back home from school, he told us that the war had begun and said to my grandfather that he would volunteer for the army. My grandfather did not say anything, but my mother stared at my uncle. Since he had already indicated that he felt elated while the communists were being killed, I felt no doubt that he would bravely eliminate them.

When it was announced that my uncle would go to war, the villagers held a great farewell party. Three youths were to go together. Soon, my house was filled with all sorts of people; it was as if we were holding a banquet. The guests lived in rather unfortunate circumstances, yet they demonstrated great concern and generosity toward my uncle. None of this, however, changed the expressions on the faces of my grandfather and mother.

On the day of my uncle's departure, we sat down together for breakfast. "Son, remember that death does not come easily. Didn't your brother come back from World War II? Even when a strong fire is set to a field, there always remains a bundle of grass that is not burnt. Likewise, the life and death of a man depends on the heavens. You just have to take care of yourself."

I cannot forget the expression on my grandfather's face as he spoke so calmly on that day. It comes back to me now as clear as a photograph.

On the day of departure, villagers and students lined up on both sides of the street, and my uncle walked in the middle. He waved goodbye to the people who were sending him off. The people waved Korean flags, and my uncle walked through the crowd in a dignified manner. The clear colors of the Korean flags that had been placed on his shoulders and around his head filled my eyes. Holding my mother's hand, I watched my uncle, who seemed to be elated. Suddenly the image of the young student who had pounded the earth, crying "I am not a communist," flashed into my mind.

After my uncle left the house, my home became quieter. There were just the three of us: grandfather, mother, and me. The house seemed rather empty. For the first several days, I was so disturbed by dreams about my uncle that I could barely sleep. However, hearing the news at school that Korean soldiers were marching onward, I was able to spend my days feeling proud of my uncle being at war. My feelings were strongest when my uncle came home on leave, ten months after his departure. I was able then to wash away the dishonor of being the son of a communist. His uniform was decorated with two chevrons and many medals, which were shining like gold in the sunlight. He was carrying a sword on his belt and a gun on his shoulder. Certainly he was a hero in the village. Once again my house was filled with people every day. The head of the village, the chief of the police station, the principal, the commander of the Civil Defense Corps—many influential people in the village visited our house and offered to treat my uncle. One day, my uncle was invited to my school to give a talk about the war during the morning assembly. The students listened with great interest to his description of a war that sounded so real. Some of the ones near me glanced my way once or twice. My uncle said,

"We are going to win the war for sure. After I return to the army, I will plant the national flag on the top of Mount Baekdu and wash my bloodstained sword in Amnok River. After that, I will come to see you again."

He then shouted "Hurrah!" three times before stepping down from the podium. We joined him spontaneously in shouting and became very excited. Everyone wanted to be a hero like my uncle. He also gave a speech at the junior high school that he had once attended.

While my uncle and I walked through the streets hand in hand during his leave from the army, the children from the village followed us. I walked more proudly than my uncle, and nobody dared criticize us or call us communists as they had done in the past.

After spending a wonderful time at home, my uncle went back to fight in the war. When he returned home the next time it was in the form of white ashes. Again, my house was filled with villagers. The funeral ceremony was held at the junior high school, and then he was buried. During the burial ceremony, my grandfather and mother did not cry.

After the Korean War armistice, we returned to our hometown and settled down. It was at that point that we realized how small the family had become. The loss of my grandmother and uncle was felt severely. However, my grandfather and mother did not mention the past; nor did they convey any hint of their feelings through facial expressions. This behavior continued even when the situation had become stable. From time to time, people talked about things that had happened during the 4.3 Incident and the Korean War, but my family was always silent on those matters. It was worse on the anniversaries of my grandmother's and uncle's deaths. It is common for people to talk about their loved ones on such anniversaries, but my family, and even my relatives, remained silent at those times. My grandfather confined himself to his room. He smoked a lot and refused to associate with other relatives. The sorrow that would come gushing out at the slightest touch was accumulating in the hearts of my family members. We held a memorial service for my father on the day of his departure from the school's residence, but we never talked about the deceased members of our family. The subject became taboo in the family.

After failing to go abroad to study, I radically changed my long-term goals. I used the knowledge that I had acquired at the university in my pursuit of wealth. I entered a trading company, learned some practical things about business, and then opened my own company, where I earned money. My simple goal was to realize my grandfather's dream. I even decided to marry and have as many smart children as possible. Many of my friends and relatives said that I had changed into a materialistic person, but after I learned of my father's life I came to think that materialistic people are the most sincere. Then I returned to Jeju Island, opened a new business, and lived what others thought of as a successful life.

* * *

Though my father was dead according to the census register, his existence was an indisputable fact, one from which I always suffered. I visited Japan several times on business trips, but the first thing I felt at those times was a fear that I might see my father. I wasn't really afraid of meeting someone who works for North Korea; rather, I was afraid of what effect my father's reappearance might have on my family. I was afraid that it might completely destroy my family. It was the fear of an evil spirit.

My mother's thoughts, on the other hand, were completely different from mine. Whereas the news of my father's existence left me feeling frustrated, it planted a small hope in my mother's heart. It seems that my mother could not forget my father even though he was the one who made her life so full of sorrow.

When my father's cousin returned to our hometown with the bewildered look on his face, I showed the letter he had brought to my mother. My mother's expressionless face became animated when she saw my father's name on the envelope. I even noticed her effort to conceal this emotion. Trying to lessen the impact of this event on my mother, I said, "Old age must have changed him."

In fact, that's what I wanted his return home to be. I hoped that his return was not some scheme, but the honest intention of an old man who wants to see his hometown one more time before he dies. I hoped that this was why he had written such a short letter instead of a long explanation.

After looking at the envelope and then reading the letter, my mother said,

"This is certainly your father's handwriting."

As she looked at me, her face began to brighten—something that I had not seen in a long time. The fact that my mother, just like my father's cousin, remembered my father's handwriting after more than thirty years of separation struck a chord in my heart. After reading the letter two or three times, my mother folded it, put it back in the envelope, and handed it to me without saying anything. She then looked up at the ceiling and heaved a deep sigh.

After receiving the letter from my father's cousin, I spent my days in anxiety, hoping that someone other than my father had written the letter as a prank. My mother and my father's cousin suggested as much. To tell the truth, I was afraid and wary of my father's return. First and foremost, I didn't want to relive the pains of the past, pains that seemed to have been almost forgotten. In addition, I could not accept my father, a man who wanted to return home now, after having lived his whole life in his own way without concern for his family.

That's the reason I couldn't talk about this event, not even to my wife. In fact, in our ten years of marriage, I had never talked to her about my father. The fact that he had been a student of Gyungsung Imperial University and that he used to ride a horse on the gentle slopes of Mount Halla wearing university garments—these facts could have been interesting topics to discuss when we were bored, but I kept my mouth shut on these matters. My wife and my children had always thought that my father passed away a long time ago. But then I had to show them a letter about his impending return and explain all those stories. That was the worst thing I ever had to do.

Then my father's telegram arrived. After receiving the telegram from my father's cousin, I said, "This might simply be a visit. Let's not worry about it." But I didn't know what to do and, to be honest, I didn't really care about what might happen next. My mother could not conceal her excitement enough for me not to notice. How could anyone not be excited about the return of someone who was considered to be dead? I was displeased with her excitement, though. It seemed wrong to be happy about this return when we did not know what consequences it would bring.

On the night that I received the telegram, I confessed the history of my family to my wife. After listening to my story, my wife said,

"I must have been a stranger to you. I guess we are not a married couple, but two strangers who just happen to live together."

She could not understand, didn't even try to understand, how I felt. And I did not have the time to make her understand. Father's cousin spent the night before my father's arrival at our house, trying to subdue his worries about the consequences of this homecoming. What would ideology mean to a man who is almost sixty? It must be that he was returning because he was homesick. With these thoughts, we decided to forget about things in the past and prepare to welcome a changed man.

I don't think we slept at all that night, but early in the morning I called the airline and inquired about the passengers on the scheduled flight. They said that there was a Mr. Park among the passengers on that flight, but they did not know for sure whether there was a passenger named Park Sung-Bin. My father's cousin said that since he had lived in Japan for more than thirty years, he had probably changed his name, and we all agreed with him.

The airplane from Osaka was scheduled to arrive at 2:15 in the afternoon. While driving to the airport with my wife, my mother, and my father's cousin, I was consumed by the image of my father, on that gray, wet evening in late fall, stepping onto the narrow porch, soaking wet. Did I stare at that dark yard on that rainy night because I, a four year-old boy, wanted to meet my father before anyone else did? As my father's cousin had said, how could a man have lived such a life of betrayal to the people around him if he were not completely mad? Betrayal of his parents who sent him to Seoul to study, betrayal of his wife who lived most of her married life as a widow, and betrayal of his son for the insults and frustrations he suffered because of his father. Could he really compensate for this life of betrayal by returning home now?

The waiting lounge for international arrivals was filled with people welcoming their friends and families. Everyone—people from the country, an old woman with a wrinkled face—looked excited and happy to see loved ones. I frequently glanced at my mother, who was sitting in one corner with an uneasy posture. I was choked with emotion, wondering whether she would make that bashful face of my aunt again when she saw my father.

Mother was watching the passengers coming out of the exit carrying their luggage. I held her arm and went to the exit to meet my father. Those who were already holding their loved ones and crying touched my heart, and I realized how selfish I was to feel hatred toward my father and how pure my mother's feelings toward my father were. My father's cousin simply stared at the exit with a stiff face. My wife stood there as if she were waiting to see something interesting.

I thought to myself: "What is family? What does it mean to be a father or a son, a husband or a wife?"

While I was thinking about these questions, a sturdy young man who was holding something caught my eye. He came out of the exit, looked around, and went to the information desk. My mother's lips seemed to be moving, as if she wanted to say something to me about him.

"Paging Mr. Park Min-Kyu. Please come to the information desk."

I was startled to hear my name called. As I approached the information desk I cast a second glance at that man. Somehow I could find my father's features in his face. Suddenly I realized that what he was holding up was a box of ashes—my father's ashes. Mother and my father's cousin were also looking at the man. I took a deep breath and continued toward the information desk, but my legs were trembling. A premonition that I might experience betrayal once again was weighing heavily on me. I walked carefully, one step at a time, as if walking on a tightrope in the air.

"Brother Min-Kyu."

I opened my eyes and it was him, that young man.

"Father said that he really wanted to return home before he died. He wrote the letter just before he passed away."

The young man said this, struggling to speak in his clumsy Korean. My father's homecoming was the final, ultimate betrayal. I looked at my mother who was standing there, completely frozen. My father's death was finally confirmed. And then I asked myself,

"What is this feeling in my heart, the feeling that had solidified there so long ago? Is it really hatred?"

As I thought about the box of ashes that was my father, my mind was consumed with that question.

Fire and Ashes

1

The reception hall was crowded with people who had come to celebrate the fact that the town of Namdo had recently been designated as a city. Congressmen from Namdo, the governor of the province, and various influential people—they all looked bright and full of vigor. The atmosphere in the hotel, which was perched on a cliff touching the sea, seemed to soar high into the sky. The sea sparkled spectacularly with rolling waves in the late afternoon light, and those sparkling ripples penetrated the hearts of the people gathered in the hotel. As I was pushing my way through the crowd, moving toward the window in order to get a better view of the sea, I was abruptly stopped by the radiant light of the sun.

"Are you enjoying the ocean view? Let's go and get a drink."

Kim Suk-Moon, one of my elementary school classmates and the head of a local agricultural cooperative, dragged me by the arm.

"How could we not drink a toast on this joyous occasion? And we have not seen each other for such a long time. Don't you get emotional seeing how our hometown has changed so much? Don't you think we ought to live a decent life as the owners of this place, freeing ourselves from poverty? Now that our town, Namdo, one of the poorest spots on this island, has been raised to the status of city, it will surely prosper. You are a special guest who has come from afar to celebrate this meaningful event, aren't you? So, let's drink a toast!"

With a rather exaggerated gesture and tone of voice, he pulled me to the bar, where we each got a drink.

"Here you are! I have been looking for you," said Kang Tae-Sam.

Kang, another friend of mine from elementary school, was the chief organizer of this public celebration. He grabbed me by the right hand and led me to a corner of the celebration hall, where several high-ranking officials were enjoying some delightful conversation. The new mayor, who was among them, began to introduce me to the others, referring to me as "the poet."

"Mr. Kim, I am so grateful for the presence of such a famous poet at this celebration," he said.

He repeatedly emphasized the word "poet."

"This is the poet Kim Hak-Chul," the mayor said as he introduced me to the others. "He wrote the lyrics for the official song of the city of Namdo. He left this native place a long time ago and now lives in Seoul. Yet Namdo is so proud of him. It is a great honor for our city that its song was written by a poet who is a native of this city and is active in literary circles in Seoul."

With the mayor's exaggerated introduction, I gave an awkward nod to each person there, and we each exchanged a few words. At the same time, feeling somewhat uncomfortable with the atmosphere, I began to experience an increasingly intense pain in my shoulders.

"We thank you for coming to the celebration," one of these people said to me, as he gestured to shake my hand. The mayor then introduced us.

"This is Mr. Ji. He is the president of a company."

Another person also held out his hand, but I had no idea who he was.

"I have often heard about you. You are widely regarded as a poet of the people. We are so proud of you," he said.

I blushed when he called me a poet of the people. At that moment Kang Tae-Sam whispered into my ear.

"Do you not know Congressman Kim from our hometown?"

Then the governor asked, "How do you feel about your hometown becoming a city?"

"I am happy about it," I said.

I gave him a prompt answer, but inwardly said to myself, "I do not know what to think. I feel possessed by a spirit."

"Mr. Kim must be more touched by this celebration, because he left this place when he was very young," said Kang Tae-Sam.

The mayor then asked, "When did you leave this place?"

I hesitated to answer, because I could not quickly estimate the passage of time.

"You probably left for Seoul when you were in the second year of middle school," said Kang, answering on my behalf.

Then I began to recollect my departure from the hometown. In fact, it was after finishing the first year of middle school, several years after the outbreak of the Korean War. I was so sad when I left my hometown. I could not understand why my father decided to leave the place in which my ancestors had lived for generations.

The mayor then said, "That span of time is enough for mountains and streams to have changed, isn't it?"

"So it is," I admitted. "Who could have thought that our hometown would have become a city?"

It was indeed hard to believe that this was the same place in which my ancestors had lived for generations.

It once was a poverty-stricken village. Although it had a harbor, it did not have a proper dock for fishing boats. Its seashore was all covered with sand and surrounded by steep cliffs. People lived on sweet potatoes, barley, and millet from the field, some fish, seaweed, and ear shells or conches caught by women divers. During the Japanese Occupation, the wasteland that spread beyond the village was used as an air force base, and that brought tradesmen to this village. However, after Liberation, the village became desolate again.

The village was severely damaged during the 4.3 Incident, an insurrection on April 3, 1948, caused by the political and ideological conflicts between the prodemocracy activists and the communists. I still could not forget those vivid scenes right after Liberation: hungry people with bloated faces lining up in front of the sweet potato storehouse of a Buddhist temple, the village in flames after the attack of the communist guerrillas, the bloody eyes of the men cursing and killing each other in the turbulence of the 4.3 Incident, and the crowds of refugees from the Korean War on the peninsula rushing to Jeju Island once the disturbance had more or less calmed down.

"This is all due to the modernization of our country," the governor of Jeju Island said with a laugh. And there was hidden meaning in his laughter. The modernization seemed tangible to me.

I was invited to this ceremony to celebrate Namdo's newly acquired status of a city because I had composed the lyrics of the city song. I arrived on the island in the morning. I had visited my hometown several times before, but not recently. The place had changed so much that it was no longer familiar to me. Newly constructed straight roads, palm trees and camellias alternately planted on the roadsides, and red and blue concrete roofs—it was quite different from the thatched-roof homes and crumbling stone fences that I was used to. The speeding cars, bars, cafés, billiard rooms, and new restaurants were all unfamiliar to me. On the sides of the circuit road of the island, three- or four-story buildings now stood where low tin-roof houses once were clustered like crab shells. Desolate cliffs and beaches had become popular swimming resorts. Around them, wonderful amusement facilities had been constructed. A small rock island about ten kilometers from the shore, which had always been desolate, was now a fishing place blessed by heaven. My hometown was now crowded throughout the year with people who came to spend money. The tangerine orchards had increased the income of the islanders during the last twenty years or so. As it is said that money tends to gather in one place, the collected funds raised Namdo from a small village of only five hundred families to a town, and then again to a city.

Kang Tae-Sam whispered to the mayor and then approached the microphone that had been placed there in advance. He cleared his voice and straightened his body.

"Excuse me, ladies and gentlemen, I thank you for coming to celebrate this historic beginning for the city of Namdo. The ceremony will now commence. First, the mayor will give an opening address."

The mayor blushed as he approached the microphone. After a few ceremonial words, his voice suddenly got louder.

"... this area, a place of suffering and tragedy in the past, has prospered with the support of the government and the villagers' spirit of self-reliance and independence. Therefore, it has been raised to the honorable status of a city. We must completely forget the pain and agony of the past, and devote ourselves to the construction of a new city, a new province, and a new country, so that our descendants will inherit this blessed land with pride. ..."

The mayor spoke with excitement. He was from Namdo. He had worked his way through high school, but had given up his dream of entering college. Instead, he passed the examination to become a fifth-class civil servant and later became a mayor. He was a self-made man. As the first mayor of the city of Namdo, it was natural for him to speak loudly about the pain and agony of the past.

After the mayor's speech, Kang announced that "Next, Mrs. Ko Young-Ae will sing our city song, which will surely become our favorite song. It is a pledge for the glorious future of our city."

When the singer appeared, the hall suddenly became quiet. People seemed to take a strong interest in her. With a slight smile on her face, a middle-aged woman in a white dress approached the microphone. Thunderous clapping shook the hall. She was a real beauty. Even though she was middle-aged, she had maintained an appearance of innocence. She looked dignified, rather than rustic or snobbish, in her florid white dress. She stood quietly before the microphone, looked around the audience, and gazed upon the vast sea in the twilight. As the pianist began a prelude to the song, Kang Tae-Sam again grabbed the microphone.

"Before you enjoy this performance, I would like to introduce our city song. The poet of the people, Kim Hak-Chul, who is also from Namdo, wrote the lyrics for this song, and Professor Meng composed the music. We wanted to invite both of them to this celebration, but Professor Meng is now abroad, so only the poet is with us today. I want you to greet him with a round of applause."

I bowed to the audience in a confused manner, for I was not expecting this introduction. I sensed the keen gaze of Mrs. Ko, who was about to sing. She nodded at me with a smile. Unintentionally, I replied with a nod and a smile, as if I had known her for a long time. The song then followed the interrupted prelude.

> Where the spirit of Mount Halla and the sea touch each other,
> A new morning for Namdo city shines.
> The history handed down in the darkness of time
> Will open a new page with our will.
> Oh, oh, Namdo City, Namdo City,

> The place that will last for long,
> Our passion will build a monument on it.
>
> People who have lived in the beautiful mountains and streams
> Have come together to build a new history.
> On the tracks of a painful history
> They gather together for a bright future.
> On the tracks of a painful history
> The light of a bright future shines
> Oh, oh, Namdo City, Namdo City,
> Our dear city, where we will be buried,
> Our love for the city will remain forever.

While the performance continued, the hall was enveloped with breathtaking silence. The melody from the piano, sometimes as if sobbing and sometimes rejoicing, penetrated each person's heart. Song lyrics usually seemed plain to me, so I could not understand why these captured my heart. Was it because I wrote the words? At that moment, a strong light shone directly into my face. When I quickly covered my face from the light, a cameraman waved at me uncomfortably, so I clumsily lowered my hand. I felt sad as I posed for the camera. The light for the camera then moved to Mrs. Ko, who was still singing.

"Isn't the song wonderful? Don't you think the melody suits the meaning of your words?"

Kim Suk-Moon whispered into my ear. He seemed to perceive that I was deeply touched by the song. Strangely, the song did move me. Some thoughts about my hometown, which I did not sense when I wrote the words, more clearly flashed through my mind and touched me.

"Is she from this place?" I asked.

I guessed that she was probably a guest from Seoul.

"You don't know her? She is Mr. Ko Jin-Kook's daughter. You know, the man who became a communist in the 4.3 Incident."

"Mr. Ko Jin-Kook?"

"Yes, he was our teacher when we were in the second year …"

Although Kim said something about Mr. Ko, I could not hear him. I was absorbed in my own thoughts. I had respected Mr. Ko as much as I hated him. He was my teacher in the second year of elementary school and a close friend of my uncle's. At that moment I was dazzled by Mrs. Ko's fluorescent dress. I closed my eyes due to a slight dizziness, and I heard thunderous applause. It seemed to come from afar. White light and clapping—they took me back a long way, reminding me of things completely forgotten.

"Bravo! Bravo! Encore!"

Those who had been immersed in Mrs. Ko's fascinating performance were now shouting and clapping for more. While Kang Tae-Sam and the singer herself did not know what to do, the mayor suddenly approached the microphone and spoke.

"Thank you, let's have an encore. How meaningful it will be for this celebration! Mrs. Ko would not mind performing an encore."

The mayor's voice was soaring high above the hall. Having an encore was exceptional, but acceptable, given that the new mayor had returned home in glory and strongly felt his own emotion in the song. Again, a thunderous round of applause shook the hall. The clapping was loud enough to shake heavens and earth.

The singer blushed as she approached the microphone. A strong light dazzled our eyes. Partially straightening the upper part of my shaking body, I closed my eyes. A middle-aged woman, whose beauty was neither vulgar nor faded—it was calm and graceful—suddenly penetrated my heart. I opened my eyes again. What kind of woman was this? She conveyed an image that did not suit this newly established city.

"She resembles Mr. Ko so much."

As Kim Suk-Moon's voice rang in my ear, I collapsed in confusion.

* * *

The school playground was tranquil in the late afternoon sunlight. In his white sports coat and white hat, the tall Mr. Ko passed through the school gate, casting a long shadow on the ground behind him.

"Sir! Sir! Siiiirrr!"

I called out to him several times in my mind. Intoxicated by the sunlight shining on his sports coat, I could not call out to him any longer. My heart was beating anxiously, and I was at my wit's end as I stared at the empty playground after Mr. Ko had passed through the school gate. My feeling toward him was a mixture of shame, envy, and hatred. When I was seven, my uncle, who had just returned from serving in the Japanese army during the Occupation, escorted me to school for the first time. Entering the school grounds, my heart was filled with excitement. When my uncle and I entered the teacher's room, the school principal, who was talking with children of my age, greeted us with a beaming smile.

"Would you come to school even in the rain?" he asked me in a gentle voice.

"Yes, I would," I answered, not knowing what to say.

"How could you come to school in the rain?" he asked again.

"I would come in my dad's old jacket," I answered.

After I spoke, a quiet laugh spread through the room for a moment. My uncle stood next to me and looked at me with embarrassment.

A teacher in white sportswear sitting next to the principal then looked me right in the face and asked, "Hey, would you come to school even if your house was on fire?"

My mind was blank. The house was on fire, on fire. As my mind was getting hazy, I could not judge what to do in that situation. I hesitated to answer and then darted out from the room. I was told later that, dashing out, I looked angrily at the teacher in the white tracksuit. That first embarrassment thrust Mr. Ko, in his white clothes, into my mind like thorns into my eyes. However, the thorns soon began to tickle my eyes and his white appearance has haunted me ever since. Some time later, my uncle left our hometown, and my affection for him brought me closer to Mr. Ko. I was completely drawn to him after I came to know that Mr. Ko was a close friend of my uncle's, that he had studied in Japan with my uncle, that he had been used by the Japanese army, and that he had returned home alive just like my uncle. My reverence for him grew even greater on the anniversary of the Independence Movement of March 1, 1919, when I was in the first grade. The men and women in our village, both young and old, gathered in the school playground. The commemoration proceeded as scheduled, and at the end of the ceremony Mr. Ko stood at the podium. His voice, roaring like a lion, caused the people in the playground to hold their breath in excitement. They clapped several times while he delivered his speech. I had never been so captivated by anyone. From that time on, the villagers considered him someone special, someone who would one day be an important person. So young men who had graduated from elementary school but could not afford to get a higher education always gathered around him. He rented a village house, which he named "The Namdo Institute for Higher Education," and began to teach classes for middle school students. When I entered the second grade, Mr. Ko became my teacher, so the uneasiness stemming from my previous embarrassment grew stronger. In those days I was haunted by dreams every night. I used to dream that my uncle who had left for the mainland was transformed into Mr. Ko, and then transformed again into me. Those dreams made me feel suffocated, and I would wake up in confusion. Whenever I would have those dreams, I would be annoyed by the difficult questions Mr. Ko asked in class, like the ones that he had asked on my first visit to the school. I could never answer his questions on those occasions; I would always recall my dreams from the night before. Then, when the questions became even more difficult, I would turn my eyes toward the playground. Feeling at a loss, the sunlight that reflected from some broken glass on the playground would always lead me into a slight dizziness. Mr. Ko not only asked me questions, he was excessively cold and strict to me. He refused to ignore anything about me, even matters that he would disregard in other children. In those situations, I would feel betrayed and depressed at the thought that I was estranged from him. Even though I, as the head of my class, took care of all his chores, I never received a word of praise from him. As a result of this unhappy situation, I became a mischievous student, always scowling.

On the last day of the second year of elementary school, Mr. Ko gave me a grade sheet and an honorary certificate, patting my head several times, saying that I should do just as well in the third grade. However, having spent the whole year in misery, I was unspeakably disappointed with him. In those days, September was the beginning of school year. During the summer vacation, I was heartbroken because of Mr. Ko. Every day I would spend long hours playing in a stream at the back of our village. After spending most of the day in the stream, I would come home, where my mother would be waiting to scold me. Yet the next day I would visit the stream again. With my body immersed in the cool stream water, I would think of my uncle and of Mr. Ko's stately demeanor. I would envision my future, as I watched clouds slowly pass across the blue sky. After the summer vacation passed and I entered third grade, I was to some degree able to overcome the effect of Mr. Ko's white tracksuit. Every now and then while I was sitting in class his clear whistle would draw my eyes to the playground, where I could see him teaching athletics to the sixth-grade students. I was slightly spellbound by him. On morning meetings for physical exercises, I used to envy and admire his white arms and legs as he stood on the platform, but he did not captivate me then as much as he did in the second grade.

* * *

Again, roaring applause shook the celebration hall. The performance had just ended. With a strong light fixed on her, Mrs. Ko bowed politely to the cheering people and listened to the clapping.

"Encore, encore!" the people cried out.

Straightening her back, she looked around the hall, bowed slightly again, and made her exit while the clapping continued.

The florid white dress stirred something in me. I was troubled by the memory of Mr. Ko, a memory I had already forgotten. Suddenly it was revived. Still feeling somewhat disturbed, I tried to collect my thoughts.

The mayor approached me, saying, "It was a wonderful song."

Mrs. Ko said, "I tried to deliver the poet Kim's intention, but …"

She looked me in the face as she spoke. It was as if she had met me before. Those eyes of hers shook my heart with fright.

"What?" I stuttered. "Your rendition was so beautiful and touching. You expressed more than I thought while I was writing those words."

But to be honest, I was only thinking of Mr. Ko while I was listening to the song.

"All right, let's have a drink," said Kang Tae-Sam.

Together with Kim Suk-Moon and Mrs. Ko, the four of us went to the bar.

"I should offer a glass of whisky to the poet," Mrs. Ko said, as she mixed a glass of whiskey and handed it to me.

"Thank you, and I should …"

Holding the glass, I did not know what to say because of the sensation caused by her white dress.

"I was rather excited to find out that the words were written by you. Furthermore, the words seemed to suit the melody so well that I was afraid and worried about whether I could sing the song well. So I practiced hard, harder than I did for my graduation recital. Now I feel ashamed that I couldn't have done better."

Her voice was soaked with sadness.

"What an honor for you two to make a song for the future of our city. And what's more, we all are from Namdo …" said Kang Tae-Sam.

"Let's have some drinks after this ceremony," Kim Suk-Moon suggested. "How about you, Mrs. Ko? Won't you join us?"

"It would be an honor. No, it will be my treat for the poet Kim …"

Kang answered for Mrs. Ko, causing us all to laugh loudly.

"It's almost time for the festival," said Kang, as he looked at his watch. He then walked over to the microphone.

"Well, thank you very much. The festival will now be held in several places around the city. Let's clean up the hall here, and then go watch the fireworks that will promise prosperity for Namdo's future."

The highest authorities left the hall first, and we followed behind, pushed along by the crowd.

Outside the hall darkness was approaching. We could immediately sense the dark blue sea with its fresh smell. In one glance, we could see the small city of Namdo. Several fishing boats with bright lights glided toward the open sea, which expanded far off into the distance.

2

In front of the hotel, a flat lawn stretched out atop steep cliffs of fantastic rocks and stones. In the cracks and crevices of the rocks, short trees—pines and others—battered by the sea wind, were perched precariously.

I used to visit this spot as an elementary school student. The open sea was a comfort to poor children. When we became hungry after playing, we would go down to the shore through narrow passages between the cliffs, gather seashells, break them with stones, and eat the meat. The seashells that gathered around rocks in the flow would remain in the ebb. A small boy could push himself under a big rock and easily catch the seashells. We would fill ourselves, climb up the cliffs again as if walking on a tightrope, and play on the lawn until sunset. The lawn was still large, and the short trees were still growing. The only changes were the new cement benches and the iron fence surrounding the lawn.

I decided to walk to the edge of the lawn and look out at the darkening sea. The sea in the evening was very lonesome and quiet. So too was the lawn, which was lit by sentinel lamps. Whenever I moved, the grass seemed to tickle the soles of my feet, even though I had shoes on. I felt inclined to remove my shoes and socks and go barefoot. When I arrived at the edge of the lawn, I found small graves scattered here and there under the dim lights. They looked much smaller under the lights than they really were.

"Here you are!" said Kim Suk-Moon. "Who would have ever imagined that this place would become the site of a five-star hotel? This is where the guerrillas were once killed. The place over there used to be covered with pine trees."

Kim pointed to where the hotel was standing. His comment reminded me of the past. After the 4.3 Incident, we were reluctant to come here. Countless rumors about this place were being spread abroad—that human bones were rolling around the lawn after the rains, that the sound of weeping could be heard at night, that someone saw the ghost of a pretty woman in a white dress waving to a fishing boat.

"Before the hotel was constructed, Mrs. Ko held an exorcism here for about ten days, and took proper care of the abandoned graves. The villagers also helped. The dead were pitiful, whichever side they belonged to. Those who survived the 4.3 Incident and now see the prosperity of our city are fortunate and happy, aren't they? That's why Mrs. Ko held the exorcism—to comfort those who had died in the Incident. She wanted all the people involved to forget the past and make a new start. Only Mrs. Ko could have done such a thing. The authorities allowed her, for certain reasons, to build resort facilities here. This kind of resort will contribute greatly to the development of Namdo."

I was not listening to him. I just stared at those quiet graves under the dim, sleepy light.

"Did Mr. Ko have a daughter back then?" I asked, moving toward the hotel.

"She was probably born after he fled to the mountains."

I barely heard his response, as it receded into the sound of the sea. The darkness grew deeper and deeper, and I caught a glimpse of the white spray from the waves hitting the cliffs. Suddenly the sound of the sea became louder. I looked at the tidy lights of Namdo city.

"She runs several businesses, including a hotel, here in the city. She reigns over the social circles, so to speak," Kim said.

"She is a brave woman."

"You may say that she is a lady above the world."

"She seems to have some money, too. Is her husband rich? Perhaps a wealthy immigrant from Japan?" I asked.

"It is true that she has much money, but she is still single. We call her Mrs. Ko, but really we should call her Miss Ko. Her father's family was wealthy a long time ago. Her father's father was the head of the village during the Japanese Occupation of Korea, and the family was rich enough to send her father to study in Japan. After the family fell to the troubles of the 4.3 Incident, relatives on the mother's side of the family took care of the family's estates and then later returned them to her. Do you know the price of land here? She is a woman of enormous fortune."

"At that time, her family members were massacred and Mr. Ko was later arrested and sentenced to death," I said.

"You remember that?"

Suddenly resplendent fireworks soared up high into the dark sky, and a loud sound reverberated into the distance.

"Wow!"

The shouts of the people fell on the city like flames. One after another, fireworks soared up into the sky, fell down toward the earth like rain, and then disappeared. As people shouted from near and far, my heart trembled. I was suffocated by the constant sound of radiant sparks descending to the ground.

* * *

It was a disastrous scene. I cried and cried, looking at our village from afar. With clenched fists, I dried the tears rolling down my cheeks. The village, all in flames, was buried under black smoke.

In the morning, sleet was swirling about outside as my grandparents and I prepared to eat breakfast. I always stayed in the main building of our house with my grandparents. They were almost seventy and loved me very much. Grandmother, who had been confined to bed for a long time, always had me near her side. Grandfather too was always nearby, and he thought much of my closeness to her. When I came home from school, I studied by my grandmother's side. Watching me study, she would forget the cares of her old age. I had my own way when I played outside, but at home I was obedient; I was like a little lamb with my grandparents. Sometimes when I did something silly or fought with my friends, they would laugh at me, saying, "How could you do such a thing?" With them I was always meek. And because of their generosity and love, I was also happy.

We heard a loud shot, but I kept on eating. I heard my father bustling around in a detached living room, and then I heard his voice outside the door.

He said, "Father, the mobs are going to attack us."

Still, I kept on eating breakfast, and grandmother just watched me eat.

"Father!" he yelled again. "Father, you have to escape!"

"You go first!" said my grandfather, as he paused from eating and opened the door.

My father said, "The situation is very serious. Please, you have to take refuge for a while."

"What would they do with old people? I have done nothing wrong to anybody," grandfather replied in a stern voice.

At that moment, another clamorous shot was heard from the entrance to the village.

"Son, just take Hak-Chul with you," he said to my father.

Grandfather then stood me up and pushed me out of the room. Out in the yard, I saw that the houses at the entrance to the village were in flames. Heavy smoke and flames were rising high in the sky, and sparks were being blown around by the wind.

"Hurry up! Don't worry about old ones like us," grandfather urged as he saw my mother and my elder brother moving household furniture into the back yard.

"I will do that, you all run away," he said.

At his insistence, the five of us just ran out of the house. Holding my brother's hand, I looked back toward the house. I saw grandfather standing in the middle of the yard, watching us, and heard grandmother coughing.

On the wide road, people were coming and going in confusion. People carrying various things on their backs were running here and there. Children were crying out as the people rushed about madly. Black smoke rose up angrily to the sky, and a strange smell gathered around the tips of our noses. We raced to the sea. Grandmother's dry coughs kept ringing in my ears.

"Boys, go to the shore west of the village and hide yourselves among the rocks!"

My father suddenly stopped and, without asking for our opinion, ordered my elder brother to go in the opposite direction and to take me with him. My parents then took my younger brother and ran the other way.

We ran as fast as we could. Arriving at the shore, we rushed toward the west side of the village as father had directed. The morning sea was quiet and occasionally we saw refugees like us. They were all moving in a hurry. They hid themselves among the cracks of the big rocks. We too hid behind big rocks. After catching our breath, we became afraid of the shots from the village. At times, we tried to stick our heads out to get a look at the village but could see nothing but thick black smoke. We wept with fear as dizzying flames soared up into the dark sky.

With the gradual flow of the tide, we started to worry about the water that was approaching the rocks we were hiding behind. If the guerrillas came down to the shore, what would become of us? A deep despair rushed over me like the tide, and I began to cry even louder than before. We remained in that situation for about half a day.

"Come out quickly, good citizens," someone yelled.

My elder brother stuck out his head to look and then pulled me by the lower end of my clothes.

"Good citizens, come out with your hands up. Come out quickly with your hands up."

The sea became noisy again as my brother watched the movements of the people, and pulled me by the hand.

When we came out with our hands held up, people were swarming about. Soldiers with guns checked the people one by one and gathered them in one place. Following the soldiers, we entered the devastated village. All the houses had been burned to ashes—only the high stone walls remained, like ghosts in smoke rising up to the clouds. Household furniture and utensils, some of them broken and others half-burned, were scattered about. As people walked around looking at the scene, their eyes began to move in strange ways. Some cried and others ground their teeth with anger. And there were countless dead bodies lying on the ground. Smeared with blood, they were scattered about in the streets, on the fences, or beside telegraph poles. There were old men and women, children, and young people. Some had been stabbed to death, and others had been shot.

Only about ten houses near the police station remained intact. All the other buildings were burned, including the village office, the elementary school, and a local historic building. The school playground was full of weeping people. Some were crying out for their family members, holding them in their arms, some were crying because they could not find their family members, and some were grinding their teeth with rage. Witnessing these scenes, my brother and I began to think of our family. We too started to weep out of fear and sadness.

On that day, Namdo and its two neighboring villages were devastated by the attacks of the communist guerrillas. It was an enormous attack that mobilized half of the guerrillas on Mount Halla. The policemen in the police substations were outnumbered, so the damage to the villages was devastating. The villagers later said that if it had not been for the support of a military squad, many more people would have been killed.

My grandfather and grandmother were also killed. Their death was appalling. They were found disfigured and covered in blood under the fence around our back yard. They looked like worn-out straw bags.

As we followed the soldiers toward the school playground, my brother pulled me by the wrist to our house. Our house was located slightly off the circular road of the island. We were greeted by a sharp smell and a dark red stone wall. Entering our house in which small fires were still smoldering, I burst out crying. My crying was a combination of surging sorrow and anger. The scene was so awful. Such a comfortable and quiet house had been reduced to nothing but blackish red ashes. The stone walls now looked like skeletons. It seemed like the end of the world for me. After searching through the house, my brother rushed to the back yard.

"Hak-Chul!" he called out, as if taking his last breath.

With tears running down my face, I ran out to the back yard and saw two bodies stained with blood. My brother, who was standing beside the bodies, looked at me vacantly. Their faces were bathed in blood, but we could still recognize them. My grandmother's chest and the lower part of her body were soaked in blood. She was clenching my grandfather's leg; he was holding a stone in one hand. Around their bodies, torn shreds of clothing were scattered about, and the ground had been dug out in several spots. When my parents arrived at the house a short time later, they looked at us in silence.

After some time, my mother grabbed my hands and said, "You are alive."

"Grandfather ..."

At my brother's tearful word, my parents discovered the death of my grandparents. My mother wailed, but my father was surprisingly calm. He looked into their bloody faces several times, and then carried their cold bodies in his arms, one at a time, into the front yard. He laid them side-by-side and covered them with his jacket. Then he returned to the backyard, collected the bloody stones and the shreds of clothing, and brought them out to the front yard.

My father later explained the event in this way. After the guerrillas arrived at the house, grandfather tried to lift grandmother over the fence in the back yard. But as they were climbing the fence, the guerrillas stabbed grandmother with spears. Grandfather tried to beat them off with stones, but more guerrillas rushed in, dragged grandfather from the fence, and hit him with stones and stabbed him with spears. Grandfather must have resisted strongly, for the torn shreds of clothing on the ground belonged to the guerrillas.

My grandparents were buried without coffins at one corner of the house. No one cried while my father and elder brother dug with burnt shovels and covered the dead bodies with earth. From that day on, I had nightmares about the death of my grandparents, and the dreadful thought that death is a trivial thing gradually took hold of my mind.

3

Brilliant fireworks soaring up into the sky shook the night. Crowds of people, intoxicated by these fireworks, were making a great deal of noise. Others had gathered in front of City Hall with torches in their hands.

"What is that?" I asked Kim Suk-Moon, standing next to me.

"Tonight they're going to have a torch procession. It will be the climax of the festival. It's an expression of the people's hope for the prosperity of the city of Namdo."

"The people might be agitated by the fire at night ..." I said.

"They should be. It's an occasion for them to release their energy."

Kim's voice was shaking.

"As for me, fires and crowds remind me of the things I experienced in my early days," I said.

"You should forget about those things. We will never have such a tragedy again," Kim replied.

* * *

On the day of the 4.3 Incident, people swarmed into the school playground in the evening. They gathered in groups around bonfires, bitterly crying and cursing the guerrillas. As the chilly late-autumn wind swept across the playground, dazzling flames like snakes' tongues darted out of the bonfires, sending sparks into the dark sky.

Suddenly people gathered around the school gate and their frantic voices filled the silent night.

"Kill, kill them! Tear them to death!" they shouted.

Those who had gathered around the bonfires began to rise up, and other desperate voices could be heard here and there.

"Be quiet, calm down," said the soldiers and policemen who were trying to stop the people from forming a crowd.

Near the gate, young men were dragging some people who appeared to be almost dead—they all hung their heads low. I could see the members of Mr. Ko's family among them. His father, almost sixty, was once the head of our village and an influential man in Namdo. I could hardly recognize his mother, who used to look like a person of noble birth from the countryside. His wife, who was well-educated and had the reputation of being a beauty, was holding her baby tightly, fearing that the child might be taken away.

"Kill the criminal's father, his mother, and his woman. Tear them to death!" someone yelled.

The soldiers and policemen were desperately stopping the people who were springing at them like mad dogs. The people threw stones or flaming pieces of wood at them. The policemen and the soldiers could not stop it. Even my father was about to rush toward them, but my mother stopped him.

"They are not to blame. They are just cursed by a bad son," she said.

Father just stood there, cursing them, and then he fell to the ground.

"There are more criminals over here!" someone suddenly shouted.

So, with similar cries coming from all around, the people became agitated once again. The policemen and the soldiers ran in the direction of the cries and helped drag more of these nearly dead people to the school gate.

"Kill them, kill them!"

People's cries filled the dark sky.

In this way, the families of those guerrillas who went to Mount Halla were rounded up and brought to one place. They were the neighbors that we had greeted on the streets every day. Almost all of their sons were around twenty years old and were followers of Mr. Ko.

"Kill, kill, kill them!"

The burning anger of the people did not subside. People threw stones and flaming chunks of wood at the families. An old woman grabbed one of them as if to bite him. Those who had been captured were already half-dead as a result of this ordeal. They were then dragged away from the school gate, while people looked on and cursed at them. Some time later, gunshots from the seashore broke the silence of the night. Those who were lying on straw bags around the bonfires suddenly became quiet.

Someone said, "They deserved to die. The other guerrillas should have witnessed their execution".

* * *

Kim Suk-Moon continued to tell me about Mrs. Ko.

"A little baby was spared. That baby is Mrs. Ko. After the disaster, she was raised by her grandparents on her mother's side. When she became of age, she left her hometown, and went to stay in her aunt's house. Even by the time she entered college, she still did not know about what had happened here in the past. When she did finally discover her own family's history, she came home, turning a deaf ear on the advice of others. She inherited all the family's property, which had been maintained by the family on her mother's side. People were initially surprised, but later relieved, by this spinster's homecoming. She started up new businesses one by one as if not knowing anything about the past. That was more than ten years ago. It is her ability that has brought her such success."

"Does she know about Mr. Ko?" I asked.

"Of course she knows."

"I cannot understand why she returned home. This really is a place of pain and shame for her …

"It is quite different from your family's leaving for Seoul. Compared to your father, who completely broke ties with this place after his departure, she is hard to understand."

What he said was true.

After the turbulence of the 4.3 Incident settled down, the Korean War broke out on June 25, 1950, and the South Korean army, which was allied with the U.S. forces, finally recovered Seoul on September 28 of that year. By that time we had already left our hometown. After having witnessed his parents' tragic death, my father wanted to leave his birthplace. Grandfather was always diligent and honest, never having done anything malicious, and grandmother was so tenderhearted that she couldn't pass a beggar on the street without giving him something to eat or to wear, like cold boiled rice or worn-out clothes. They were brutally murdered and, what is worse, murdered by their fellow villagers. After that incident people exchanged murderous glances with each other. All of these things caused my father to distance himself from his native town.

"You are here! How do you like seeing this new city of Namdo at night?" Mrs. Ko whispered into my ear, as she approached me.

"It is so beautiful," I said.

I rose up from my seat as I answered her awkwardly. With a great bang, the final round of fireworks produced a gorgeous flower in the middle of the sky, came down slowly, and finally disappeared. The people who had gathered in the public square then began to disperse.

"The torch procession is probably about to begin," she said quietly.

Someone then interrupted our conversation, saying, "The spirit of this procession will never die."

I wondered to myself if the fire of anger had really been extinguished: "The fire that wandered about wherever the wind blew—did it really die?"

As I asked myself this question, I walked toward the shore to shake off the smell of that burning fire. The fresh smell of the sea flooded my nostrils. Suddenly the sound of waves hitting the cliff rang in my ears like Mr. Ko's clear whistle during those morning meetings.

"Come on, let's go downtown," said a friend of mine, as he dragged me by the arm.

Just then a horn sounding like a boat whistle blew from the hotel yard.

"Let's go watch the torch lights," he said.

Mrs. Ko, sitting in the driver's seat, was smiling as she held the steering wheel. Kang Tae-Sam was seated in the front seat, and Kim Suk-Moon and I were in the back. Her car gently made its way downtown.

We parked the car near the central traffic circle, where people had gathered. There were about ten thousand young people gathered there, each holding a torch that lit up their faces. It seemed that something was about to happen. A young man with a torch approached the crowd and read what he had written on a piece of paper. The people were somber, as if listening to a prayer.

"On this night, at this historical moment, the birth of the city of Namdo, we will proceed with the eternal torch to proclaim our desire to live in harmony, to devote ourselves to building this newly established city, and to make this a wonderful place to live. This procession expresses our intention to bring everlasting prosperity to Namdo and to lighten the dark world. Therefore ..."

The words that were bubbling from his mouth were a repetition of the same idea. I was more surprised by the organization committee, who had planned to read such a speech before the procession, than by the actual content of the speech. And I was appalled by those who were listening to that speech so seriously. The people then began to move along, holding their torches. Their procession looked like the flames of a fire that moved with the wind. The scene was so horrible that I turned my face away. Intoxicated by the flames, people looked at the scene absentmindedly.

After watching this sight for a good while, we drove the car in the opposite direction of the procession. We decided to go around the downtown area. There were celebrations on every street, and every house was gorgeously decorated with ornaments. The new city flag and the Korean national flag were hung on the poles of streetlights, and the celebration arch was standing majestically. Crowds of people swarming about in the streets wouldn't get out of the way of the cars. Even the policemen who were controlling the traffic with big smiles on their faces didn't care about the traffic congestion. Sitting in the back seat, I nearly suffocated with a sense of strange despondency while watching the soaring mood outside.

"There will be a party tonight at ten o'clock. Let's all go together," Mrs. Ko said.

When she mentioned the party, Kim and Kang asked her to stop the car. They wanted to go and get their wives since, as Kang explained, this celebration was Mrs. Ko's first work for the new city of Namdo. It was to be a grand party for those who had made a special effort for the celebration ceremony as well as for the higher authorities in this province and their wives.

"If you do not have your wife along, you will not be allowed to enter the party," Mrs. Ko said.

"But you don't have to worry about it. I will go with you on behalf of your wife."

I could see her through the rear view mirror smiling as she spoke.

"Mrs. Ko. Don't be too elated because you are hosting this grand party," I responded bluntly.

Even though a poor village had become a prosperous city, the reception, the fireworks, the torch procession—all these did not suit this city's standing. And now a grand party? That was going too far! I felt utterly alone, thinking that I had no relevance to these events.

"Do not blame me. You think that building great hotels and establishing amusement quarters sicken the city, don't you? But the city will inevitably need those things."

I had many things to say to her, but I held my tongue.

All I said was, "Nevertheless, these works do not suit you, the daughter of Mr. Ko." However, even that was not exactly what I had intended to say.

"There are many things in the world that are not suitable. I have thought that it was not suitable for my father to have become a communist and then a guerrilla. I do not know anything about my father, but how on earth could the son of a country landowner, the son of one of the pro-Japanese group, who was the chief of a village under the Japanese rule, become a communist? It has always been a mystery to me. I have come to accept it by thinking that anyone in his unique situation would have done the same thing."

Holding the steering wheel, she spoke cautiously and dryly. Her manner of speaking displeased me.

"To be honest, I was attracted to, but at the same time hated, Mr. Ko. I always had strong feelings when I saw the sunlight on his white tracksuit. My feelings were a mixture of respect and envy. But after the 4.3 Incident I felt mostly hatred. It was not a simple sentiment, but it is the truth. Just as he had me under his control, so too he controlled the souls of the other senseless youths in our village. He set a fire in their hearts. He succeeded in making them childish communists. I hated his conceit and his air of being a forerunner. He controlled other people's lives through his will, and violated them. He was, in other words, a spiritual tyrant of the youths of our village. I hated his arrogance. He was always trying to be a leader, opening up a new way for others."

I chattered away as if venting my anger for no particular reason. Whenever I thought about the fact that in that time of darkness he led the young people, and not only on ideological issues, I hated him for the arrogance of his heroic attitude. He wanted to rule over the villagers because he was raised as the son of an influential man in a small town.

* * *

When spring arrived, I did not see Mr. Ko anywhere. Various rumors about him were being spread on the streets, in the classrooms, and throughout the school. One day, while I was half asleep, I heard a conversation between my father and mother.

Sighing, she said, "What is Mr. Ko making such a fuss about? He should respect his father's honor as the head of the village. He will not get any particular profit from those communists."

"He is the only son, and he has caused trouble since he entered middle school. Even when he was in Japan, he made his parents and relatives worry. His family members were so happy when he came back alive from the World

War II, but his heart was not at home. He wandered about outside. After marriage he seemed to be settling down, but …"

Father continued to talk about what had happened in Mr. Ko's family. When he went to college in Japan, he frequently got into trouble, so the military policemen and police investigators visited his house often. That is why his father was reluctantly entrusted as the head of village. And because of his father's status, he had to volunteer for military service as a student soldier to fight for Japan in the Second World War. After Liberation he returned home and expressed open animosity against his father, who had been the head of the village under Japanese rule. So his house was always turbulent. After he married, he seemed to be settling down a bit, and he worked diligently at the school. However, he opened an educational institute for middle school students and taught those who could not receive middle school education. That was a prelude for bigger troubles.

"That's how the family was ruined. Were it not for Mr. Ko, his father, the head of our village, would have had no worries … well, I just hope that things turn out okay for everyone."

As mother spoke, father lit another cigarette. Pretending to be asleep, I listened to every word my parents said.

* * *

"My father was drowned in the raging waves of history. Don't criticize him too much," Mrs. Ko said.

With her words, I was brought back from the past, and the phrase "raging waves of history" touched my heart.

She said, "Let's just forget about it. Let's bury all past events in this newly established city. Once they are buried, they will decay and become manure."

She then stopped the car, got out, and opened the back door for me.

I was thinking to myself: Whenever I thought of those events of the past, those nightmares, I felt sorry that people took them as their destiny. They said, "Let's forget about all of it. It's all in the past now. What's the use of mentioning it again?" However, whether we knew it or not, those events of the past continue to affect the present. Given that this too was another one of those turbulent times in history, the people carrying those torches must also have been following some power. But when they become lost and confused, they attribute their confusion to those raging waves of history.

I was thinking about this while drinking a cup of tea in a hotel coffee shop. This issue truly perplexed me. Whenever I thought about my hometown, I was disappointed by the fact that people simply buried the events of the past.

* * *

It was a little after the student demonstrations on April 19, 1960. I was a college student and I felt that since a new era had begun I needed to know about the 4.3 Incident, which had been buried in the past. I felt that whatever the cause and result might be, the facts needed to be collected—that otherwise the truth of the situation might be lost. So, with several friends, I formed a group to study the 4.3 Incident. That summer we went back to our hometown, visited each village, and began to collect the testimonies of those who experienced the Incident. We chose to investigate the areas that were damaged by the guerrillas and some villages in the mid-area of Mount Halla that were, at the time, regarded as having been liberated by the communists. Our investigation was made difficult by the fact that no one would reveal his or her own story. In addition, our project ran into trouble when it caused misunderstandings among the citizens of Jeju Island. People thought that we were trying to justify the 4.3 Incident by taking advantage of the current political situation, in which negotiations between North and South Korea were scheduled to take place. Our investigations also provoked a movement in Jeju to know the truth about the 4.3 Incident. I was surprised when things went in this unexpected direction. Furthermore, on May 16 of the next year, there was a coup, and our work was misunderstood as communist activity. Since my origin was so obvious and my family members were victims of the 4.3 Incident, I could escape from that misunderstanding, but those who worked with me received a restraining order. What was even more upsetting was that we had no way to prove our innocence.

The confusing atmosphere surrounding the 4.3 Incident continued. Everyone remained silent about the Incident. Those who had accidentally participated in the left-wing activities in those days now felt that their actions were dishonorable. And those who had supported the right-wing, prodemocracy activities were ashamed by the brutal suppression of the people. So both parties wanted to bury the past. People asked, "Why are you digging up what was already forgotten? Why are you opening up wounds again?" Since they had interpreted the Incident according to their interests, it was possible that in the future it would be remembered only from one perspective. In that case, the truth would be lost forever. Nevertheless, they wished to keep it covered up. There was no change in attitude on that issue even in this newly developing city.

* * *

While I was thinking these fretful thoughts, not knowing that my tea had gone cold, Mrs. Ko approached me. She was wearing a gaudy dress and smiling at me.

The party was grand. The lounge on the rooftop had been designed for many functions. The reception hall of the hotel had been turned into a ballroom. Dancers danced on a stage, singers from Seoul sang, and men and women in formal dress watched this wonderful show in amazement. They danced and drank together. The young businessmen from the city were happier than the higher authorities and thoroughly enjoyed the feast. It was an expression of pride that they themselves had built this city, a city that was comparable to Seoul. Music, wine, dancers, and singers—all were judged to compete with the cultural standards of Seoul. The party was not just for their amusement, but also for their self-esteem. It meant a vigorous beginning.

Mrs. Ko and I sat face to face as we drank together, and though I am a clumsy dancer, I also danced with her. But I could not enjoy the party. I was entirely rustic and did not belong here. In such an awkward mood, I thought of my childhood. My grandfather loved me so much, always taking me with him to the fields. He let me gather grains of barley or millet or sweet potatoes after the harvest. He made sure that I collected all the grains that had fallen from the loaded wagons. He was considered by the villagers to be rich but he was very strict about the grain. He would not leave any grain on the floor or in the yard. He harshly scolded any member of the family that did not finish their meal. His strong attachment to even a handful of barley or one sweet potato still impressed me, though I was now over forty. I had a habit of never leaving my meals unfinished wherever I ate, and when a grain of boiled rice accidentally fell from the table, I would put it back into my mouth without shame. Because of these thoughts, I felt stifled and left the party hall.

Even outside the hall I could hear the strains of the entertainment inside. It seemed to be part of a world that was irrelevant to me. I felt lonely looking at the sky, which was beautifully sprinkled with stars. Whenever I heard the mirth of the party, I felt like drifting about in the night sea, with the devastated scenes of my old village plainly visible in the darkness. The stories of that time that tightly bound my mischievous childhood with a mixture of loneliness and hatred, stories that had been hidden somewhere in a disheveled way, had been unraveled again tonight.

4

After the entire village was devastated in the fire set by the communist guerrillas, the villagers spent several days sleeping under old straw bags near the police substation and on the playground of the elementary school. Then they began to build stone walls around the police substation and the school to protect themselves from the further attacks by the guerrillas, and they dug out huts called *hambas* to stay in. The huts were one-room shelters with walls made of stones and roofs made of pinewood and covered with thatch. They provided minimal protection from the wind, rain, and snow. The problem was how to pass the winter. Boys of my age went beyond the stone walls to gather firewood—that was their duty. The young men who were capable of work participated in the suppression of the communist guerrillas, and the women and the elderly helped build the stone walls.

My family spent several days in one corner of the school playground and then went back to the site of our house. Red stone walls and burnt red clod greeted us in silence. When we entered the remains of the house, we found red stains all around; it looked like the blood of my grandparents. They lay silent in a small grave. Upon seeing the graves, I burst into tears. Quietly my mother went to the garden and grabbed some Chinese cabbage leaves. My father and my elder brother took the remnants of burnt pieces of wood to one corner. Everyone moved quietly and vacantly, like shadows. As she was collecting the leaves, mother looked about the front and back yards of the house, trying to find anything useful. She took broken vessels, farming tools, and pieces of furniture that were still functional to another corner. I became angry at the sight of my family's feebleness. Determined to kill the communists and their children, a strong hatred toward Mr. Ko surged within my heart.

My brother, then a middle school student, received military training for several days. Then, with an iron spear, he went to the foot of Mount Halla every day to fight against the communist guerrillas. At that time, I turned into a mischievous boy and became a very different person. Singing a military song that went "Let's seize the traitors, the communists, the criminals in the mountain" until my throat became hoarse, my friends and I pretended to be soldiers when we played. School was closed for a while, and during that time we always played as soldiers, trying to kill guerrillas.

When the full-scale suppression of the guerrillas began, the villagers of the mid-areas of Mount Halla who could not evacuate themselves to villages near the seashore were either caught or surrendered. Those who surrendered carried little white flags and had to go through a police investigation. They were held in some of the *hambas* in front of the police substation. I began to target and attack the children of those who had surrendered. Whenever I could, I would call them out from those shelters and humiliate them. However big a boy might be, he would feel defeated when I called him "a son of a guerrilla." When we played as soldiers in the school playground, I always played the role of the captain of a punitive force, and children from the villages in the mid-areas of Mount Halla were forced to play the role of guerrillas. Whenever they did not accept that role, I would bully them. It was a thrill to oppress them. And although it was just play, I could dominate them, pretending to inspect, and then brutally execute, the captured guerrillas.

Playing in the school playground, anyone who first spotted a defector would cry out, "Look at the communist!" Then we would climb over the school fence shouting, "You bastards, you're dead." We would throw stones or clods of earth at the defectors who, with bags on their backs and their heads held low, already felt totally defeated. If we were not satisfied with that, we would roar at them in a loud voice, "Let's go and kill the communist traitors." However, they just passed by with their eyes closed as if they were deaf. Whenever I came across the defectors, which happened several times a day, my rage would explode. It was thrilling. Not only at school but also at home, I was always the boss among children of my age and a formidable force to children from the villages in the mid-areas of Mount Halla.

When spring came, school went well, but I became even more mischievous. Children from the villages in the mid-areas of Mount Halla joined our school. Because the school had been burned in the fire, we gathered boards that lay around the school fence and made small desks out of them. There was an insufficient number of desks, and I was in charge of distributing them to the students. So I became even more tyrannical. I picked on the boys who were rather big and likely to be troublesome, and I was hard on them.

One day, my mother and I went to a pine grove near the seashore to gather firewood. Exuberant pine trees that used to block the sky from sight all had been cut down by the military during the suppression of the guerrillas. The once lofty trees had been chopped down and placed crosswise and lengthwise. Nimbly wandering among their stumps, I chopped off thick branches with a sharp-edged axe to use them as firewood. I felt so excited when I was roaming about, stepping on the stumps of fallen trees, as if trampling upon fallen guerrillas, so I was happy to gather firewood. When I would strike a pine tree oozing resin, I would get a great feeling as the wood split. I could easily split a field-length piece of wood. It gave me a strange but pleasant sensation. My hatred of the guerrillas diminished to some degree through this kind of labor. So I once wrote a poem about how I felt doing that work.

> With cracks, cracks
> A tree is cut
> By my powerful axe
> As if a guerilla's head were chopped off.
> With rips, rips,
> Firewood is split
> By my sharp-edged axe
> As if a guerrilla is shot to death.
>
> With cracks,
> With rips
> Firewood is piled up
> With bangs,
> With thuds
> Guerrillas are dying.
> It's good to see them die.

This poem surprised my third grade teacher. The school principal and all the other students at school admired my literary talent, and I once read the poem aloud to the entire student body during a morning meeting. My face became red-hot with anger as I read the poem. But later, when I became a professional poet and thought about that poem, I felt ashamed of that dreadful image of myself. I was so choked by the image that I could not write at all for some time.

On that day, I was so excited. I hummed as I chopped the branches off trees and split them into firewood. As I was placing an A-frame with a half bundle of branches on my back, my mother urgently said,

"Let's go quickly!"

Just as we were leaving the grove, we heard the sounds of other people nearby.

"Let's go!" she said again.

In spite of mother's command, I was inexplicably attracted to that sound, so with the A-frame on my back I approached a clearing in the forest. On a flat area, by a precipitous cliff touching the sea, some people were sitting, and others standing. They were leisurely smoking and looking at the sea as they chatted. They looked like policemen and members of the militia. I hesitated. I also saw other people who were tightly bound to several pine trees standing on the lawn. Judging from their drooped heads, messy hair, and tattered clothing, I soon realized that they were guerrillas. There were five of them.

"Son, let's go quickly. Hurry up!"

I heard my mother call me again. Pretending not to hear her, I moved closer to the clearing. One of those on the ground ordered the rest to move. With the order, they extinguished their cigarettes on the ground and dusted off their pants. Some of them were holding spears. They again gathered and whispered to each other, without doing anything. The long hair of those bound to the pine trees was fluttering in the sea wind. At that moment, a couple of the militiamen approached those bound to the trees. I thought that they would execute them, but they didn't. They put cigarettes in the teeth of those who were bound, and lit them.

"Ha, this is unusual," I thought.

I had never seen this sort of thing before. Guerrillas were sometimes executed in the school playground. After cursing and abusing them, the villagers would stab them to death with spears. Whenever I saw those scenes, my heart began to simmer with indignation. I felt such resentment that I wanted to snatch a gun and shoot them at once.

Sometime later I heard gunshots. The heads of those who were smoking dropped. I felt as if something that had been grabbing me by the chest was suddenly released. I also felt the weight of the A-frame on my back. I was exhausted; all the strength of my legs was gone. Besides, the shots kept ringing in my ears. I heard something. Was it the sound of the sea wind, the shot, a tearful voice, or the screams of the guerrillas? But it was none of these. As I listened to that sound, I could not move. It was not the first time that I had seen people killed. Sometimes guerillas were bound on wooden targets that had been prepared for weapons training in the school ground and then stabbed to death. Whenever I watched those executions, I felt more enjoyment than fear. If somebody had given me a gun or a spear, I could have killed guerrillas with pleasure.

A couple of days later, I went out with my mother to pick up firewood near the seashore, and I visited the clearing again. When my mother asked, "Where are you going, son?" I pretended not to hear her. I made my way to the lot, but there was nothing. I had an unsatisfied feeling because I was expecting to see another execution.

"Son, what are you doing here?"

My mother was already looking at me from behind. I saw countless small graves in clusters in the clearing. They looked just like the graves of babies, and there was no turf on them. Only small amounts of earth were covering them. Suddenly I thought of the graves of my grandparents.

My mother said, "Let's hurry up!"

Just as I was about to turn around, I saw a huge grave. Glancing at the grave, and seeing something that she should not have seen, she pulled me by one end of my clothes before I could approach it.

I was told later that the small graves were temporary ones for the executed guerillas and the big one was for the family members of Mr. Ko.

* * *

I came back to the present again. With a desire to disentangle these thoughts, I moved closer to that clearing. The lawn was well kept and tastefully decorated with benches and sentinel lamps that suited the atmosphere of the sea. At the farthest end of the lawn, there was an extraordinarily large grave. It was obviously well taken care of. As I was about to approach the grave, I heard a person moving behind me.

"You don't like the party?" Mrs. Ko asked, as she approached me, smiling.

"I just keep thinking of the past," I replied.

"Are you thinking of my father?"

"No, I'm thinking of myself. I hated Mr. Ko Jin-Kook."

"Do you hate me too?" she asked playfully.

"I hope so. Not only you, but I'm beginning to hate all the people of this new city," I said.

"That's strange. You wrote such earnest words for the city song."

"I feel betrayed."

I did not think of the real meaning of betrayal, but I said the word as if to spit.

"You are sentimental. The world is changing. There is no time to look back. You might be left behind."

As she continued to speak, I heard the sound of some cars. The party was probably ending. The front entrance of the hotel was crowded with people. Mrs. Ko excused herself with a slight nod and returned to the people. I was thirsty and I felt like drinking, so I left the hotel grounds.

Suddenly the surroundings became quiet. Sparsely spaced street lamps lit the dark ground. The sound of the wind, of the sea, the headlights of cars passing quickly, and the streets lights from afar made me feel very lonely. I walked aimlessly toward the center of the city.

5

My ankles were aching from the walk by the time I reached the downtown area. I dropped into a bar to have a drink, and suddenly I missed my old house. I wanted to see it in this new city, but I had lost my way. So I asked for directions from some people who were passing by.

"Do you know where Kim Chul-Geun (my father's name) used to live? The place that was called Joong Dong Nae in the past."

No one knew it. The people I approached regarded me as a drunkard. While I was looking around in the downtown core, trying to find my way, I met Kang Tae-Sam. After the party, he had taken his wife home, and then dropped by the ceremony headquarters to join in the end of the torch procession. Coming out of the headquarters, he saw me in the distance and ran to meet me. At first he too thought I was drunk. I asked about my old house, and we searched for it together. It was near the central roundabout, which had become the center of the new city.

Kang said, "This is prime real estate. If your father had continued to live here, he would probably be the richest man in Namdo now."

He again said that it was wrong for us to leave this place. However, I was not interested in the value of the real estate. I felt empty and I wanted to cry when I found no trace of our house. Perhaps because he sensed my emotions, he took me to a nearby bar, where I proceeded to drink heavily.

After that, my memory failed me. I had a heavy headache and was thirsty. Looking around, I found myself lying in a strange room. There was a wardrobe, a TV set, a sofa, a table, and a phone. I sobered up when I discovered I was lying in some sort of motel room.

I heard someone splashing water in the bathroom, so I got out of the bed, and found a woman's clothes nearby. My heart sank, and my whole body stiffened. "Was I at the house of Mrs. Ko Young-Ae?" I wondered. I was ashamed of the thought. "Did I have some obscene thought about her?" I became more thirsty and my headache grew more severe as I heard the leisurely sound of water coming from the bathroom. I had an impulse to open the bathroom door, but the more strongly I felt that impulse, the more disheartened I became.

Humming and drying her body, a young woman came into the room and was surprised to find me awake. She turned back and said,

"My goodness. Turn your face away from me."

She pretended to be greatly surprised, yet the tone of her voice did not indicate surprise at all. I looked away—not because of her request, but because of my own feeling of shame. I was relieved that she was not Mrs. Ko, and then I recovered the presence of mind to smile at her feigned surprise.

"Did you have a good sleep?" she asked. "What kind of man are you only to sleep? Did you take me with you so that I would be your sleeping companion?"

After getting dressed, she came and sat next to me, smiling the whole time.

"I can't remember anything," I said, turning toward the wall.

"You are shrewd. Men usually say that. Are you making up a story because I may hold you responsible for me?"

She would not believe me.

"Don't worry," she said. "You didn't do anything that you should be responsible for."

Her voice was strange but clear. I turned to her and found that she had extraordinarily fair skin and small eyes.

"Your drunken rowdiness was a great scene. You pressed the man with you, first for your grandmother, then for a woman called Ko Young-Ae. Therefore, I came in on behalf of some woman named Mrs. Ko."

My face felt hot, so I lay in bed facing the wall. It was natural for me to have looked for my grandmother when I visited the site of my old house, which had vanished without a trace, but I felt uncomfortable hearing that I had also sought out Mrs. Ko.

"Is she your ex-girlfriend?" the young woman asked.

Her teasing somehow relieved my disturbed heart, so I continued to talk with her.

"Get up and take a shower. Wash out all the drink from last night," she said.

I did not feel like getting up. I wanted to sleep until sunset.

"You are not from this city, are you?" she asked, "Are you from Seoul? Are you a tangerine trader? You do not look like a trader. Ah, the president of a company must have sent you. I am sure. Are you the secretary of a Chaebol? You came to inspect the boss's real estate? Did you buy it from the man that you came with last night? He is somebody here …"

Without giving me any chance to ask a question, she chattered very quickly and kept smiling. Her talkative nature made me feel better.

"At any rate, I am very concerned for the city of Namdo. People from Seoul are drooling over anything valuable. Their greed has no bounds …"

I could not just listen to her, so I asked, "Are you from Seoul too?"

"Yes. Not originally, but I stayed there for a while. So you might say I am from Seoul."

"What brought you here?" I asked.

"What have I come here for? We are here for the same reason. I came here to make off with money from the pockets of rich men in this suddenly prospering city. But they do not take my bait so easily."

The young woman frankly opened her heart.

"Thieves are not a different species," I said cynically.

"Nevertheless we are not thieves. We are paid for our labor."

"For your labor?"

"Yes, we sell smiles. And if offered a better price, we sell our bodies too. We earn money by selling. We do not ask for anything free."

"You sell smiles and bodies?"

The young woman told me frankly about her situation. She had come here with three others because people said that Jeju was a good place to live. One of them had worked as a masseuse, another as a hairdresser in a hotel, and she herself had worked as a waitress in a coffee shop. She said she later changed her job because she was so sick of the country folk who behaved rudely over a 500 won cup of coffee.

She said, "Go to the sauna in the Tourist Hotel. Girl number thirteen is a real good masseuse."

I just laughed. This woman sounded so friendly. "Was it because of the scent of the soap on her body that I smelled a little while ago?" I wondered. The scent swarmed into my nostrils and made me very comfortable. The bitterness attached to the thought that I had spent the night with a woman disappeared, and her clear voice enabled me to feel a certain amount of intimacy with her. It was as if her heart were also transparent. I felt free because she revealed everything about herself. Impure thoughts in my mind seemed to be washed away one by one, and my heart was made transparent. The fear and hesitations that I had about the fireworks and the excited people at the reception hall were all washed out as I was listened to her. Then I gradually became hungry.

"Miss, is there any good restaurant around here for getting rid of a hangover?" I asked.

I wanted to have breakfast with her in a restaurant.

"Yes, of course. A woman I know very well opened a restaurant with the help of her lover. The soup in that restaurant is cooked like Chung Jin-Dong's broth in Seoul. It's famous here."

The phone rang loudly as the woman prepared to go out in a hurry.

It was Kang Tae-Sam. He asked me to give a short speech at a student literary contest at 11:00 A.M. that morning.

"But I was drowned in a liquor jug last night. How could I give a speech at a literary contest for innocent students?"

I said this, not conscious of the fact that the woman was still there. After hanging up the phone, I turned around and found her smiling.

"You are not the president of a company, but a literary man. Are you a poet or a novelist?" she asked, smiling at me.

"I know nothing about literature. I am a real estate trader," I said. "Let's go out quickly."

After hastening her along with my awkward mumbling, she looked at me more suspiciously.

She said, "If you walk with me, you may feel uncomfortable. So you should follow a few steps behind."

I did as she advised, and I laughed while I walked, thinking of the situation.

The nondescript marketplace was crowded. Some old women were sitting with baskets of tangerines that they had picked in their own yards. Their tangerines were not like the ones in ordinary stores; they had stems and green leaves on them. These natives of Jeju were not doing well in their business. Their wrinkled faces looked pitiful in front of the unsavory and unseemly fruits. A couple of steamed sweet potatoes, a few radishes, and some unknown fruits picked from trees on a mountain were also on display. These old women were swatting away weak flies from the fruit. As I passed them by, I felt as if they were my relatives, so I wanted to buy all of their goods.

When I approached the middle of the market, a stout young man whistled loudly from afar. He was walking along the market road, kicking at low benches with his military shoes. He was behaving like a crazy man and walking in my direction. The old women, who were frightened, scattered about, wrapping up their displayed goods in their skirts. I was astonished by this unlikely scene. The young man was wearing a pair of black sunglasses, and a yellow armband with the word "Order" written in red. My heart was beating fast as I glared at him. I wanted to fight him.

"If you are a vendor, keep order. What is the use of the market if it is such a mess?" he said.

After yelling at some of the vendors, he turned back. The vendors who had hidden themselves here and there crawled out, rearranged their goods, and sat on the road again. They looked calm, as if nothing had happened. I could not understand their easygoing attitude.

"Do they really work in such conditions?" I asked the young woman I was with.

"They come and sit everyday because they want to sell," she responded.

"Who is he, the man with the whistle?"

"He is a market inspector. He earns his living this way. His job is to scream at the vendors every half hour."

I could barely understand the situation. People here lived in such a way. Like a stranger from a distant country, the scene was strange to me. It was an image of my birthplace that I had never imagined. That young man said that the town of Namdo was changing into a city. Now this city had become one in which old folks sitting on low benches could be kicked at by a pair of boots.

"The young man should strike them with terror to get rid of the illegal vendors. The more disgust he draws from the people, the more successful he will be."

I was bewildered at this woman's explanation.

"He makes a living by selling disgust?" I asked.

"That's right. He is a strange vendor. There are many ways of making a living in the world."

Smiling, she pointed to a shabby restaurant.

* * *

After having some soup to get rid of the hangover, I entered a coffee shop on the second floor of a motel. I wanted to have a cup of strong coffee.

The shop was half-full, and at one corner some young men were sleeping. They were stretched out, as if still recovering from last night's excitement. An employee said that she had stayed up all night.

At that time, two young men of just over thirty with drunken-looking faces entered the coffee shop and sat down in the middle of the room.

"Have you already been drinking this morning?"

A female manager, wearing traditional Korean dress, dragged her skirt as she walked over and sat next to the smaller one of these two men.

"Already?" the man said. "Are you making a fuss about it? It's more honorable to drink during the daytime than all through the night."

"That's right," she replied. "There's no doubt about it."

"Lady, don't patronize me," the skinny young man replied. "I am not a rich man. Bring two cups of hot coffee and go away."

The woman then stood up promptly.

"No. Even though we are not rich, don't go away," said the short man, as he grabbed her roughly by the hand and forced her to sit down.

"Two cups of coffee and one juice here," the woman ordered, as she sat down next to him.

"Madam, you are such a favorite in Namdo. People say that the rich owners of tangerine farms follow the edges of your skirts," the short man said, teasing her.

"Oh, no, don't talk like that. I'm known, and I do a good business. Why are you trying to bother me?"

With smiles in her eyes, she sat closer to the man.

"Don't do that! Don't ruin innocent rich men in this countryside with your pretty face. Why have you come down here and put fire in the hearts of innocent people, rather than robbing those blackmailers in Seoul?"

Though the skinny young man was rebuking her, she still smiled.

"What? Did you say the rich men here are innocent? They are the stingiest in the world. There is no way to rake money from the rich here," she replied.

"No wonder they are stingy: garbage in, garbage out. They are more honest than stingy. They mean to pay the fair price. Don't obsess over the money of the innocent tangerine farmers. If you do not listen to my warning, I'll kick you out of town."

The skinny man squinted his eyes as he threatened her.

Coffee and juice were then brought to them. The two men slurped them at once, and slammed their cups down on the table. At the same time, the sound of drums and gongs could be heard in the streets.

"There's the damn *gulgoong!*" one of the men said.

They spat out curses with angry looks in their faces.

"Wow, what a row! Look out the window!" the woman said, as she approached the window and shouted.

A person carrying a picket with the name of each district on it was followed by other people holding various signs. The signs read, "Creating an Advanced Country," "Building a Modern City," "Developing Namdo City for the Prosperity of Our Country," and "New City, New Heart." Each sign was followed by a different masquerade group or *gulgoong* team. They were striking gongs and dancing. Each district had made its own street procession as part of a competitive performance. Citizens who were watching them in streets also joined in the procession, dancing alongside them. The most remarkable masquerade was the one that was performed by male and female tourists who had dressed in the costumes of various countries around the world. They were passing by, making strange gestures, and saying to spectators in streets that Namdo was the most beautiful city in the world. The streets were filled with the *gulgoong* teams and spectators.

6

The view of the autumn sky entered my eyes through the window. It was so high and clear, something that you could never see in Seoul. I remembered the time when, as a child, I would search for wild fruits during the autumn harvests. I would search for them beside the stone walls that bordered the fields. Once, while collecting berries, I suddenly looked up at the blue sky and felt my eyes go watery as I became dizzy.

Pedestrians jumped in amid the *gulgoong* teams and the groups of masqueraders moving around the traffic circle and danced with them. Though the guards tried to stop them and the policemen whistled, the people didn't pay attention. They were excited and elated to see the traffic jam—cars were backed up in rows. It seemed as if the people were possessed by spirits. I looked at the four-story building that was standing on the site where my old house used to be, and laughed at the thought of the room where I had spent the previous night with a strange woman. The third and forth floors of this building were an inn; on the second floor there was a billiard room and a coffee shop; there were stores on the ground floor, and a bar in the basement. On this very site, my grandparents had died. This was where we had swallowed tears of anger. A building, utterly indifferent to things past, was now standing on the ground where their bodies had been temporarily buried. With shaking legs and a throbbing heart, I wanted to fall onto the ground. My body felt helpless and heavy. I wondered if this feeling was the result of having spent my anger.

I left that place in order to escape from people. I wanted to leave this newly established and exciting city as soon as possible. Namdo Village, which remained in my heart as my birthplace, had never made me feel so lonesome and desolate. All things now were trying to deceive me. Elated *gulgoong* teams and intoxicated people were dancing in order to conceal a big plot. They were bragging in order to hide something deep within themselves. I wanted to leave, as quickly as I could, this new city where lies and deception were dancing wildly.

My one-day stay in this city inflated the shame of my life. For a moment, I was excited by a grand celebration for this new city, elated by rhetorical flourishes, and intoxicated by fireworks, a torch procession, a wonderful show, and the sweet voice of a beautiful woman at night. Following others, I was excited, drunken, surprised, and moved. I listened to a song whose lyrics I had written and harbored a wicked interest in the daughter of my old teacher—I had spent the day in this way. However, this city was not able to wash away my painful and bloodstained memory. Rather, it etched the memory deeper in my heart.

Since so much time had passed, I should have been able to love my birthplace again, but I couldn't shake off a sense of betrayal about it. I wondered where my disappointment and anger with this newly established city came from. The atmosphere that Mr. Ko had long ago brought to this place was once again flowing within it, and that made me depressed. Imagine a balloon high up in the sky being swept away by a strong wind and ending up in a strange place. My fate and the fate of this newly established city seemed like such a balloon. I wondered if I too would wander about, imprisoned in the pain and indigestible anger of the past, never finding a place in which to settle down.

* * *

One day, we gathered some nails from the school that had been burnt and were playing a game with them at one corner of the school playground. In this game, nails were stood up in a circle on the ground. Each of us would take turns throwing nails at the circle, and whoever knocked down an opponent's nail would keep it. After the village was destroyed by the fire, children would pick up nails from the residential sites that had been burned down and play this game. We used to scoop out the red earth with our hands to find nails in the lots of burnt houses. We would pick up those that were not so burnt and straighten them out with stones to use them in the game. In the distance that day, a man from the village office was walking around the *hambas* excitedly ringing a bell, the lower edges of his dirty overcoat flapping in the wind. The sound of the bell also fluttered with the hem of his garment, spreading into the sky.

He shouted, "Come quick. Gather in the school playground as soon as possible."

"Jing-a-ling, jing-a-ling, jing-a-ling," the bell sounded.

The children suddenly became quiet and looked in the direction of the sound. The school playground was higher than the other areas. From there, all the houses in the village could be seen.

"Hurry up. Come together."

Someone said, "Something is going to happen. One of those bastards was caught. He must have been a bigwig."

Something terrible always happened after we heard that tofu-seller ring his bell. In the school playground or in the back yard of the police substation, captured guerrillas were executed with villagers standing around in a circle. Though the prisoners were already half-dead, people would shout at them with scorn. Then young men with spears would dash at them and stab them to death. I had already begun to enjoy those events. Whenever I watched an execution scene, that bitter resentment was naturally revived, the resentment that had been smoldering in my heart ever since I witnessed my grandparents' tragic death.

People began to come together in the school playground. The sun hid its face behind the dark clouds. The fragments of glass that used to dance with the sunlight were inert, and the school grounds became gloomy. The back of a half-burnt old pine tree, a thick stump of a cherry blossom tree, broken exercise bars, signs used for weapons training—these were the dismal surroundings of our village. Except for a few trees in front of the teacher's office, the trees in the playground had all been chopped down. Trees around the village had also been axed. When I went out to pick up firewood in the pine tree grove, chopped trees lay scattered about. I was just as appalled by the trees as I was by the dead bodies lying on the street the day the guerrillas attacked the village. But now I could happily wield my axe on the stumps of those big trees.

More and more people gathered in school playground.

"Wow, something is going to happen."

The children looked at each other with excitement and expectation. Still, the school playground was gloomy. Low clouds imprisoned the sun. I suddenly missed the sunrays that would jump up and down, reflected by fragments of glass. I wished the sun would quickly come out of the clouds. I said to myself, "Come out, sun, come out with dazzling smiles!"

The sound of the bell was not to be heard any more.

"Hey, something is going to happen soon," someone said.

The children pulled the nails out of the ground, scrubbed them on their pants to get rid of the dirt, and then put them into their pockets. They suddenly lost interest in their nail game. They were looking forward to something bigger, but it was not the killing of a couple of guerrillas. Something bigger and more exciting was waiting for them.

Suddenly the playground became bright. The sun had emerged from the clouds, and the fragments of glass scattered on the playground began to dance again. The sunlight leaped on the fragments of glass with excitement. They were dazzling, so beautiful. People came together in the playground, trampling over those radiant fragments of glass. The sunlight screamed under their feet.

"Beep ... beep ... beep."

A military truck slowly entered the playground with its headlights on, even though it was daytime. Standing aside, people made way for the truck. Police officers and soldiers were in the truck.

"This is nothing," someone said.

The children were disappointed. Standing on both sides of the truck were soldiers with guns and police officers.

"Get out of the way," shouted the chief of police, with a gun at his waist.

The people moved. And when the truck stopped at one corner of the playground, the chief police officer shouted loudly.

"Come over here!" he said.

The village head and the principal went forward, and militiamen prohibited others from approaching the truck. A lieutenant colonel got out of the truck. He also had a gun at his waist, and he was wearing black sunglasses. The other soldiers then got out of the truck.

"Quiet, quiet!" someone shouted.

The children pushed themselves through the crowd to get closer to the truck.

"Quiet, quiet!"

Not listening to the chief of police, the other people also tried to get a little closer to the truck, sticking out their heads to see what was inside it. A young man was crouching inside. He must have been a guerrilla. He must have been a bigwig since they were making such a fuss about him.

"Quiet!"

Still, people were making noise. They were curious about the young man in the truck.

"Get out!" the lieutenant colonel shouted at the truck.

A policeman in the truck, holding his gun with both of his hands, kicked the young man.

"Get out!" he yelled.

The soldiers on the ground glared at the young man. With his head hanging low and his arms bound with a rope, he got out the truck. Soldiers with guns quickly surrounded him.

"Hey, that son of bitch is Ko Jin-Kook," someone shouted.

At first I had no idea who Ko Jin-Kook was.

"Be quiet and listen to me!" the chief of police yelled.

"Kill that son of bitch!" someone shouted.

The people were already disturbed.

"Hey you, you son of bitch," someone said quietly.

Long messy hair, dirty worn clothes, a dark bruised face—he was surely a communist guerrilla. He was no longer a slim young man in a white tracksuit that reflected the sunlight. I rubbed my eyes. It looked like him, but it was not him. It couldn't be him. People shouted at him. The police officers tried hard to stop people from rushing to him.

"Kill him! Beat the son of bitch to death!" someone yelled.

"Kill him, kill him!"

People were agitated, shouting as if the playground were shaking and the earth was collapsing.

"Give me back my dead son!" an old woman screamed, as she approached him, swinging her arms and sobbing wildly.

Men with guns blocked her and moved her to another corner of the playground.

"Son of a bitch! Bring back my dead son!" she shouted again.

The old woman then fell down and cried, beating the ground.

Guarded by men with guns, Mr. Ko mounted the platform and knelt down on his knees so that everybody could see him. People became strangely quiet.

"You all know who this man is. He is the marrow of the vicious communists. He is the one who led young men to communism and brought them to the mountain. Ever since returning from the Japanese army after Liberation, he has continued to try to turn Jeju into a communist island. He is the most vicious of all communists. It was he who threw this village into a pit of fire and he who burned to ashes the very school in which he worked, where his innocent students studied."

While the speech was delivered, the people did not show any sign of disturbance. They waited for more from the prosecutor.

"All of you, look at his face! You have heard of a wolf in sheep's clothing. Here is such a one. These communists, disguising themselves as sheep, sneak in and make wolfish plots."

"Kill him quickly," someone said. I couldn't bear to look at him any longer. My teeth were grinding.

People started shouting. With my eyes wide open, I looked right into his face.

"Mr. Ko. Mr. Ko!" I said to myself.

An image of the dead bodies of my grandparents appeared before my eyes. Suddenly I was disgusted at the name that I had repeatedly called out with infinite longing and respect. I felt suffocated.

"Hey you, criminal of the mountain, traitor! You enemy!" I screamed.

Shouting from the pit of my stomach, I unconsciously rushed to the platform. I grabbed a hard stone and threw it as hard as I could at the drooping head of Mr. Ko Jin-Kook. Everyone looked at me. He too raised his head and looked at me. With my eyes closed, I threw another stone at him. His face was distorted and he hung his head again.

"We should kill him ourselves," someone yelled.

Suddenly stones flew at him. It all happened so quickly.

"Everyone please calm down. Be sensible!" the lieutenant colonel shouted, while waving his hands.

But the people had already lost their senses. The men with guns surrounding the platform were at a loss, and Mr. Ko had already fallen down.

"Trample him to death. Tear him to death!"

Shouts continued to ring out, and people threw things at him.

Like a fire fanned by the wild wind, the crowd flew out of control. After seeing Mr. Ko's dead body, people withdrew, licking their dry lips. I also withdrew from the scene with great satisfaction. I felt as though I had participated in a glorious event. Gradually, all of the rioting and shouting people withdrew, quietly, gently, weakly. I too felt exhausted and wanted to fall down on the ground.

* * *

I was surrounded by the excitement of the people on the street, just as I had been surrounded by the excitement of the people that day in the school playground. I grabbed a cab and went back to the hotel. Though the agitations of history remained with me, others had carelessly thrown the past into the ground and buried it, pretending to forget about it. These people were soaring up into the sky with the fever of a new start. Some day when enough time had passed, all of them would feel empty and fall back down to the ground. I wanted to leave this city before seeing that emptiness.

I packed a small bag and was about to come out of the hotel when I suddenly heard a woman's voice.

"Are you leaving this way?" she asked.

It was Ko Young-Ae. I felt ashamed. It seemed as though I were running away.

"When you return, after a long absence, you may be able to understand the people of this city."

She thought that I was leaving without settling a big quarrel with myself.

I thought that I should say something, but I couldn't open my mouth. I just nodded and turned away from her as the taxi driver started the engine.

"I will give you a ride to Jeju City," she said.

Pretending not to hear her, I got in the taxi. As it began to move, I waved goodbye to her.

"I'll never come back to this city again," I said to myself.

However, it wasn't long before my thinking changed. After leaving the city, I couldn't help but feel homesick.

Dead Silence

1

"Great comrades of the commando unit fighting for the liberation of Jeju Island!" These first words of the chief commander reverberated loudly into the forests of Bulgunorum, an inactive volcano on Mount Halla, located some eight hundred meters above sea level. The echo of his words pierced like daggers into the hearts of the young men gathered there.

The chief commander's speech continued.

"Great comrades! You who have decided to risk your lives in this struggle to build a new society! Today, Mount Halla and the people of Jeju give you an important mission—to defy those punitive units, the subordinates of the counterrevolutionary, antinationalist imperialists, who obstruct our fight for justice."

His impassioned speech was so full of anger that the mountains and the stars hidden in the darkness trembled with fear and the sharp December winds did not blow.

The chief commander of the Jeju commando unit, Lee Duk-Gu, began scrutinizing the eyes of the hundred or so young people gathered in front of the caves in the crater of Bulgunorum, a safe haven for the commando unit of the southeast area. The chief commander wanted to confirm the resolve of those youths, whose eyes sparkled even in the darkness.

At the top of Bulgunorum, located in Somang Village, in the district of Namwon, there is a unique crater that looks like an iron rice kettle with the top open. Because the crater continuously emits warm air, snow does not accumulate on the hill, even in the middle of the winter. Around this area there are naturally formed caves in which ten or so people can sleep and eat comfortably. It's the perfect place for a hideout.

"Dear Comrades! The time has finally come. The people of North Korea and our revolutionary comrades in Japan have promised to support us fully in our heroic battle on Jeju Island. Our fight against the antinationalists will intensify in the near future. Some time ago, Comrade Kim Dal-Sam left for Haeju, in North Korea, to participate as our delegate in the National Convention of the People's Representatives. At that meeting, he reported on the progress of our heroic fight and received offerings of support from the other comrades there. The time is near when the invincible Soviet warships in the Pacific, sent by the leader of the Soviet Union, Great Comrade Stalin, will fire against the national army and the police force of Rhee Syngman, the subordinate of the U.S. imperial forces. The day is near when these warships will salute us for having fought and risked our lives at the foot of Mount

Halla. Rhee Syngman's national army and police force, which are now surrounding us to begin their scorched-earth strategy, will soon be trembling in front of the Soviet warships. A two-sided operation—our comrades on one side of the great Mount Halla and the Soviet warships on the other—will force our enemies to flee. Comrades! Let's remember our efforts so far, our anger, and the comrades who died before of us, those whose blood was spilled at the foot of Mount Halla. The day will soon come when we take up guns, swords, and spears and go forward to attack the enemy with shouts of victory. Tomorrow's early morning surprise attack will be a prelude to that glorious day. It is a great honor for you to participate in this mission, which will be recorded in the history of the communist revolution and remembered forever."

His passionate speech reverberated through the dark forest surrounding the large crater and stirred strong emotions in the hearts of those young men. Their cheering continued until the echo of his words dissipated in the darkness and the crater was once again filled with silence.

"This mission will be directed by Oh Gyu-Min, the vice commander of the southeast commando unit. Comrade Oh will now explain the tactics of the operation in detail. Let's give him a warm welcome and pledge to follow his instructions in order to win this battle."

The chief commander began clapping as Gyu-Min came forward. Again, the soldiers filled the silent darkness with cheers that shook the mountains.

"The southeast commando unit is honored to participate with the people of Jeju in this holy fight."

Gyu-Min stopped his speech for a moment. As the cold silence rushed in, goose bumps spread over the backs of the soldiers.

"On April 3 in the year 4281,[1] the people of Jeju arose courageously with revolutionary flags to realize the unification of Korea and build the People's Democratic Republic. But the imperialist U.S. and its followers brought about a division in the nation and set up a puppet government in South Korea. That's why we are here. The imperialists, scared of our resistance, mobilized the army and police forces of Rhee Syngman's government and committed acts of brutality, murdering innocent people, setting fire to people's homes and fields, and forcefully seizing their harvests, the products of their sacred labor. The shared resentment against these acts of brutality stirred up a combative spirit and revolutionary ideas in the people of Jeju and inspired them to endure the cold and hunger in the caves of Mount Halla and to fight relentlessly. Now Rhee Syngman's government

---

[1] According to Korean legend, the nation was founded in 2333 B.C. by a mystical figure named Dan-Gun. Some Koreans count years from this point in time as a way of emphasizing the independence of Korea. The year 4281, according to this system, corresponds to 1948 A.D.

is conceiving other tactics of inhumanity and wickedness. They plan to slaughter us all like dogs and pigs with modern weapons, to destroy our strategic points, the inner villages, and to seduce the Korean people with honeyed words so that they abandon their revolutionary ideals. During the last few months, many comrades and villagers left the mountain because of those seductive words, but they were murdered mercilessly with the guns and swords of the army and government police. They have designated the area around the districts of Pyosun and Namwon, where the most humble and honest people live, as their strategic area. So that place is now suffering greatly in terms of human lives and material damage. To make matters worse, the puppet government is determined to evaluate the success or failure of their strategy through their operation in the area of Namwon. So they stationed an infantry company at the Eugwi Elementary School in Namwon and carried out a full-scale scorched-earth attack against the people two days ago. In that attack, those living in the inner villages were captured and are now being held at the school. We must rescue these people, wipe out the punitive unit, and neutralize the subordinate forces of the American imperialists. This mission is the historic beginning of the ultimate independence of Jeju Island. For this mission, the commanding unit has set up a detailed plan, based on our best information, and has sent fifty comrades from a special attack unit to support us."

The vice commander took a deep breath and then continued his speech:

"Comrades of the southeast commando unit! Do you remember your family and friends who were killed at gunpoint by those wicked people? The fires they started burned down the houses in which we had lived happily for generations and destroyed the crops and livestock that we value like our own children. Through this mission, we will vent the anger and hatred buried deep in our hearts. Comrades! Courageous revolutionary comrades! It is an honor to spill our blood on Jeju Island for the liberation of the Korean people! Our red blood will remain here as long as the mountains and the rivers of Jeju exist, and the island will remember us eternally by decorating itself with flowers and trees every season."

His speech began to falter with the trembling in his voice.

"It is a little past midnight now. Let us go. I am confident that this mission will be a successful one."

As Gyu-Min finished his speech, the wind blew, shaking the forest. The soldiers slowly began moving in the darkness, and the sound of their footsteps dissipated in all directions.

The chief commander held the cold hands of Gyu-Min for a long time.

"I pray for your success."

Their eyes glittered as they met. Gyu-Min turned away first and started to follow the other soldiers, who were climbing up the mountain, out of the crater.

2

The size of the troop put into this operation was about that of an infantry company—it included three platoons and one reconnaissance squad. Most of the commandos were from the districts of Pyosun and Namwon; they were members of the People's Commando Unit of Southeast Jeju. An additional fifty commandos, selected from the headquarters, joined the mission as well.

The reconnaissance squad led the way, followed by two platoons whose squads were ten meters apart. Behind them was the commanding unit under the direction of Gyu-Min, and at the very end of the line was another platoon. The squads communicated with each other by means of a rope they were all holding.

The wind that night in December was as sharp as a razor. Though everyone wore hats and washcloths over their ears, the biting wind froze their ears and noses. Thick snow hit their faces as they were pushed along by a strong wind blowing on their backs.

When they entered the village, having passed the pasture of communal ranches in the village of Sumang, the wind abated slightly due to the sheltering trees. But the loud noise of the wind rustling in the trees created a gloomy atmosphere. Even in the darkness, some red stone walls could be seen in a burnt-down area. Shivering, the commandos tried to look away, but the images of their scorched hometown flashed across their minds, appearing more clearly than ever.

Since late fall, the government forces had been carrying out full-scale punitive attacks in the district of Namwon, located between the seashore and Mount Halla. Operating on the pretext that the villages in this area could be hideouts for the communist guerillas, the government army designated the area as an operational zone and indiscriminately set fire to all of the houses there.

One day, a punitive unit came to the area and torched a thatched-roof house. With the wind blowing from the northwest, other thatched-roof houses quickly caught fire. The villagers who had not yet been evacuated ran out of their houses, at which point they were shot by soldiers in the punitive unit who had been waiting for them. People were killed and houses in which families had lived for generations were instantly reduced to ashes. The punitive units also set fire to the crops that had just been reaped, the product of a summer of hard work in the fields. The burnt grains gave off a strong smell.

Gyu-Min bit his lips on seeing the remnants of his village in the darkness. There was no reason why his village should have suffered this ghastly fate. No one from his village was a major figure in the communist movement. Many of the villagers who had gone to the mountain did so only because they could not be evacuated to the seashore villages earlier.

The rope that connected the various squads vibrated once or twice. The squad in front stopped slowly and hid beside the stone wall on the roadside. They were at Nopunmaru, a hill between the villages of Sumang and Eugwi. From there on, it was a steep road downhill.

On the right side of the hill was a field, and beyond the field there was what used to be a forest of pine trees. There once was a forest on the left side of the hill as well, but the trees on both sides of the hill had recently been cut down. Even in the darkness, one could see that the area had been cleared. From that location, the whole village was plainly visible.

After the government army had stationed itself in the village, it cut down all of the trees along the streets for strategic reasons. Looking at the ruined forests, Gyu-Min felt such a surge of anger inside him that he was left gasping for air. All of the commandos went into the pine tree field and hid behind the tree stumps.

The school in which the army was stationed, the very one in which Gyu-Min had worked for more than two years, came into view. Because it was a tall building, it could be seen clearly even in the darkness. However, the inside and the area surrounding the school were only barely visible.

Just after 2:00 A.M., Gyu-Min summoned the platoon leaders.

"We will depart in thirty minutes. It will take twenty minutes from here to reach the school. The operation will start at 3:00 A.M. sharp, when the guards are likely to be drowsy."

Then he went over the details of the mission once again.

"Two days earlier, the punitive units searched through the farms of Sumang and Eugwi and arrested two hundred people who had gone to live in the mountains with the communist guerillas. Members of the Civil Defense Corps and policemen also participated in that operation. Since they were strangers to Jeju and the weather was bad, the punitive units had a difficult time. After the operation, they decided to take one day off to rest, but they are probably still tired. If we take advantage of their fatigue with a surprise attack, there is a good chance of success."

Gyu-Min continued:

"The government has set up combat headquarters in Jeju City and has begun executing plans to exterminate the communist guerrillas. They have stationed punitive units at every strategic position at the foot of Mount Halla and in the inner villages. They have also planned a 'deer hunting' mission in which soldiers will surround the mountain and then ascend it on all sides at the same time. A punitive unit the size of an infantry company has been stationed in the village of Eugwi to carry out this mission. Depending on its success or failure, the government will decide whether or not to continue this type of operation. If we strike a blow tonight, the government will be forced to modify or abandon its so-called deer hunting tactic."

* * *

Recently, the government had begun a two-pronged strategy: pacification of the villagers using various forms of propaganda and, simultaneously, suppression of the communist guerrillas. With the arrival of winter, it had become difficult for people to live in the mountains. In addition to this, the suppression activities of the government had become increasingly severe, and this was weakening the fighting spirit of the guerrillas. Because the government's propaganda work was very effective on those villagers who had gone to live on the mountain, the number of civilian defectors had increased. Since they were civilians, there was no real damage to the fighting power of the guerillas, but it nevertheless had a subtle demoralizing effect on the fighting forces. Furthermore, a strange rumor was spreading that all of the soldiers and policemen in South Korea would gather on Jeju Island, encircle Mount Halla, and climb up to Baegnok Crater at the top. The American warships in the sea, airplanes in the sky, and a punitive unit on the ground would simultaneously attack the guerrillas and turn Mount Halla into a blazing inferno. With rumors like these flying about, the guerrillas had become rather despondent.

In order to change this depressed atmosphere and bring about a turning point in guerrilla activities, the commando unit had begun planning a sneak attack one month earlier. While they were drawing up their plans, a punitive unit attacked the village and captured some of the villagers. Since it was urgent to free those who had been captured in the government attack, the commando unit designated this day as D-day. The commando leaders estimated that there was about a seventy percent chance that this mission would be successful. They thought that their success was almost certain if the villagers who were captured and being held in the school were to join them in this fight.

***

"How do you feel about this mission?"

Gyu-Min's voice was rough and trembling as he asked this of one of the platoon leaders. He was irritated by the fact that his emotion was always reflected in his voice.

The platoon leader, who was from that village, had graduated from the same elementary school as Gyu-Min, two years after him. Since he had fought for the Japanese in China, he was skillful in guerrilla warfare.

"It looks like a dead village," the platoon leader answered.

Gyu-Min wanted to say that it might be a dead village now, but that soon it will be bustling with vigor and activity. However, the words never came out of his mouth.

"There are three guard posts around the school. One at the front gate on the southeast side, another at the rear gate on the north, and another on the west. The first platoon will depart first and …"

The duty of the first platoon was to kill the guards and to secure the guard post. While the first platoon was doing this, the other soldiers were to enter the school.

"Since the wall of the school is low, it's easy to jump over it. The second platoon will ..."

While soldiers in the first platoon were fighting with the guards, soldiers from the second and third platoons were to jump the wall and then hide beside it, where they would not be easily noticed due to the darkness.

"Do not waste your ammunition. That will determine our success or failure."

Thirty cartridges were given to each soldier. Since there were a hundred and thirty-five soldiers, a total of four thousand cartridges were distributed. This meant that with only four thousand cartridges they had to kill an entire infantry company.

"If this mission is successful, we can liberate Jeju Island."

He emphasized this point one more time and then said no more. He was sure that the commandos knew what he wanted to add.

"Let's go!"

The platoon leaders, who were listening without speaking, stood up and walked away slowly, with slightly bent postures. Soon the sound of the commandos' footsteps filled the dark silence of the night.

Gyu-Min was trembling. Cold air rushed into his chest. Tall trees on the sides of the street were swaying to and fro and hissing in the strong wind. This strange sound disturbed him and caused him to tighten his muscles. He felt as he used to when he heard an old cow lowing early in the morning. It was the same feeling he had experienced one afternoon in the fall when he saw an old man on top of a roof, waving some clothes, calling out for the spirit of a loved one who had died. These feelings made the coldness even more intense for him.

As the commandos moved silently in the darkness toward the school, Gyu-Min heard the sound of a rooster and wondered where in the village there could be a rooster. For a moment he thought he was hallucinating. This village used to be full of the cries of roosters at dawn. If one rooster started to crow, the others would also crow competitively. Women, when they were awakened by those sounds, would immediately prepare breakfast for their families.

Suddenly there was a jerk in the rope. The commandos in the front unit stopped and hid themselves on either side of the street. After a while, they continued on.

The school now filled Gyu-Min's view. There was a large flowerbed on the east side of the school. On the south and west sides there was a playground, and beyond that there was a large field. Since villagers had been unable to farm during the winter, Gyu-Min guessed that the fields would probably be empty. He thought that the commandos should attack from the south and west since these would be the overlooked spots.

The commandos in Gyu-Min's unit, a unit the size of a platoon, hid themselves beside the wall of the field on the opposite side of the street from the school.

The entire area was silent. Only the school building was readily visible in the darkness. The wall surrounding the playground appeared as a thin line, and the three guard posts were only faintly visible.

Gyu-Min was worried. The guard posts were more heavily armed than he had guessed; it seemed that they would not be easy to attack. By now, the commandos would be creeping toward the guard posts, he thought.

Gyu-Min closed his eyes gently and took a deep breath. His heart was pounding loudly. He wanted to leap over the wall right away and attack, disregarding the original plan.

At that moment some soldiers from the guard post at the front gate of the school began walking along the wall in the direction of Gyu-Min and his unit. It looked to him as though there were two or three of them, but there were others also patrolling the school.

The soldiers walked to where Gyu-Min was hiding and then stopped. The area was silent except for the sound of the wind rattling the windows of the school. The soldiers remained still for some time, and Gyu-Min wondered if they could smell something.

A gunshot suddenly shattered the night silence. The shadow in front of Gyu-Min immediately disappeared and wild footsteps rumbled along the earth, while more gunshots rang out.

Gyu-Min quickly climbed over the wall of the field and made his way to the wall surrounding the school grounds. He realized that the sound of the gunshots could not have come from the old-fashioned guns the commandos were carrying. The clear, sharp sound could only have come from M-1 rifles. So the commando unit, he thought, must have been spotted by the guards. The sound of gunshots seemed to be coming from the guard posts.

He carefully surveyed the playground. He could see that the commandos were already over the school wall and inside the school grounds. Then he saw dark shadows moving near the flowerbed where he was hiding. He thought that they must be soldiers from the punitive unit.

"Kill them first," he calmly ordered the other commandos in his unit.

The guns, which were used by the Japanese army, made a dull sound as they were fired. The shadows did not move anymore. At the same time, the commandos started firing their old-fashioned guns from all around the school.

"They must have taken our gunshots as a signal for a fight," said one of the commandos.

Gyu-Min, however, did not hear what the commando said. He thought that it was useless to fire on the school building from the wall, but since the fighting had started already, they would have to charge the enemy. The distance between the school and the wall on the perimeter of the school grounds varied: it was greater on the south and west sides than on the east and north sides, but most of the commandos had been placed on the south and west sides to attack the guard posts.

It was still completely silent inside the school building.

"We shouldn't delay any longer. We should charge in right away," said the platoon leader.

"Attack!"

At that very instant, shots were fired from inside the school, and a strange fire suddenly lit up the sky over the school grounds. Gyu-Min could see some of his men crawling on the playground.

"It's a flare!"

The bright light exposed the commandos.

"Attack!" yelled someone from the northwest side of the school.

During the brief moment of darkness after the light bomb went out, the commandos moved swiftly. Gyu-Min realized that this was going to be a difficult fight even with the surprise attack: they had to strike fast before the counterattack began.

Gyu-Min jumped over the school wall and hid at the foot of a tall tree. His guards quickly followed him, protecting him. Again, a flare was fired and loud gunshots followed.

"There's a machine gun on the roof."

"A machine gun!"

Gyu-Min never expected this. He wondered how they could possibly have set up a machine gun on a roof with such a steep slope.

Gyu-Min stuck close to the foot of the tree. This was the place he had often used as a teacher for outdoor classes. It was cool there, even in midsummer. The tree was older than the school.

Again a flare exploded and the playground was brightly lit. At the same time, fires broke out in the classrooms and on the roof. The commandos that were already inside the playground couldn't move at all. In the darkness that followed the blast of light, they advanced on their hands and knees toward the school. During the brief flashes of light, they were fired on. Gyu-Min thought that if they could advance a little further, they would reach a blind spot from which the machine gun on the roof couldn't hit them.

"Shouldn't we retreat?" asked the platoon leader, standing next to Gyu-Min.

He was one of the guards for Lee Duk-Gu and had participated in this fight to support Gyu-Min. He was an expert in guerrilla warfare. But Gyu-Min could not order a retreat.

"What are you saying? They're surrounded. We just have to wait for them to run out of ammunition."

Gyu-Min said this angrily, but he too wondered whether his soldiers could put up with the machine gun fire. However, he couldn't retreat now.

Again, a flare lit up the playground. The entire building suddenly appeared before Gyu-Min's eyes and his throat was choked with a lump of sorrow.

* * *

Eugwi Elementary School was an unforgettable place for Gyu-Min. He had graduated from a college of education during the Japanese Occupation of Korea. A year after his graduation, the country was liberated from Japanese rule. At that time, he was happy that he could be a teacher in an independent country. The flowerbed near the tree behind which he was hiding was decorated with smooth stones that he and his students had carried. He had divided the flowerbed into several sections and had instructed the students to plant different kinds of flowers there. When looking at the blossoming flowers each season, he had been intoxicated with happiness over his country's freedom. Each fall, he organized a field day, which became the village festival; each winter, he put on a school play depicting the people's joy at being liberated. He also regularly taught the female students how to dance.

As a teacher, he always came to school early in the morning and returned home late in the evening. The school was his life; it was full of joy. Sometimes, he spent the night talking with students at his house. After one year of this, he found another joy—that of teaching revolutionary songs to the students, who worshiped him. He invited not only his own students but also other young people to the school to talk about politics and to encourage them to be active in leading the country.

* * *

Those happy moments kept flashing through his mind during the intermittent blasts of light from the flares.

The tall tree that stretched upward split into two main branches. Through the opening between the branches, he glanced at the dark school, which was being pounded with bullets.

"Let's retreat and return another day," urged the platoon leader once again.

This was not the attitude a subordinate should show to a commanding officer. However, this commando was under the direct control of the chief of the headquarters. Since the life and death of the commando unit depended on this operation, Gyu-Min could not flatly ignore his advice, but he felt that he could not retreat after having witnessed his men bleeding in front of his eyes.

"There is another machine gun on the back side of the roof," said another commando near the platoon leader.

This meant the platoon in charge of the back side must have been unable to attack the enemy.

Gyu-Min estimated that the distance between the tree and the school was about 80 meters. Since it was midnight, it would be difficult for the machine gun to hit the commandos at that distance. He hoped that his men would gain time by staying out of the range of the machine gun. However, each time the light bomb faded, he saw his men on the ground advance a little closer to the outer range of the machine gun that was hungry for human life.

"Order a retreat," the platoon leader urged him again.

But Gyu-Min had by now lost all of his will to command.

A flare lit the sky, and shots rained down on the commandos with thunderous noise.

3

As the darkness of the night began to fade in the eastern sky, the sound of gunshots ceased. Even though it was winter, it was quite warm. Heavy silence filled the playground, and there was no wind. A strong smell permeated the entire area, the smell of burning bones or some mixture of explosives and blood.

"Everyone has retreated," shouted a soldier, as he stood up from behind the sandbags on the school roof.

Armed soldiers carrying guns came out of the school, making some noise. They were scattered around the school in groups of five or six. One group came to the middle of the school ground and tapped the dead bodies with their feet.

The dead bodies were scattered on the ground, their heads pointing in the direction of the school. They were still holding their old-fashioned guns and had blood-stained earth in their mouths. Some of their fur hats had fallen off, revealing their short, bloody hair. One of the dead commandos looked like he was about eighteen or nineteen years old. Evidently he had been struck by two bullets: one knocked his fur hat off; the other one took his life. A bit of the ground was dug out near the hand of one of the bodies, whose fingernails were filled with earth. It seemed that he had dug his fingers into the earth in severe pain. Some of the bodies were already frozen and did not budge at all when kicked. Their faces were stuck to the ground; they had been killed while crawling toward the school on their hands and knees.

After confirming the death of the guerrillas, the government soldiers gathered in the middle of the playground. A captain wearing a steel helmet came out of the school with a tense expression on his face. The soldiers fell into formation as a second lieutenant shouted out orders. While they were lining up, the captain stood in front of them and watched the sun rising in the east. He then gestured to the second lieutenant.

From the classrooms of the school, civilians came out in two lines. Soldiers holding guns followed them. Looking like convicted criminals, the civilians hung their heads low as they walked. Old people and women could be spotted among them.

The civilians gathered together in front of the soldiers who were already lined up. They were wearing soiled clothes and their faces were swollen and yellow. It was obvious that they were the ones that had left their villages to go live in the mountains.

The civilians were then ordered to move the bodies of the dead commandos and place them, one by one, beside the drill platform. The bodies of the government soldiers who had been killed were placed in front of the flag platform. Worn-out straw bags were placed under their bodies and blankets were placed on top. The other bodies were dragged and left on the bare ground, their heads pointing toward the north.

There were eight dead government soldiers and about eighty-three dead guerillas.

The captain yelled in the direction of the headquarters of the infantry company and a sergeant rushed forward. After the captain ordered him to hoist the national flag, the sergeant looked at his watch, thinking that it was too early to raise it.

"Just hoist the flag. Don't worry about the time."

While two privates were raising the flag, the captain bowed his head in front of his dead men. The playground was filled with warm sunlight. The civilians looked at the captain out of the corner of their eyes and became nervous.

The captain slowly walked toward the front of the line of soldiers. Choked with emotion, a first lieutenant reported the number of dead soldiers.

"… and eight soldiers were killed in action."

The lieutenant tried to finish his report by saying "over," but his words were slurred. The captain looked at his men, the dead ones lying on the old straw bags in front of the platform, and then turned his face toward the sky. Other soldiers who were staring at the dead bodies of their fellow soldiers also turned their eyes toward the empty sky. Dead silence reigned over the frozen playground. Even the white sunshine seemed as cold as ice.

The captain turned toward the soldiers in line and gestured to the first lieutenant. The lieutenant then ordered the civilians to form two lines.

"Look at the faces of these communists carefully. Look at each of them one by one. They said they attacked to kill us but they intended to kill you as well. Since more and more civilians are defecting these days, they attacked us to prevent further defection. They wanted to set an example. Look carefully at these communists who intended to kill you."

The first lieutenant spoke calmly as he said this to the civilians, who held up their faces to look at the lieutenant.

The civilians walked along, looking at the dead commandos. Some of them could not bear the sight and turned their faces away. The soldiers, who were following behind them, forced them to look at the bodies carefully. Some civilians, when they recognized an acquaintance, frowned, turned away, or expressed surprise by opening their eyes widely. Most of the dead commandos were familiar to them. They were the youths of the nearby villages; they were sometimes seen near the stream at the foot of Mount Halla. However, with their blood-bruised faces, bloodstained clothes, and dirt-covered bodies, they no longer looked like human beings.

After looking at the dead bodies, the civilians lined up again. The captain came forward, and following him were the first and second lieutenants.

"So, did you take a good look at them? They are the bastards who were going to make Jeju a communist island. They were in the same party with you once, but when you defected, they didn't like it. So they attacked us early this morning. They intended to kill you as well. Since you have had a good look at them, I will ask you one question now. Answer me honestly."

Slurring his words, he looked at the people, and they looked back at him. Their life or death depended on his words at that moment.

"Answer me frankly. If you lie, it will be the end of your life."

The civilians held their breath.

"Raise your hands if you know any of the dead commandos."

The captain glared at the civilians with angry eyes. The civilians looked around at each other, but they hesitated to raise their hands right away.

"Not one of you knows any of these communists? Aren't they all from around these villages?"

The first lieutenant yelled at those who were studying the expressions on the others' faces. Only then were hands raised, one by one. Eventually, almost all of them raised their hands.

"Those of you who did not raise your hand come forward right now."

As the captain gestured, the first lieutenant started wading his way through the civilians, trying to find those who did not raise their hands. At that point, those who had raised their hands reluctantly lifted them up again, this time higher than before.

"Come forward right away."

The captain spoke bluntly, but no one came forward.

"Go to the front," said the first lieutenant as he pushed an old woman.

The old woman said, "I have bad eyesight so I could not recognize anyone."

"Where are you from?" the captain asked the woman rudely.

"What did you say?"

The old woman shook her head, as she struggled to adjust her gray, disheveled hair.

"Where are you from?" he asked again.

The captain then gestured to a sergeant, who came forward and moved the old woman to the side. Everyone focused on the woman.

"So, all of you know the communists. Then move their bodies over there. Since they are your acquaintances, you should move them."

The captain spoke in an abusive tone, with a frown on his face.

Following the first lieutenant's order, the civilians began moving the bodies of the commandos to the empty field west of the school grounds. The field, where sweet potatoes were once planted, was rather muddy. After the fall harvest, the field had been left empty. With the sunshine, the frozen field had thawed and the mud now stuck to the shoes of the civilians.

* * *

The conditions in this area had begun deteriorating earlier that fall. The schools closed down and many young people left the village. However, most people were unable to evacuate to the seashore villages. They knew that it would be dangerous to remain in their villages, but they could not leave their crops in the field, after having worked so hard during the summer. So they remained in the villages and finished their harvest. The rice stalks were cut, tied up with ropes, carried into their homes, and turned into stacks of grain. The sweet potatoes were harvested and placed in storage pits in the ground. They thought that they would be able to evacuate once they had planted barley in the fields, but just as they were doing so the punitive unit attacked the village.

To escape the attack, the villagers went to the mountain, but all they thought about during that time was getting back to their fields to sow the barley. Even during the riots, they only thought about their farming. So their hearts sank on that day when they looked at the burnt-out field with no barley in it. What a disaster, they thought. They wondered how they could survive.

* * *

It was difficult for two people to carry one dead body, so they dragged the bodies along the ground.

With the wind blowing through this open field, it was quiet cold, even though the morning sun was shining. After all of the bodies were placed in the center of the burnt-out field, the civilians shook the dirt from their own clothes, and looked at the bodies. The faces of the dead, now covered in mud, were difficult to recognize. Soon they would be buried in the ground and slowly they would decay. They wondered whether the families who would return after the fighting was over to claim the remains of their loved ones would be able to identify the bodies. Soon they began to feel an enormous sadness for the deceased.

The government soldiers then came into the field with the children and old people of the village, those who did not help carry the dead bodies. Following them was the captain.

4

Oh Gyu-Min climbed up a camellia tree and hid. From his hiding place, two fields away from the school grounds, he could see the school. The sun rose higher in the sky and the sunshine felt warm and friendly, as if it would talk to him, there in the burnt-out yard of his house. Drowsiness gradually overcame him since he had not slept well for the last several days.

Earlier, while bullets were raining down on the tree Gyu-Min was hiding behind on the school grounds, the platoon leader ran away since Gyu-Min did not listen to his plea to retreat. Trying to escape, Gyu-Min also climbed over the wall of the school, but there was no place for him to go. Even if he returned to the mountain, there would be no way to avoid his responsibility for having lost the fight. And the faces of the soldiers, as they crawled toward the school, knowing that this was a losing battle, kept returning to his mind and tormenting him. It was at that point that he thought of his home. It had already been burned down, but he thought that there might be someone there waiting for him.

His scorched house was in a neighborhood close to the school.

As he approached the street leading to his house, he felt comfortable, as though he had already returned there. He then entered the passageway, which led to the front yard of his house. On the sides of the street, there were thickets of camellia trees, just as before. When he entered the house, the straw on the ground welcomed him with crackling sounds.

The old house was completely burnt, but the high stone walls enabled him to recognize the original shape of the house even in the darkness. As he entered the house, a strange but familiar smell, the smell of roasted grain, rushed into his nostrils.

When day broke, the entire site was fully exposed: only red walls remained where three houses had once stood. However, he waited there for a long time since he thought that someone, perhaps someone hiding behind a wall, might come out to greet him.

He then climbed up the old camellia in the backyard of his house and hid. There was no place else for him to go.

He could see the entire school grounds from the tree. While observing what was going on outside the school, he thought about his family members—his father, who had been captured and killed by the policemen because of his son, and the other family members, who had taken refuge at Seogwi port, where his maternal family lived. These thoughts lasted for only a brief moment and then his attention was drawn to a strange sound. He listened to the speech, which sounded like a roar, while hiding in the camellia tree.

"My beloved fellow soldiers! ... My beloved fellow soldiers!"

The speech bounced off the mountain and echoed through the fields around the village. The voice of the captain of the punitive unit was trembling, and filled with pure hostility. Suddenly, the speech that Lee Duk-Gu gave inside the crater of Bulgunorum flashed across Gyu-Min's mind.

"We joined the army, risking our lives to build a new country. We came all the way to Mount Halla on Jeju Island to defeat the vicious political maneuvering and communist obstructions at the foundation of this country. We fought against communist guerrillas, enduring the cold and hunger, and we made remarkable military gains. If we restore peace on Jeju Island, this will mean peace in Korea, and it will quickly lead to the establishment of a democratic country in Korea. The cowardly communists attacked us in the middle of the night while our fellow soldiers were sound asleep. That's how we lost eight fellow soldiers. However, your brave counterattack, in which you risked your own lives, put an end to eighty-three communists. This is an unprecedented event in the historic battle against the communists on Jeju Island. We should solemnly pledge at this time, by the lives of our fellow soldiers killed in action, that we will never give up in our fight against the communist guerrillas."

The captain then paused, and the soldiers, who were shouldering their guns, surrounded the civilians. He then continued.

"They are all communists. Last night the communist guerrillas made a surprise attack to rescue them. We just confirmed the fact that these people all knew the dead guerrillas. That proves that they are communists as well. I order you to shoot them on this spot."

The chief took a few steps backward, and then gave the following order:

"Ready, aim, fire!"

The sound of the gunshots shook the entire village. Not one bullet missed its target. The people who had gathered in the middle of the playground dropped to the ground, one by one.

The muzzles of the guns emitted puffs of white smoke, and the smell of the gunpowder soon entered Gyu-Min's nostrils.

When the soldiers finished firing, they lowered the guns from their shoulders and walked slowly toward the school.

After they were gone, dead silence and sunshine filled the empty field. The village, the thick forest, the field, and even the sky that was looking down on them all sank into desolation.

Crows soon flocked to the field, stirring up a whistling wind. As they descended upon the dead bodies, they began to caw. Gyu-Min closed his eyes. The cawing of the crows, which ended the dead silence, reverberated throughout the village and beyond.

Chronology

The 4.3 Incident—"4" refers to the fourth month of the year; "3" to the third day of the month. The "4.3 Incident" is the Jeju Massacre, a complex series of events on Jeju Island that began on April 3, 1948. On that day, approximately 1,500 armed civilians launched an assault on the island's police stations and other institutions that were regarded as protecting Japanese interests during the Occupation of Korea and American interests in the years following the Occupation, while the U.S. Military Government controlled the nation. Syngman Rhee, the leader of the right-wing provisional government at the time, backed by the U.S. Military Government, responded to the civilian uprising by ordering a brutal crackdown on all those involved in or in any way associated with it. The weeks and months following April 3 were a period of enormous social chaos on Jeju, during which at least 30,000 people were killed—many of them innocent civilians. The massacre was carried out by the combined forces of the Korean military and national police units and directed by the American military. The governments of both Korea and the United States have claimed that the Korean Communist Party supported the uprising on April 3. In November 2003, some 55 years after the bloodbath on Jeju, the Korean government expressed its first formal apology to the victims of the massacre and their families.

The 4.19 Revolt—also known as "The Revolt of April 19," refers to the massive student demonstrations that took place on April 19, 1960, in response to the unfair election, one month earlier, of Syngman Rhee. This revolt led to the downfall of Rhee, the first president of the Republic of Korea. However, the social and political confusion that ensued paved the way for a military coup on May 16, 1961.

The 5.16 Coup—On May 16, 1961, Park Chung-Hee led a military coup, which resulted in the downfall of Yun Poson, the newly elected president. Through this coup, Park Chung-Hee became the third president of the Republic of Korea.

The Japanese Occupation—the period from 1910 to 1945, during which Korea was occupied and controlled by the Japanese. During the Occupation, the Japanese government forced Korean citizens to adopt Japanese names and become citizens of Japan. The occupying government also prohibited the use of the Korean language in all public and private places.

Liberation—Korea's liberation from Japanese rule, which coincides with the end of WWII. With its defeat by the Allied forces in WWII, Japan lost all of its former colonies, including Korea.

Glossary of Korean Terms

Gisaeng—female entertainers, the Korean equivalent of the Japanese *geisha*. They were originally trained and maintained by the royal court, and were skilled in the traditional arts, such as music, dance, and poetry.

Gulgoong—a local event on Jeju Island in which villagers dress like servants or shamans and walk around the village with gongs, doing acrobatics and collecting donations for a feast or for public expenses.

Hamba—makeshift huts, one-room shelters with walls made of stones and roofs made of pinewood covered with thatch.

Hanbok—traditional Korean clothing.

Hanja—the characters of the Chinese script. Even in contemporary Korea, Chinese characters are used frequently in official or academic contexts and are an essential part of formal education.

Jeonbokjuk—rice porridge with ground shellfish, commonly eaten when one is ill or hungover.

Jongjobu—the brother of one's paternal grandfather. English lacks a specific term for describing this relationship. The closest English synonym is "granduncle," which refers to the brother of any of one's four grandparents.

Pungsusa—a spiritual guide who helps people find propitious burial sites. Those who practiced *Sundo* were especially concerned with finding such burial sites for deceased relatives.

Seonbae / Hubae—In Korea, students who attend the same school or university, but in different grades, form hierarchical senior / junior relationships that continue throughout their lives. Junior students (*hubae*) are expected to show respect toward their seniors (*seonbae*), while senior students are expected to take care of their juniors. Students in the same grade are considered equals and so do not form hierarchical relationships, except when there is an age difference.

Sundo—a traditional Korean method of training the mind and body to preserve health and achieve longevity. Some adherents have imbued it with spiritual beliefs and practiced it as a religion.

Yut—a traditional Korean board game played with four wooden sticks and beans.

Glossary of Other Terms and Names

Amnok River—one of the main rivers along the border between North Korea and China.

Bulgunorum—an inactive volcanic hill on Mount Halla, which is itself an extinct volcano.

Civil Defense Corps—During the turbulent times prior to the Korean War, Korean villages that lacked a police force often had a Civil Defense Corps, made up of volunteers, to maintain order. The Korean term is *Minbodan*.

Degrees of Kinship—In Korea, relations between family members are counted as follows: children and their parents are related to each other by one degree of kinship, while the relation between a child and either of his or her grandparents counts as two degrees, as does the relations between siblings. Therefore, the relation between a child and his or her uncle or aunt is three degrees, and first cousins are related to each other by four degrees, and so on. The Korean term for degrees of kinship is *chone*.

Head Family—In traditional Korean culture, family lineage runs, from one generation to the next, through the "head family," the family formed by the first-born son in each generation. The head family bears the principal responsibilities for ceremonies involving the extended family, such as those for worshiping the family's ancestors.

Inner Villages—the villages on Jeju Island in between Mount Halla, where the communist guerrillas were based in 1948, and the seashore villages, which were controlled by the Korean military.

Mount Baekdu—the largest mountain (2,744 meters) on the Korean Peninsula, located along border between North Korea and China.

Mount Halla—a huge inactive volcano that occupies much of the surface of Jeju Island. At 1,950 meters, it is the highest mountain in South Korea.

Topknot—In traditional Korean culture, the topknot of hair on a male represents the fact that he is married. During the Japanese Occupation, the Japanese government forced all Korean men to cut off their topknots. They also forcefully set an example by removing the topknot of Korea's King Ko-Jong, an event that is a perennial source of shame and outrage among Korean people. For many Koreans at that time, the topknot was regarded as a symbol of Korean independence.

DEAD SILENCE

And Other Stories of the Jeju Massacre

Hyun Kil-Un was born in 1940 on Jeju Island and has lived the greater part of his life on the island, attending Jeju National University as a student and later teaching there from 1979 to 1986. He began his literary career in 1980 with the short story "Sounds of a Collapsing Castle," and his first collection of stories, *The Dream of a Dragon-horse*, was published in 1985. Since the early 1990s he has written several novels, including *Transparent Darkness, The River of Women, Halla Mountain, Invisible Face, We Forget Too Easily,* and *Nail Marks.* Hyun is well known in Korea and highly regarded as a writer, especially for his fictional accounts of the Jeju Massacre. He has received several Korean literary awards for his short stories and novels, many of which have been translated into foreign languages. In 2004 he retired from his position of Professor of Korean Language and Literature at Hanyang University.

Kang Hyunsook teaches at Hanyang University.
Lee Jin-Ah teaches at Hankuk University of Foreign Studies.
John Michael McGuire teaches at Hanyang University.

EastBridge
Signature Books
Doug Merwin, Imprint Editor

The **Signature Books** imprint of EastBridge is dedicated to presenting a wide range of exceptional books in the field of Asian and related studies. The principal concentrations are texts and supplementary materials for academic courses, literature-in-translation, and the writings of Westerners who experienced Asia as journalists, scholars, diplomats, and travelers.

Doug Merwin, publisher and editor-in-chief of EastBridge, has more than thirty years' experience as an editor of books and journals on Asia and is the founding editor of East Gate Books.